LIVING SPRINGS PUBLISHERS PRESENTS:

STORIES THROUGH THE AGES
BABY BOOMERS PLUS
2024

Compiled and edited by:
Henry E. Peavler, Dan Peavler, and
Jacqueline Veryle Peavler

Introduction by: Henry Peavler and Dan Peavler

Short Stories by:
Samuel George Tooma, Geoffrey K. Graves, Amy Lauer Goldin,
Jacqueline Bassan, Michael Jefferson, Bill Weatherford,
Deac Etherington, Kevin L Hostbjor, Bridgett Kendall,
Neil McKinnon, Cat Funk, CM Kelly, J Craig Dix, Brian Kelly,
Elaine Thomas, Luanne Castle, J.R Reynolds, Scott Winkler,
T. Dan Nelson, Ken Sutherland

Copyright 2024
by Living Springs Publishers LLP

Paperback ISBN: 978-1-953686-41-1
Paperback ISSN: 2770-0178
eBook ISBN: 978-1-953686-42-8
eBook ISSN: 2770-0194

www.LivingSpringsPublishers.com

"You are never too old to set another
goal or to dream a new dream."
–C.S. Lewis

Contents

Synopses

Protector: First Place: A wonderful story set in the Middle Ages. Author Michael Jefferson has created a marvelous fantasy that is both a love story and adventure. Will the hero and heroine find love or immortality, or are they destined for something much worse? The Lady of the Lake is irreverent, funny, and determined and she demands that you read this story.

Unknown Caller: Second Place: By Samuel George Tooma. A couple learns that the wife has contracted a rare and deadly disease and that she has less than a year to live. Her only hope is if she can be accepted into an unsanctioned, clinical trial of a high-risk expensive drug. With little hope of being accepted into the program and with no way to pay its cost, all hope seems lost. Then, a mysterious woman resolves all the issues, and the wife is accepted into the trial with all expenses paid. Who is this woman? What are her motives? The husband soon finds out to beware of strangers bearing gifts.

Just This Once? Third Place: The author, Brian Kelly, provides a splendid glimpse into cultural differences in Ireland during the 1960's. Humorous at times, yet distressing in the cruelty practiced against those considered to be 'different'. Our hero finds himself the victim of childhood taunting and ridicule but realizes that others face far worse. We can only hope that in the end he will 'do the right thing.'

Night Song: By Jacqueline Bassan. A third-year medical student, still glowing with the idealism of her youth, is faced with the stark realities of life on the children's ward of a hospital. Where expectations of coughs and colds are blunted by cancer and other life-threatening diseases, she must face close-up as a professional, while pushing emotion aside. All the while, the pop music of that era is a part of the story.

Mother of Two: By Luanne Castle. Jeannie, a young mother of two children, goes about her life with a loving husband and a bright future. Suddenly, disaster strikes in a most unfortunate way. Who is at fault? What are the horrible consequences? A must read to find the answers.

How I'll Miss Paris: By J Craig Dix. For a change of pace, we find an exciting mystery, set in Paris in the early 1950's. Henri Gaspard is a special operative whose task is to 'confront' those deemed unwanted by "The Directors". Ready to retire he's convinced to take one more assignment. This well-written story isn't what it seems in the beginning and the ending is both surprising, yet inevitable.

Lean Away from the Night: By Deac Etherington. A wonderfully crafted story about a young would-be writer who finds love, then loses it only to cross a continent to try and find it again. The characters are well defined and true to their personalities, which may or may not be a good thing. Our hero doesn't necessarily find what he was looking for, but he's probably better off with what he gets. Don't miss reading this one.

Almost Intact: By Cat Funk. The laws of the land were handed down over centuries dictating how one behaved in the circle of life. All of that changed as the new creatures moved into the forest. Creatures on two legs. Would they honor the code or not? Regardless, life goes on and we adapt, or we don't survive. An excellent story with an emotional ending.

The Shadow Girl: By Amy Lauer Goldin. Set in the 1960's, this story is about a little girl and her mother who set off on an adventure, but she doesn't know what it could be. It isn't her birthday or Christmas, but something is in the air. What is it? Suddenly a pleasant outing turns sinister, and her world is threatened by something she doesn't understand. A must read.

He Called It a What?: The author, Geoffrey K. Graves, has created a humorous reflection on what 1960's life was like in the Biology Lab of his high school in California. The students participate in the standard dissections of lowly earthworms and frogs while anticipating the inevitable charts of human anatomy. What ensues is a funny tale about how one biology teacher pronounces certain body parts during his lecture.

The Hindenbug: Author Kevin L. Hostbjor's story of an ant colony at war with various enemies in their territory is surprisingly touching. The hero and heroine find love in a most unlikely way and together vanquish their foes against overwhelming odds. We discover, that while love triumphs, the forces of nature prevail, as they must to preserve the colony.

It's Called SPAM: A large family moves from the big city to a farm, or ranch, leading to many unfamiliar adventures on a plot of land the mother names 'Windrift Acres'. Author CM Kelly recounts the many problems associated with guiding a large family through everyday challenges, with little money to ease the burdens. The title will be misleading to those born after a certain age. Read the story to discover why.

Best Beloved: This story is set in England where our heroine suffers at the hands of her abusive husband and his family. The author, Bridgett Kendall, weaves a bittersweet story of the narrator losing her baby with no one to share her misery and no prospects for the future. The characters are all victims of the times they live in. The ending will surprise you as we discover the strength and wisdom that she eventually exhibits to resolve the matter.

Some Things Cannot Be Fixed: By Neil McKinnon. Noburo is a young Japanese boy whose family lived in western Canada. He learned respect from his father and grandfather, played in the creek and learned about birds. Then the bombs fell on Pearl Harbor. The family is forced to move to Alberta and work on a farm there. Read the story to find out how it ends.

Special Delivery: By T. Dan Nelson Two mischievous young boys unknowingly, or should we say innocently, wreak havoc on their rural neighbors by pretending to be mailmen. The special delivery packages they leave are most unwanted causing the neighborhood to organize vigilantes to catch the culprits. The surprise ending is humorous and lucky for the boys.

Lesson in Pie: This excellent story by J.R Reynolds creates the mystery of what is a 'BetterBilt Pie'? Dwight is curious to find out more about his grandfather. In the search he comes across a riddle that seems impossible to solve, but through luck and perseverance he solves the mystery and finds much more. Read the story to see for yourself.

Balance: Ken Sutherland has gifted us a marvelous story. Michael a young Irish lad who, along with his father and brother, immigrate during the Irish Potato famine. They look for work in Canada then, finding none and facing starvation, they choose to cross the frozen Detroit River to try and find work in the USA. This is a story of the struggle for survival by people with indomitable spirit but little in the way of material comforts.

Love & Apples: By Elaine Thomas. A young girl is left in the care of her grandmother and aunt while her parents are on a business trip. Grace tries her best to be 'good' but temptation is too much to bear and she comically succumbs. She fears the consequences only to find that the adults aren't as bad as she anticipated. This is a fun story.

Swampin' in '63: By Bill Weatherford. The son of the owner works alongside the migrant workers picking fruit in California's San Joaquin Valley. Leo, the true hero of the story, is a laborer, or trajabador, yes, but he is also a philosopher, mentor and professor to the young boy who is trying to find his way in the world. Excellently written and full of lasting memories, this is a must read.

Winter Squall: By Scott Winkler. In this story, the father, Eugene, can only be described as a despicable narcissist who horribly mistreats his wife and daughter, bringing serious illness upon the former and chasing the latter away from the family home in fear and disgust. He presents himself to the outside world as a virtuous philanthropist but in the end, karma wins out. He perishes in a morbid comeuppance that many will find satisfying.

Introduction

"That's what we storytellers do. We restore order with imagination. We instill hope again and again and again."
~Walt Disney

Living Springs Publishers is proud to announce the winners of our "Stories Through the Ages Baby Boomer Plus 2024" short story contest. This is our eighth annual contest which is open for stories 900-5000 words in length, restricted to authors born in 1966 or before. We place no restrictions on the topics our storytellers wish to write about. It is truly an international contest with many stories originating in countries other than the United States. These stories coupled with stories by authors from every corner of the United States, makes our contest extremely competitive.

By writing about and learning from our past we develop a better understanding of our dreams for tomorrow. We can always find hope even during the most trying of times. Creative is the one word that comes to mind in describing this year's group of stories. From a king's protector to an Irish legend, to stories of how it used to be, our authors used imagination to tell captivating stories with gripping narratives. The transformative stories in this book will inspire and entertain all readers.

It always amazes us at Living Springs Publishers that there are so many talented and gifted writers who are willing to bring their brilliant works of prose to the public forum. There are countless people in the world with original ideas for drafting a short story, poem, or novel, but only a select few have the patience, fortitude and courage to bring their tales to life. We want to thank all the authors who took the time and effort to send in their short stories to our contest. And, of course, congratulations to the prize winners and those who are being published in this year's book.

Protector
By Michael Jefferson

Sir Morpheus' eyes flutter, then open, "Again?" the knight asks.

"Again," the Lady of the Lake replies.

With amber hair cascading down her shoulders, shimmering green eyes, and an enticing figure, the Lady of the Lake is an enviable beauty. But she exists as a transparent apparition and is believed to be a witch.

"How did I die this time?" he asks.

"The fire-breathing dragon of Ergon swatted you with her tail. She broke all your ribs. One pierced your heart. Couldn't save you, buddy."

Morpheus slowly sits up, groaning. Sir Morpheus has dark, swarthy features with thick, braided hair, high cheekbones, and bottomless black eyes. His strength, skills, and seeming immortality have made him the most feared knight in the kingdom.

"Sometimes you speak so strangely."

"You have to have a good sense of humor to live in this disease-ridden, dung-filled excuse for a kingdom," the Lady of the Lake replies.

"How many deaths does this make?"

The Lake of the Lake's transparent visage drifts closer. He feels comforted by her smile.

"I believe this makes eighteen in forty-five years,

but you've had two in the last six months. You've got to be more careful, Morph."

"Or what? I will die?"

"Relax, Morph. It's King Harold who's dying. He promised to release us from our vow, and unlike us, he can't live forever."

"We should never have made such an agreement," he says.

"We didn't have a choice."

"I believe in keeping my word. But I want to die like everyone else."

***

Bellamy, Sir Morpheus' eighteen-year-old squire, rushes down the corridor to Morpheus' room. Boyish, brave, and eager to be a knight, Bellamy is wary of the Lady of the Lake's hold over his master.

He frantically bangs on the door. Getting no response, he bursts in.

The Lady of the Lake confronts him, baring her teeth like a protective lioness, her hair flowing like flames, and her eyes burning with anger.

Bellamy stumbles backward, cowering and covering his eyes.

"Stop frightening the boy," Morpheus calls out.

"Please forgive my intrusion," Bellamy says. "King Harold is dead, and your Queen demands your immediate presence."

"Spoiled brat," the Lady of the Lake comments.

Morpheus quickly dresses. "Stay here," he says to the Lady of the Lake, who quietly fumes as they leave.

***

"She hates me," Bellamy laments as the two men walk toward the throne room.

"The Lady of the Lake hates everyone."

"Not you."

"We have a bond."

"Then she is a real woman?" Bellamy asks.

"She is to me."

"You once told me you are not of this land, Sir Morpheus, but not how you came here," Bellamy says. "How is it you came to serve the House of Astley?"

"I found myself in a lake. I do not remember how I got there or anything before that. I quickly became aware that I could not swim, so I thought it would be in my best interest to get to shore. I was wrong. I encountered four of King Eric the Bold's knights. I managed to get a sword away from one of them and killed all four of them."

"And so, King Eric knighted you and made you his protector."

"No. The King saw what happened and sent four more men to kill me. I killed two more, but one of them came up behind me and put his sword through my back."

"And when you recovered, the King made you his protector."

"No. I died."

"For the first time," Bellamy says.

"I was told later that was when the Lady of the Lake fell from the sky and into the water. When she emerged and saw me lying there dead, she became enraged, threatening to kill the King's entire army. But King Eric the Bold was unafraid. He told her he had seen her kind before, and he knew how to destroy her. She resurrected me, and in exchange for her life, we made a pact with King Eric that we would serve the House of Astley until they set us free. That is when the King made me his protector."

"You sound as if you regret your agreement. I cannot think of any greater gift than being immortal."

"Really, Bellamy? Would you like to watch everyone you know grow old while you remain young? And if you had children, could you face burying them? Would you like to suffer the most grievous injuries possible, die in agony, and then wake up whole again…and again…and again?"

"So, you have given up the right to die because you honor your word?"

"And for love, Bellamy. The love of a woman I cannot touch."

They paused at the throne room door, "Do you think the Queen will grant your freedom?" Bellamy asks.

"I am hopeful. You are ready to assume my duties."

They bow as they enter the throne room.

Queen Hester is sitting on a large gold throne.

With her feet in the air, the twelve-year-old monarch resembles a doll seated in a highchair.

Small and slight with curly blonde ringlets and innocent pale features, Hester is often perceived as a child, but her intelligence, maturity, and piercing blue eyes say otherwise.

"Leave us," she says to Bellamy.

Relieved, Bellamy exhales, quickly exiting.

"I remember when I realized you were the most powerful man in the world, Sir Morpheus. I was four. It was after the Battle of Chelsea Woods. You had single-handedly saved thirty of our men trapped by the Barbarians, and you were sitting proudly on your horse. You picked me up and sat me in front of you and said, 'All is safe now.' We rode through the village together and everyone was throwing flowers at the future queen and her protector."

"It was a very satisfying moment."

"Now, as I ascend to the throne, I want to feel safe again. And I will when you take your place beside me."

"Your father promised me that upon his death the Lady of the Lake and I would be free of our vow."

"It was not his promise to make. When my grandfather, Eric the Bold died, your services were passed on to my father. Now, with King Harold's death, the decision to end or continue your service passes to me."

"So, you will not honor your father's dying

promise?"

"You can never be replaced."

"I am training my successor."

"Bellamy? He is a boy."

"And you are a twelve-year-old queen. But because you were properly prepared, you will be an even greater leader than your father."

Queen Hester sighs. "You deserve to hear the truth. I am frightened, Morpheus. Duke Typhon Ruthven of York has openly said he feels a child should not reign. I know he is plotting against me. I may be murdered before I even take the throne. I need you, Morpheus."

***

The four conspirators meet at Duke Typhon Ruthven's castle, intent on ending Queen Hester's reign before it begins.

Short, squat, and pampered, the inky-haired, flinty-eyed Typhon Ruthven owes his riches to his cunning nature. He has convinced his compassionate, blonde-haired brother, Duke Willem Ruthven of Driffield, to join him, claiming Queen Hester's overthrow will benefit the peasants. Enticed by the promise of gold and land, Corson and Cameron Mammon, a pair of bearded, unsmiling, brutal cousins from Leeds, have also pledged to help Typhon Ruthven overthrow the new Queen.

"You have not been very subtle about our intentions," Willem says.

"I believe it was Sir Morpheus himself who said,

'The easiest path to victory is the obvious one,'"
Typhon replies.

Cameron agrees. "Now is the time to strike, before the people rally around the child."

"But how?" Willem asks. "She has Sir Morpheus and the Lady of the Lake, the two most powerful weapons in the kingdom, at her disposal. How do you defeat creatures that cannot be killed?"

Typhon smiles confidently. "We do not have to kill them, only neutralize them."

***

All the nobles in the kingdom attend Queen Hester's lavish coronation. A massive dining table with fresh fruit, bread, meat, and exotic flowers dominates the room. The walls of the room are decorated with the colorful family crests of the attending families. A band of minstrels quietly performs in the background, while the Queen's guard, dressed in polished silver armor, stands at attention near the door.

Queen Hester moves about the room, her flowing white gown attended by two slouching female servants who appear embarrassed that they tower over her. Bellamy is by her side as she talks with the noblemen and their wives, his eyes darting around the room, his hand poised on his polished sword. The Ruthvens and Mammons occupy a corner of the room, cautiously greeting and speaking with potential allies.

The massive doors open. Sir Morpheus stands in

the doorway, resplendent in black.

The guests gasp and gape at the sight of the Lady of the Lake.

"She is as beautiful as I have heard. More so," says Willem.

"Do not let her splendor put you under her spell," Typhon replies. "She is an apparition. A trick perpetrated by Morpheus."

"Are you certain? Perhaps it is the other way around," Willem asks.

"What I know is our plan will succeed. That is all I need to know."

Sensing the Lady of the Lake's reluctance to enter the room, Morpheus extends his hand.

"No! Remember, we must never touch!"

"Sometimes there is nothing I would rather do," he says.

The guests back away from Morpheus and the Lady of the Lake as they move around the room.

A comely raven-haired servant girl crosses their path, holding two steins.

"Gimme," the Lady of the Lake says. "I get nervous in front of crowds. And when I'm nervous, I turn into a sponge."

The servant smiles. "I do not understand you, my lady, but if it is drink you require, I am at your service. But can an apparition hold a stein?"

"No problem, homegirl. And I'm not a ghost," the Lady of the Lake replies.

The stein floats from the servant's hand into her

fluttering grasp. She takes a long drink.

"Mmm. Have some, Morph."

The Lady of the Lake finishes her drink as Morpheus takes his first sip. She floats the empty stein back to the servant. "More please."

She notices Morpheus' sullen expression. "Still sulking over Hester's decision? It's a party, Morph. Pretend you're having fun."

Noticing how quiet the room has become, the Lady of the Lake turns, glaring at the people around her. The guests cringe, looking away.

"You medieval morons! Am I showing too much decolletage? Am I speaking too strangely? Then why is everyone looking at me?"

"Perhaps because they can see right through you," Morpheus whispers.

"I'm not a curiosity. I'm not a ghost. I'm a woman!"

"And a beautiful one at that," Morpheus says, hoping to appease her anger. "But we must face the truth, my lady. There is no one like you in the Kingdom. And no one like me."

The servant girl returns. "Then let's drink to being outcasts," the Lady of the Lake says. Whisking the stein from the servant's grasp, she quickly downs it.

Typhon turns to the others. "It is said that the power to destroy The Lady of the Lake is passed from one Astley to another. Now we possess that power."

Typhon moves toward Sir Morpheus and The Lady of the Lake, bowing.

"On behalf of myself and the other guests, allow me to apologize for our behavior."

"Accepted. I would offer you my hand, but…"

Typhon laughs. "That is not necessary, my lady. It is a pleasure to have you present for this historic event."

"I didn't have much choice. Little Miss Muffet ordered me to come."

Typhon gives her a confused look.

"She occasionally speaks in her native tongue," Morpheus offers.

"Curious. I have heard you will be continuing in your role as protector, Sir Morpheus," Typhon continues. "You never seem to age. May I ask what your secret is?"

The servant girl returns with two new steins for the Lady of the Lake and Morpheus.

"Avoiding drink," Morpheus jokes, taking a gulp.

Typhon holds up his stein. "A toast then, to a long and healthy life."

They drink. The Lady of the Lake shakes her head, causing her transparent body to disappear and reappear.

"I hear you are planning to overthrow the Queen," she slurs.

"What? No!" Typhon replies nervously.

"Then you'll be loyal to Queen Hester?"

"Of course!"

"Good. Then repeat the sacred oath of loyalty and say it loudly... Zippy-do-dah."

"ZIPPY-DO-DAH!"

The guests look at Typhon strangely, laughing.

Embarrassed, Typhon storms off.

"That was small of you," Morpheus says.

"That fop had it coming."

The Lady of the Lake hiccups, her body fading in and out of focus. "This mead is very strong."

Her body fades, returning as a blur.

"Oh. Oh."

The Lady of the Lake disappears, her stein hitting the floor.

Morpheus wobbles, feeling ill. Bellamy catches him as he passes out.

Typhon turns to his fellow conspirators. "The poison has done its work. Now we must do ours. We will move against the Queen's army in the morning. By this time tomorrow, I will be King, and you will all be very, very rich."

***

Queen Hester and Bellamy watch the Dukes' forces set up camp in the valley only a mile away from the castle.

"The combined armies of the four Dukes have routed our men," Bellamy says.

"How many men do we have left?"

"Perhaps a thousand against four times as many."

"You have acquitted yourself well against overwhelming odds, Bellamy. Sir Morpheus was right; you are ready to protect the throne. Unfortunately, it appears there will soon be no throne to protect."

"How is Sir Morpheus?" Bellamy asks.

"Still unconscious. Perhaps dead. I cannot tell. And the Lady of the Lake has forsaken us. I thought of them as gods, Bellamy. They proved to be all too human."

"If it is any consolation, the court physician said one drop of poison should have killed them," Bellamy says. "They each drank two or three cups of it."

"It is of no consolation at all. And the serving girl?"

"She is how we found out it only takes one drop."

***

The Lady of the Lake can feel her body winking in and out of focus.

Concentrating, she forces her transparent form to stabilize itself.

She quickly finds a chamber pot, throwing up in it.

Clutching her throbbing head, she looks around the room.

Morpheus lies motionless on the bed.

"Dead again," she mutters.

***

Queen Hester and Bellamy continue to watch the activities of Typhon's army in the valley.

"Is that music I hear?" Queen Hester asks.

"Bagpipes. I hate bagpipes."

"Perhaps Duke Ruthven's celebration is premature," a voice behind them says.

***

The Ruthvens and Mammons click their glasses together.

"To King Typhon Ruthven," Corson says. "Long live the King!"

As the men cheer, Willem looks up at the hill overlooking the valley.

"I think you need another plan, Typhon," he says.

The other men look up at the horizon.

Sir Morpheus is sitting on his horse, looking down at the celebrating army.

Fear whispered on the lips of uneasy soldiers, spreads throughout the camp.

Typhon's men drop their weapons and flee.

Sir Morpheus raises his sword, charging down the hill. A thousand vengeful soldiers follow him.

***

Bowing, Sir Morpheus enters the Queen's throne room. The Lady of the Lake glides in behind him.

"You sent for us, my Queen?"

With a wave of her tiny hand, Queen Hester dismisses her court. Only Bellamy remains by her side.

"Typhon Ruthven and his fellow traitors are hanging in the village square. He did have a final message he asked to be conveyed to the Lady of the Lake. He said, 'Zippy-do-dah, indeed.'"

Smiling, the Lady of the Lake says. "A personal gag between us, your majesty. Looks like the joke was on him."

"Well said, I think… Sir Morpheus, you rallied our men and saved the kingdom. Your actions are worthy of the greatest reward I can give. You asked me if I would release you and the Lady of the Lake from your vow. Do you still wish to be freed from our agreement?"

"Yes, Your Majesty."

"I am grateful for your friendship, guidance, and heroism. I free you and the Lady of the Lake from your obligation to the House of Astley."

***

Morpheus packs his belongings. Turning, he looks at the shimmering vision of The Lady of the Lake.

"You are free to return to the ether."

Despite her watery, transparent appearance, Morpheus can see she's crying.

"I'm staying with you."

"Why? Our duty to the House of Astley is finally over. The next time I die, you will not be able to bring me back."

"Then I'll die with you."

"But you are immortal."

"No. In fact, you and I are very much alike," she says. "I'm an exile sent from the twenty-fourth century."

Morpheus looks at her suspiciously. "It would explain the way you speak. Why were you sent here?"

"I dared to love a man. And in our time, that's against the law."

"Who was it?" he asked.

"You! And I still love you. Your real name is Adrian Archer. And I'm Anne Lockhart. I came up with the name Morpheus because you put your enemies to sleep…permanently."

The Lady of the Lake's transparent visage begins to solidify.

Their eyes lock. She moves toward him and kisses him.

"I thought you said we could never touch?"

"It was part of our punishment when we were sent here. You were banished first. Your memories of our life together were erased, so you wouldn't know who I was, and you'd never realize you have the same powers that I do. We were supposed to be separated, but I begged our supreme leader to be sent here with you. He agreed, but only if we never touched. I wanted to be with you, so I said yes, knowing if we touched, we would no longer be immortal."

He holds her close. "Now we'll both grow old and die."

"Yes, but we'll do it together."

"Yes, but we'll do it together."

Michael Jefferson

Michael Jefferson has been writing books, articles, short stories, and scripts since he was 12. His first novel, *Horndog: Forty Years of Losing at the Dating Game*, was published in 2017. He is also the author of more than forty short stories in virtually every genre. His scripts include "Hell in Little Heaven," a western, and "Foul Ground," a baseball treatment.

Plucked from the chorus to be a featured soloist at age 9, he successfully maneuvered through "They Call the Wind Maria." As a teenager and adult, he fronted a variety of acts that have toured the East Coast, including art rockers THC, The O'Donnell Gang, a 12-member classic rock outfit, Brass Monkey, a rock and blues quartet, Unzipped, a Ska and 80s influenced group, and R & B shouters Frankie Noire and the Blackhearts. For the past twenty years, he has been the lead singer for the Holy Innocents, making over 500 appearances with the band.

His second career as a singer led to his writing articles and reviews about numerous artists, including Traffic, Spooky Tooth, The Band, Tony Joe White, Jim Capaldi, and the Moody Blues. His extensive review of Spooky Tooth's "Lost in a Dream" CD is a permanent feature on Goldmine Magazine's website. He was the primary reviewer and writer for Coffeerooms.com for a decade, penning over 80 DVD and 120 CD reviews. He was a researcher and interviewer for "Rock Dreams," a documentary tracing the Yonkers rock scene and the emergence of Steven Tyler as the area's biggest star.

Among his many independent projects, he wrote an all-encompassing paper on the building, peacetime record, and ultimate destruction of the battlecruiser H.M.S. Hood, the pride of the British Navy. He was the managing and contributing editor for Con Edison's Bronx Division Magazine, writing as many as half a dozen articles per issue, and served as editor/writer for numerous not-for-profits, including the Will Rogers Institute, Hudson River Museum, and the Westchester Philharmonic.

A former amateur boxer, he was 11-0 with 11 knockouts. An avid softball player, he played leftfield for numerous teams for 35 years.

Unknown Caller
By Samuel George Tooma

"Mr. and Mrs. Pierce. Please have a seat."

"Thank you, Doctor." I helped my wife Lisa into a chair facing Dr. Wright's imposing desk.

When we were settled into our chairs, Lisa asked with a quiver in her voice. "Do you have the results of the two days of tests, Dr. Wright? It's been two weeks, and I haven't had a good night's sleep since."

"I understand, Mrs. Pierce. This must be very hard on you."

I saw Lisa lower her head until her chin hit her chest.

"Many of the tests have only recently been developed and are quite complicated, Mrs. Pierce. Especially the lab analyses, which must be run several times to be sure the results are consistent. Also, ..."

I interrupted, "That's all well and good, Dr. Wright. But what are the results? Where does my wife stand?"

He looked at us with a serious, somber expression on his face. Finally, he said, "I'm sorry. But the results are not what we had hoped."

Lisa looked up. "Then I do have ALS?"

"Yes and no, Mrs. Pierce. At first, I thought you might have Bulbar onset ALS. This is a very aggressive form of the disease. But what the tests have confirmed is that you have a very rare form of ALS. We don't even have an accepted name for it. It's being referred to as Bulbar onset ALS-X, or BOAX."

I asked, "What does that mean? What can we expect? What can we do?"

"I'm afraid that I don't have comforting answers to those questions."

We stared at the doctor as he sat there slowly shaking his head.

"Mrs. Pierce. I'm so sorry to be the bearer of this news. But I must tell you that from the very limited number of cases of BOAX diagnosed in the United States, once diagnosed, the survival time has always been under a year."

Lisa gasped.

In a croaked whisper, I asked. "There's no hope at all?"

Dr. Wright looked at me for at least ten seconds. "There is just one very small hope. Very small." He paused, then added, "And expensive."

"What is it...What is it?"

"I hesitate to say this because I'm not even sure the hope exists."

"What do you mean?"

"We have a very highly respected physician on our staff that specializes in treating the standard form of ALS. In fact, I have consulted him on your case. He recently heard about a drug trial in Brazil that might be successful in treating BOAX."

"Is the drug available here?" I asked, looking at Lisa hopefully.

"No, Mr. Pierce."

"Then why did you tell us if it we can't get the drug?"

"Dr. Rodriguez, the doctor I mentioned, told me that they are conducting an unsanctioned trial of this drug in Rio de Janeiro. They have recently diagnosed three cases of BOAX in Brazil. The experimental drug to be tested is extremely expensive, and it is unlikely that the Brazilians will allow any outsiders into the test trial. Also, chances of success are low, and I hate to say this, but possible death from the drug itself is high."

"I repeat, why did you tell us?"

Dr. Wright hesitated. "Dr. Rodriguez is from Rio, and he knows several of the doctors conducting the trial. He might be able to convince them to accept Mrs. Pierce into the trial."

"Have Dr. Rodriguez ask right away."

"We can ask, Mr. Pierce, but I must warn you, the Brazilians will probably refuse to accept any patients other than Brazilians."

"Why?"

"The drug is extremely expensive, about $500,000, and it could be fatal. The Brazilians may not accept the liability."

My jaw dropped. I looked at Lisa and her mouth was agape. We knew that we didn't have more than $10,000 in the bank. A half million was out of the question.

"What can we do, Doctor?"

"I honestly don't know. The trial is not sanctioned, so no reputable organization will put up that kind of money to support you. It will fall on you to come up with the money. But we can explore the possibility of them accepting Mrs. Pierce into the trial."

Later that day, I said, "Even if Dr. Rodriguez can get you accepted into the clinical trial program, how are we going to raise a half million dollars?"

"I don't know, Daniel. It seems hopeless."

"There must be some way we can raise the money. Bring it up to our church congregation?"

"Daniel, our church is small, and it is made up with ordinary people like us. Poor."

"Then what can we do?"

"I don't know...I just don't know."

I smiled. "Lisa, we can pray."

"That we can do, Daniel. Let's pray right now."

I sat next to Lisa on the couch, tenderly took her hand in mine, and we prayed.

Later, my cell phone chimed.

"Mr. Pierce? This is Dr. Wright. I have some news."

"Yes."

"Dr. Rodriguez called his contacts in Brazil. He told me that they will accept your wife into the trial if she signs a document releasing the Brazilians of any liability should the test fail. Dr. Rodriguez also said they would reduce the cost to $300,000 if he would come to Rio and help in conducting the trial."

"Dr. Wright. Unfortunately, $300,000 is still way above our means."

"That's unfortunate. Dr. Rodriguez also told me that the trial starts in four days. Mrs. Pierce must be in Brazil by tomorrow afternoon."

Crestfallen, I thanked him and ended the call. I hugged Lisa, and we began crying in one another's arms. As we hugged, my phone chimed again. I looked at the screen. 'Unknown Caller'.

"Hello?"

"Daniel. I suggest you look in your mailbox."

"Who is this?"

"Look in your mailbox now." She ended the call. I looked at Lisa with a puzzled look.

"A woman just told me to look in our mailbox."

"Who was it?"

"She didn't say, but she called me by my first name."

When I returned, I placed a cardboard box on the table.

"Who's it from, Daniel?"

"No clue. No address. It's just hand-written and addressed 'To: Mr. and Mrs. Pierce'. It wasn't mailed. Someone must have put it in our mailbox."

"Open it, Daniel."

I opened the box and took out two standard size business envelopes and another cardboard box. I opened one of the envelopes, and it contained a first-class airline ticket for Lisa Pierce to Rio de Janeiro, Brazil.

"What the hell!" I exclaimed.

Lisa took the ticket and stared at it with a puzzled look.

I opened the second envelope and took out another piece of paper. I studied it for a few seconds then dropped a cashier's check for $300,000 on the table.

Lisa picked up the check. "What's going on here?"

I opened the cardboard box with shaking hands. Inside were three stacks of one-hundred-dollar bills. I counted the bills in one of the stacks.

"Lisa, there is $30,000 here."

"Daniel, who has done this for us?"

"I have no idea. But what's bothering me more than anything is who knows about the details of our situation? Rio de Janeiro, the cost of the experimental trial, when the trial starts. We only found out about all this a few hours ago. And, what's the extra $30,000 for? Lisa, none of this makes sense. All this stuff is impossible."

She nodded in agreement and asked, "My reservation to Rio is tomorrow morning. Should I go?"

"Of course. We now have the money, and you have to be in Brazil tomorrow."

"The ticket is for me. Why not you too?"

"I don't know, Lisa. Like I said, none of this

makes sense."

My phone chimed. I looked at the screen, then to Lisa. "'Unknown Caller' again."

Lisa gasped.

"Hello."

"Hi, Daniel. This is your friend again."

"Who is this? What's your name?"

"I hope you like everything I sent you."

"How do you know about me and my wife?"

"Daniel, here is what I want you to do with the thirty thousand. Call Maximillian Brown Investors. Purchase thirty thousand dollars' worth of common shares of BioAI. Do this right after we end this call. Listen carefully. Two days from now, sell all your BioAI shares, first thing. You'll be happy. Daniel, be sure your wife is on the flight to Rio in the morning. She'll be fine. Trust me. Bye."

Before I could say another word, she ended the call.

* * *

As I drove home the next morning from the airport, I had mixed emotions. Everything had been beautifully arranged at the airport. Wheelchair assistance was waiting at curbside, and we were assured that a wheelchair would be ready for Lisa in Rio. Also, transportation would be there to take her to the hospital. Saying goodbye to Lisa was very difficult because her battle was our fight, and I felt that I should be with her during the difficult and dangerous trial. The kiss goodbye was very emotional. I had purchased the BioAI stock as my mysterious woman 'friend' had instructed. The financial advisor commented on the newness of the stock's availability and its low price per share. But he seemed pleased with the $30,000 purchase.

However, this whole experience had me greatly puzzled. Who was this woman benefactor and why was she doing this for us. It was impossible for anyone to know all the details of our needs. We had only known them for a few hours. Minutes, really. How would we pay her back? How could we ever thank her? Who could possibly gain from helping us? Then it hit me! Dr. Rodriguez! Fame and fortune could be his if the trial were a success. He and Dr. Wright were the only people that knew of the clinical trial, its cost, Brazil, and the need to get there by this afternoon. It must be Rodriguez and Wright.

I must confront them.

When I got home, my cell phone chimed.

Unknown caller.

"Hello."

The familiar voice of my female 'friend' said, "Everything went well at the airport, I see. Your wife should be in Rio in a few hours."

"Yes, everything was perfectly arranged. But tell me. Who are you and why are you doing this for us?"

"I'm glad to see that you purchased the BioAI stock. Remember to sell all your shares tomorrow morning. First thing."

"Again, I asked, "Who are you? What's your name?"

"Daniel, I'd like to meet with you."

"When? I want to see Lisa's doctors today, and I'm working tomorrow."

"How about tonight?"

"Who are you? Is there something you want from us?"

"How about eight o'clock at the Grape and Olive restaurant? Your favorite food is Greek."

"How do you know that? Who are you?"

"See you at eight. Dinner is on me. Bye."

I stared at the phone and thought, *who is she? How does she know I love Greek food and that the Grape and Olive is my favorite restaurant?*

* * *

With trepidation, I walked up to the maître 'd, a tall distinguished black man.

"Yes, Sir. How can I help you this evening?"

"I'm meeting a woman for dinner at eight o'clock. I don't know her name."

"Ah, yes. You must be Mr. Pierce. She's expecting you."

"Do you know her name?"

"No, Mr. Pierce. I do not. Please follow me."

As we approached an intimate table located in an alcove in the back of the restaurant, I was stunned. There sat the most incredibly beautiful woman I have ever seen. Ever!

"Daniel. It is so wonderful to meet you."

I tried to utter a reply, but only incoherent grunts came out of my mouth. I was absolutely speechless. She took my breath away.

The maître 'd said, "Enjoy your dinner, Mr. Pierce." He looked at the woman, looked at me, shook his head, and said with a smile, "I'm sure you will."

I sat opposite her and stared into her extraordinary dark brown eyes.

She smiled and said, "I hope you don't mind, but I took the liberty of ordering your favorite Greek wine, Vincento. Santorini's best. She signaled the sommelier to fill our glasses."

I finally got control of myself and said, "Vincento is my favorite wine, but I seldom get it because it's a little pricey."

"Well, I don't think cost will be an issue for you any longer. I'll see to that."

Then I asked for perhaps the eighth time, "Who are you?"

She looked at me and smiled.

Perfect smile. Perfect lips. Perfect teeth.

"Daniel, how would you like to be famous and fabulously wealthy?"

Perfect black hair. Perfect skin. Perfect breasts.

"Let me tell you, Daniel. The thirty thousand you invested in BioAI this morning is going to triple in value by the end of tonight. Then it's going to crash tomorrow. That's why you must dump all your shares tomorrow morning. Before the crash."

"How can you possibly know this?"

"Daniel, the ninety to hundred thousand you make on this stock market venture is only the tip of the iceberg. I can make you famous and rich beyond your wildest imagination."

"How? Why?"

"Let's enjoy our dinner. You can sleep on what I've said tonight and give me an answer tomorrow."

When we had finished our entrée and were waiting for our after-dinner coffee to be poured, I heard a familiar voice. "Hi, Daniel. Surprised to see you here. Where's Lisa, and who is your friend here?"

"Pastor Freud. Hi. Lisa is in Brazil undergoing some medical treatments. And this is uh…."

"Cherise. Nice to meet you, Pastor."

"Cherise. The pleasure is all mine."

I noticed that Freud was visibly shaking as he took her offered hand into his. He held her hand, for what seemed to me, longer than necessary. He finally broke his stare at her and released her hand. He half looked at me and said, "In Brazil? Medical treatments? I know she is having problems. I hope it is not serious."

He kept glancing at Cherise as he spoke to me.

"Hopefully, we'll know in a week or so."

"Good. Good. Well, I'd better get back to my table. Nice meeting you, Cherise. Hopefully, we'll bump into each other again."

"That would be nice."

As Pastor Freud walked away, he stubbed his foot on a nearby table chair.

I looked at Cherise who was smiling coyly. "Cherise, huh. Can I call you Cher?"

"I prefer Cherise."

"I finally have a name to call you. What's your last name?"

"Do you like Jim Freud as your Pastor?"

"Cherise, why don't you ever answer my questions?"

"Do you like him?"

I shook my head. "Yes, he's a nice guy. A good pastor."

"Would you be surprised if I told you he was a hypocrite?"

"Yes, I would. Why do you say that? And how do you know him?"

"He doesn't practice what he preaches. He's also a womanizer. In fact, he's having affairs with three women in your congregation right now. It was four women until four months ago. He found out the woman was having health problems, and he ended the affair."

"How do you know this? How do you even know his first name is Jim?"

She smiled.

When we finished our coffee, Cherise stood up, came over to me, and kissed me gently on the lips. I was shocked at this unexpected act.

"I'll call tomorrow. We need to talk."

She started to walk away. Then she turned and said, "By the way, Wright and Rodriguez told you the truth today. They don't have any ulterior motives concerning Lisa." She came back to me and kissed me again. She said, "Can't wait to see you tomorrow."

I was in a euphoric daze as I left the table. I decided to make a 'pit stop'. When I entered the men's room, I saw Pastor Freud drying his hands. Although I still did not trust what Cherise had told me about him, I did look at Freud in a different light. What he said next convinced me that she was right.

"Daniel, who is that woman you had dinner with? She is the most dazzling woman I have ever seen. Beautiful long, blonde hair, blue eyes, tall, long legs. Who is she?"

"Wait a minute, Jim. You said she was a tall blonde?"

"Yes, blonde. I'm not sure how tall she is, but her legs looked incredibly long. She has to be nearly six feet tall. She's perfect."

"Pastor, I know that you are married. I'm a little surprised at your reaction to this woman."

"Daniel, yes. I'm a pastor, and I'm married. But I'm also a man. I still notice women. Especially one that looks like that."

"I guess so. I'll see you in church on Sunday."

As I was leaving, the maître 'd wished me a good night. I turned to him and asked, "Sir, you saw the woman I had dinner with tonight. Can you describe her?"

"Why, of course, Mr. Pierce. And I must say she is beyond beautiful. She had light brown skin, lighter than mine. She was probably about five foot five, and her hair was black and tightly curled."

I stared at him trying to process what he had just told me.

I drove home in a very confused state. This night had not gone like anything I could have imagined.

Later, I tried to sort these crazy things out.

How did she know who Jim Freud was? That he was a hypocrite. A womanizer. Having relationships with multiple women at the same time. The reason Freud ended an affair four months ago. How did she know that I confronted Wright and Rodriguez? And they were not in a conspiracy concerning the clinical trials? And the most puzzling thing of all, was how could three men describe the same woman so differently? The woman I had dinner with most definitely had long brown hair and radiant brown eyes. Freud described a tall, blonde, and the maître 'd described a light-skinned black woman. All three of us thought that she was extremely beautiful. This is not possible. Why doesn't she answer my questions? Why did she kiss me? On the lips, even. Twice. And the second kiss was very passionate. I'm a happily married man to a woman who really needs me right now. Yet, I very much enjoyed the touch of her lips. I feel that I could fall in love with her. Can't let that happen. What are her plans for me? Rich? Famous? How? Why? Can I trust her?

How can she look so different to three different men?

* * *

"Hi, Daniel." Cherise said when I opened the door for her. She came in and immediately put her arm around my waist and kissed me. Although surprised, I did not resist. I hated myself for not turning away. She took my hand and led me to the kitchen.

"Sit down." She said, "I'll get us some wine."

She went over to a cabinet and took out two wine glasses. She opened the refrigerator, and took out a bottle of vincento red wine. How that bottle of vincento got in my refrigerator I do not know.

She opened the bottle and poured the wine into the glasses with a flourish and said, "To us. "She held up her glass. We clinked glasses and took a sip.

"Later this afternoon, your financial advisor will notify you that your thirty-thousand-dollar investment has turned into ninety-three thousand in just one day. How does that feel?"

"Great, but how is this possible?"

"That's nothing compared to how much you are going to make. Interested?"

"Yes, but how? What's in this for you?" If you know so much, why don't you just do it yourself?"

"Daniel, you ask too many questions."

"Why don't you answer them?"

"I've got big plans for you, Daniel. Important plans. And we need to start now."

Cherise stood up and came over to me. She

tousled my hair and moved her lips toward mine. Oh, how I wanted her lips to be pressed against mine. My heart began beating at a rapid rate.

At the last second, I pulled away. "I'm married Cherise. You know that."

She looked at me and smiled. "You are perfect for what I have for you to do."

I was relieved that she didn't push the intimacy issue. But, at the same time, I berated myself for not taking advantage of the situation. She was so desirable.

"Okay, Daniel. It's time that I tell you what we are going to do."

We sat down comfortably in the living room, and Cherise refilled our wine glasses.

"I told you that I was going to make you rich and famous. I'm going to help you do this far beyond your wildest dreams."

"How can y...."

"Let me talk, Daniel. Just listen."

The power in her voice severely frightened me. She stared at me, but this time I didn't see any beauty in her eyes. I saw power, control, and evil.

Cherise stared at me. I said nothing.

"In the next year, you are going to write a book that's going to skyrocket to the top of all the best seller lists. You will be invited to be a guest on all the late-night talk shows. They will be fighting to have you on their shows. Oprah Winfrey will dedicate an entire show to you. All the major TV networks and magazines will feature major stories about you. Your fame will quickly spread throughout the world. You will be invited to speak to huge audiences all over the world. Movie producers will be bidding to get you to agree for them to make movies and documentaries of you and your book. This is just the start. Do you follow me so far?"

"Cherise. How can I do this? I'm not an author. I'm terrible at public speaking."

"I will tell you what to write. I will be speaking for you."

"If you are writing the words and speaking for me, why don't you do it yourself?"

Cherise just stared at me with an icy, demeaning look.

"What's this famous book going to be about?"

"The purpose and meaning of life."

"What! This doesn't make any sense."

"Your book will open the eyes of everyone who reads it."

"I can't imagine how I could possibly write that."

"Daniel. You don't have to know anything. I'll do everything. Haven't you been listening?"

I couldn't answer her.

"Here's where we go next. You will become the most sought after and trusted man in the world. You will be extremely wealthy, but you will also be the most generous philanthropist the world has ever seen. You will be loved by everyone. In the second year, you will write the penultimate book."

Cherise's eyes widened, her nostrils flared, and she said, "Your second book will turn the world upside down."

The wild expression on her face was frightening. I was too scared to ask the obvious question. She answered it for me.

"Your second book will renounce God. It will debunk the Bible, show that Jesus never became more than a poor carpenter, that the crucifixion is just fiction, and that His resurrection was a hoax."

I stood up and turned my back to her. I said, "You are crazy. I'll never do that."

I turned around quickly to confront her, and what I saw for just a fraction of a second terrified me to my very core. I did not see the beautiful woman I fantasized making love to. What I saw was a hideous beast with leathery reptilian skin. It had fiery red eyes and stood about seven feet tall. It wore no clothing, and there were many horrible bone-like protrusions sticking out from its body. It was more terrifying than anything I could have imagined. Then, in a blink of an eye, Cherise was once again standing in front of me.

"Daniel, Daniel. Calm down. Think about what I've promised you. And to sweeten the whole thing. You can have me."

Cherise looked like Cherise, but I didn't see her as beautiful anymore. In fact, I feared her more than anything I had ever feared. She was a demon. Perhaps even Satan himself.

Got to think this out. Don't challenge her. She can probably kill me right here. Right now. Think. Think.

"Okay, Cherise. Say I agree to this crazy scheme of yours. Will you finally agree to answer some questions I have?"

"Try me."

"Who will believe this crazy idea?"

"The humans in this world are so gullible. They are easily influenced by movie and sports stars and the rich and famous, which you will be. You will be the most famous and believable person in the world. People will listen to you, doubt their faith, and turn away from God. You'll see."

She reached out to take my hand. I pulled my hand away. "That's the other thing, Cherise. I'm a happily married man. My wife is fighting for her life. I want to be at her side."

"That's very admirable, Daniel. But I hate to say this. If you don't agree to do this, your wife, Lisa, isn't going to survive the clinical trials."

I gasped in horror. *That monster just threatened me. Can she do this? Kill Lisa? Kill me if I refuse? She referred to people as humans. Think. Need time to think. Got to get out of this horrible situation. But how? Stall her. Buy time.*

"Okay, Cherise. You've made your point. But this whole thing goes against everything I stand for. I'm a believing Christian. This is not an easy decision for me. Can I think this out and let you know tomorrow?"

"Tomorrow morning, Daniel. You've got until then. But tell me. You don't really believe all that Christian nonsense, do you? The Son of God? Virgin birth? Dying on the cross to pay the ransom for your sins? Rising from the dead? Come on, Daniel. You are an intelligent man. You can't believe all that rubbish. It's all made up to make you feel better about dying. A crutch. Let's do what I say and have some fun together. Real fun. I'll be back in the morning. We'll get started then."

Good. Got until tomorrow to pray and think.

When we reached the door, she tried to kiss me. I turned my head, and her kiss fell on my cheek. I thought of the hideous monster I had seen, and I felt nauseous.

As soon as I closed the door, I fell on my knees. *Was she really a demonic monster from hell? Had I imagined what I saw?*

My question was answered when I looked out the door's sidelight. She should have been walking from the porch to her car. But there was no one there. She and her car had disappeared.

I prayed for guidance and help for nearly an hour.

No doubt. She's Satan or one of his demons. More powerful than me. Can't fight her alone. She can do things. Make things happen. Can she kill me? Lisa? This is spiritual warfare. I need divine help or I'm dead.

I wish I had paid more attention in my Bible studies. But I do know that Jesus quoted Scripture when He confronted the devil in the wilderness. Also, the apostle Paul wrote about spiritual warfare and how to deal with it. He said, with the full armor of God, I can withstand the devil. With the sword of the Holy Spirit, which is the Word of God, I can defeat him.

The apostle James said, submit yourself to God. Resist Satan, and he will flee.

"Yes!" I now had a plan. *Please God, let it work.*

* * *

When the doorbell rang the next morning, my heart started racing in terror. I knew that this could be the last hour of my life. I opened the door and Cherise came in smiling.

"Hi, Sweetheart. Ready to get down to business?"

"I believe so, Cherise. I've been thinking very hard on what you promised me. Before I say 'yes', I have one question to ask you, and you've got to promise me right now that you will answer me. Agreed?"

"Sure."

"First, I need to show you something."

I turned and walked toward the desk. Cherise followed me.

Stay calm. Voice stay strong. Lord, be with me.

With my back toward her, I asked, "When you said that I could have you, did you mean sexually?"

"I most certainly did. We'll devour each other."

I removed the sheet of paper covering my Bible,

grabbed it firmly, spun around quickly, and threw the Bible right at the monster from hell that was facing me.

"Well devour this shithead."

The demon did not have time to react, and the Bible hit it in the chest. It screamed hideously as the Bible struck. Flashes of searing flames shot out of its chest. Acrid smoke filled the room. There was a loud crackling noise followed by an explosion. The demon blew apart into a million pieces, then it was gone. Ashes floated in the air, and the room reeked of rotten eggs. I stood alone in the room. My Bible was on the floor unscathed. I noticed that it lay open, and I picked it up. It was open at John 10 verses 27-29. The verses glowing visibly. 'No one can snatch those that believe out of God's hand. No one is stronger than Him'.

Despite these comforting verses in John, I still feared that Cherise or another demon would seek retribution and kill me and Lisa.

Two days later, my phone chimed.

Dr. Wright.

"Hello, Dr. Wright."

"Hello, Mr. Pierce. Dr. Rodriguez just called me from Rio. He gave me wonderful news."

Samuel George Tooma

Samuel Tooma worked for the US Department of Defense as a civilian physical oceanographer for over 36 years. He worked on submarines, navy, coast guard, and civilian ships, and navy aircraft, and spent time in scientific camps on the Arctic Ocean ice pack. Mr. Tooma spent 2 years as the Environmental Science Advisor to the Commander of the Submarine Forces in the Pacific, after which he was awarded the Meritorious Civilian Service medal. During his professional career, he published 6 scientific papers in peer reviewed journals. His primary scientific areas of study include the Arctic Ocean environment, seafloor properties, and the use of aircraft and satellite mounted sensors to determine environmental properties of interest. All these studies were applied to the environmental impact on navy systems and operations. In 2021, Mr. Tooma published a fiction novel entitled "The SOOF", and in 2023, he published a sequel entitled "Assassin's Revenge". Both these novels have won literary awards in competitions. In 2023, Mr. Tooma entered a short story entitled" Eden's Rain" into a best writing contest. This story won first place and was published in an anthology entitled "Finding the Good Through the Rain published by Indignor House Publishing. His professional website is www.samuelgtooma.com.

Just This Once?
By Brian Kelly

The "Welshies" - first came the Welshies. Back to Belfast in the summer of 1967, when I was eight. Our family had lived in Swansea for three years due to my dad's job. In truth I was the only 'Welshie', having gone to primary school in Swansea for those three years. My parents still spoke in broad Belfast tones while my one-year-old sister gurgled indecipherably in possibly many languages or none. We'd moved back to live temporarily with my maternal grandparents in working class South Belfast. I knew things would be different – just not that I would be different. But then there's the different, and there's different …

My accent, with its rounded vowels and sing-song lilt was a source of great amusement to extended family members and their friends. Saturday evenings saw a crowd of these descend on my grandparents' terraced house, some to savour my granny's home-made soup and some of the men to appease their wives. These men would have spent the afternoon at a home game of the local football team (nobody called it 'soccer'), Linfield. In practice most of them would have been more ardent supporters of Guinness, having spent most of their time in the stadium bar...before, during, and after the match. While waiting for their turn to be served soup they would dangle sixpence pieces in front of me.

"Go on, son. Pretend you're cheering on Linfield. Say, 'Come on the Blues!'"

"Come on the Blows!"

"Again!"

"Come on the Blows!"

"Ha, ha! Brilliant! Here you go – here's a tanner for you!"

That really was the extent of the teasing I faced that summer but by the beginning of September it was time to start my new school.

"You'll be fine son," said Mum. "Sure, your cousin Joey is three years above you and he'll keep an eye out."

She said this while walking me round to Joey's house which was at the top of the next street to ours. The school was at the bottom of that street. A tall, square Victorian building, so unlike my modern school in Swansea.

*****

"Don't even think about looking for me! Not in my classroom. Not in the playground. Not on the way home from school. Unless your head is hanging off. On both sides. I'm taking you in today...and that's it. Once. Just this once."

"But can you tell me ...?"

"Oh, for God's sake! Put away that gurning puppy face! All right. Three questions. Just this once."

"What floor are the toilets on?"

"Floor? Floor? You're a scream. The toilets are the floor. Well, there's a bit of a drain. Look, over there - to the left."

"But there's no roof on that building?"

"That's right. They're all-weather toilets, so you don't hang about. Next question …"

"Where's the refectory?"

"What do you mean - refectory? Some sort of religious thing? We're all Presbyterians - no Papish stuff here. Why do you speak like that anyway? It's like you're singing. Like my Ma in the bath. Only better."

"No, refectory. Like the canteen."

"There's no canteen. Everybody goes home to their Ma's or Granny's at lunchtime. Didn't they tell you that?"

"Maybe. I find people here hard to make out."

"Right. I'm off for football with my mates."

"I've a third question to use up."

"Hurry up!"

"Where does my class play football?"

"You don't. We've the main yard, then the next two years have the side yards. You and your class just have to wait and get bigger."

Bang! Or was it thwack? Or whack? All I knew was that a stray football hit me flush in the face - an errant shot from one of Joey's class. I didn't fall, but my face froze - as if attacked by a mob of manic dentists...from my mouth to my nose, across my cheeks, into my ears and up to my forehead.

"Bloody hell! Why didn't you duck? Or swerve? Instead of standing there like an eeejit! And whose idea was it to put a white shirt on you? There's blood everywhere. They'll blame me you idiot."

He used the cuffs of his jumper to try and stem the blood. At least it was a red jumper.

"Is my head hanging off?"

"Not yet, not yet."

*****

"This is Brian. A new boy. It's his first day at our school."

That was Miss Henderson. She looked younger than my mum, so I guessed she was in her twenties. She wore what was almost a mini skirt, a plain blouse, and kept her long fair hair tied back in an Alice band.

"… was at school for three years in Swansea, that's in Wales."

"Ah - the Welshie. I heard about him," barked a big boy called Billy.

"I heard he talks funny!" scoffed an almost as big a boy called Tommy.

"Sshh … Now class - say hello to Brian."

The response was a disinterested mix of grunts and mumbles.

"Now Brian - you say 'Hello class!'"

"Hell -Oh -Oh class."

"Oh-oh! Posh boy. Sounds like the Duke of

Edinburgh."

"Billy, stop that! Now you say 'hello' back properly."

"We don't say hello in our street Miss," said Billy. "We say 'Bout ye!' or 'What about ye?'"

"Yes, well, we'll move on. Now Brian, have you done anything nice since you moved back to Belfast."

"I've been to see the Blows."

"The blows?"

"Yes Miss. Linfield. The blows."

With all the grace of inebriated synchronised swimmers the class cackled, banged their desks, punched each other on the arms. I wilted in my chair. The classroom clock showed it wasn't even 9.00 am.

*****

At lunchtime I ran all the way back to my granny's. Even though it was a short distance it seemed like a marathon.

"How was school?" shouted Mum from down the hall.

"I hate it! I don't ever want to go back!"

"It's only your first day, it's bound to be … Oh my God! Mummy - come and see this! Who did that to your nose?"

"Nobody."

"Don't you go defending any bullies. Tell me the truth," said Mum.

"Yes, son - tell us. I'll know his family," said Granny.

"Nobody did it."

"They must have," said Mum.

"Well, yes. But not on purpose. It was a ball - you can ask Joey."

After Granny's minced steak, carrots and onions, made in her pressure cooker which often had the temperament of an angry wasp, all to soon it was time to head back to school.

"I don't want to go."

"It'll be better this afternoon," said Mum.

"They make fun of the way I talk."

"Remember," said Granny. "Sticks and stones may break my bones, but names will never hurt me."

"Yeah – but you don't get called names. Anyway, I'm sick."

"What's wrong with you?" asked Mum.

"My nose. It still hurts and it's all blocked up."

"It's something and nothing. Now away you go!" said Granny.

*****

"Miss, miss!"

"Yes Tommy?"

"My Uncle Ernie was in our house at lunchtime. He says they're not 'Welshies', they're 'Taffies.'"

"Ha, ha! 'Taffies!' Or is it 'Toffees'?" shouted Billy.

There was more desk banging and shouting, accompanied this time by the throwing of used bubblegum and the launch of paper planes across the room.

"Calm down everyone. It's not 'Toffees.' It's

'Taffy' or 'Taffies.' The nickname comes from the River Taff which runs through Cardiff, the capital of Wales."

"Imagine being called after a river!" laughed Tommy.

"No more smart comments class. Brian, can you tell us something that was different in your old school?"

"It was newer Miss."

"Ok. What about something a little more different?"

"We walked into class holding hands, Miss. Boys holding hands with girls."

"Weirdos! Holding hands with girls!" barked Billy,

"Yuk! Touching boys!" screamed a pretty girl called Frances.

However, the uproar became more muted. The class quietened down. Curious looks were exchanged. Young minds wandering. And wondering. Musing at the maybe.

Miss Henderson tried to take advantage of this relative calm, pushing further.

"Brian, any other differences you'd like to share?"

"On the first of March, St David's Day, we all wear a flower on our jumpers."

"A flower? Bet it was a pansy!" roared Billy.

"Ha, ha! Flower power Welshie!"

"Stop that, Jimmy!"

"Oh yes, sorry Miss. I meant flower power Taffy."

"Was it a daffodil Brian?" asked Miss Henderson.

"Yes, Miss."

And I longed for that school and even the daffodil.

*****

Everyone seemed related in Belfast...more so than in Wales it seemed. The closeness of the community here and the relative lack of travel meant there were connections everywhere. Uncles, Aunts and cousins I had known about, but a whole new population emerged of more distant relatives, second cousins, first cousins once removed, first cousins twice removed. I struggled to keep up. Some were regarded less fondly than others.

"Don't be talking to them. Never mind first cousins once removed...more like first cousins well removed!"

"Have nothing to do with those ones living over the bridge! I lent that Sammy a bike 20 years ago and it still hasn't come back."

It turned out Joey wasn't a first cousin after all, but one of the more tenuous types. In fairness he did intervene a few times in the early days when I was getting picked on in the playground. A shove, or even a look, was enough to get my tormentors to back off. Gradually I made some friends in my class. Not the big boys who still scared me. Not the "squirts", as Joey called them, the odder-looking boys who always got top marks in class tests and presented Miss Henderson with homework she hadn't asked for. I made friends with, I suppose, the more ordinary, less visible types. Making friends with girls was never considered, although there were two girls in my class, Frances and Donna, whom I thought were really pretty, like something from a washing-up liquid TV commercial. However, it turned out they were both distant cousins of some sort, so I doubted that I'd ever get to marry either of them.

*****

My new gang introduced me to street games, the norm in this part of Belfast, whereas in Wales we'd played in back gardens and parks. The back yards of houses here were small, cobbled stone or paved areas, but the back entries or alleys were used as makeshift football pitches. The streets themselves offered good spaces for games as cars were rare in Belfast in the mid-60s.

The most popular street game was "kribbie", which consisted of throwing a football aimed at the opposing kerb so that the ball bounced back into your arms. A successful catch allowed you to move halfway across the street for the next throw, and a further successful effort enabled progression to the other side.

I was spectacularly rubbish. My norms, rather than hitting that sweet spot between kerb and road, were to lob the ball into a neighbour's front passage or startle a bemused passing cat.

"You stupid wee Taffy! The ball's gone into Bilko Benson's. He always takes our balls and bursts them with a big nail."

(Bilko Benson looked like Sergeant Bilko the American TV character but never exhibited any of the humour).

"I'll go and fetch the ball."

"Of course, you will," said Jimmy, the leader of our gang.

"When it gets dark?" I pleaded.

"Now!"

Bilko Benson's front gate creaked and groaned as I pushed it open. I heard husky coughs from inside the house as I crawled on my hands and knees along his front garden, an unruly mess of grass, nettles and rhubarb leaves. I spotted a ball, but it, like my spirits, was sadly deflated. A second ball was in a similar state. I heard the coughs becoming louder and a fiddling of the front door handle. I grabbed the next ball, which was gloriously plump, and scampered out of the garden towards my mates who were cowering behind the nearest street corner.

"You got the ball."

"He got the ball."

"I got the ball...here's the ball."

"You got the ball. Wait...it's the wrong ball!"

"I'm not going back there!"

"You won't have to...it's a better ball."

*****

It was another Saturday evening at my grandparents' house, filled, as ever with uncles, aunts and cousins. Landing in after the football match were some of my uncles' mates, red and ruddy from their match-time Guinness. Before long one of them resorted to the tiresome ritual.

"Kid! Say, 'Come on the Blues!'"

"Come on the Blews …"

That's rubbish – it's nearly right! No sixpence tonight.

*****

Another game I was introduced to was 'Hide and Seek'. The starting point was an area behind some sheds and warehouses a few streets from school.

"Have you played this before?" asked Jimmy.

"No. My mum said I might get lost."

"Never mind, you're on it."

"On it?"

"Yes, we hide, and you find us. Cover your eyes, count to a thousand, then come and get us. We'll make it easy since it's your first time. But no peeking!"

I covered my eyes and started counting. "1,2,3,4,5…"

It was getting darker, and the sheds and warehouses were giving up strange sounds.

"301, 302, 303, 304, 305."

It was now becoming windier, and the unknown noises were getting louder. I clenched my eyes even tighter.

"535, 536, 537, 538, 539 …"

"What the hell are you doing?"

I opened my eyes. It was Jimmy, with the other boys behind him.

"I'm counting."

"Why are you still counting?"

"You said count to a thousand. I've only reached, em, five hundred and forty, em, fifty-seven."

"Are you for real? That's not how you count in 'Hide and Seek.' You go 5,10,15,20 – and so on!"

"Oh, I see. I'm sorry. Can we start again?"

"Nah, it's too late now. My tea will be ready," said Jimmy.

"Mine too," said Sammy.

"Do you think they have any fun in Wales?" mumbled Jimmy.

*****

"This is Ajibola. A new boy. This is his first day at our school."

She'd welcomed me similarly on my first day, but everyone knew it was my first day, just as we all knew this was Ajibola's first day. He was a dark-skinned boy; the rest of the class was all white; about my height but with a wirier physique.

Miss Henderson continued her welcome speech, however, unlike my introduction, her voice was stuttering; strained; nervy.

The class was different also. There were no paper planes whizzing around the classroom. No slamming of desks. No ear lobes being flicked by the classmate behind. Instead, there was, simply, silence.

Miss Henderson seemed relieved to end her monologue, pulling down the large map of the world in front of the blackboard. And it was "blackboard" back then, not "chalkboard", not "whiteboard." Using the long wooden window opener as a pointer, Miss Henderson directed the hook end towards Africa.

"This is Ajibola. Ajibola is from Nigeria."

Ajibola stood rigidly, albeit his head was slightly bowed, facing the class yet shunning any eye contact. Miss Henderson ushered him to the only spare seat and desk, at the front of the classroom, beside me. I was reminded of my first day and the sheer relief of being able to face forward. This time I looked over my shoulder, seeing faces that stared and stared, and some that stared and glared.

I nodded to Ajibola, and offered a mild smile...I didn't want to appear over-friendly. After all, he was my likely escape route from the teasing and taunting which I had endured over the past two months. My Welsh accent, albeit diluting by the day, would probably be of little interest compared to whatever foreign one he may have. I realised that Miss Henderson had forgotten, or perhaps avoided, asking him to introduce himself to the class.

*****

That had been a Friday. The following evening Granny's house was more crowded than ever. The biggest loudmouth, he of the sixpences, and his cronies were congregated in the front hallway.

"I see some darkies moved into the next street," bellowed the loud one.

"He's a doctor, I heard," said another

"He wouldn't be touching me! "retorted the boorish one. "I've seen him, he's not just black, he's navy blue!"

I made sure I stayed away from him and his rotten sixpences for the rest of the night.

*****

One Monday morning, as with every school day, breaktimes were staggered by class. Five minutes to drink the one third of a pint bottle of unrefrigerated milk – at best lukewarm, sometimes sour – then five minutes to go outside to the damp, dank toilet block. Most days I tried to hold everything in until lunchtime at Granny's, but on this day, I really needed to go. Usually, the big boys in the class made sure they got to use the toilets first, but this time they held back, only joining the queue after Ajibola had entered, just ahead of me.

"Do you think his Charlie, his wee man, will be the same colour as the rest of him?"

"Dunno, it might be whiter if it's out of the sun."

"We'll soon find out."

Four big boys grabbed Ajibola, tugging his shorts down as he fought and flailed to no avail.

"It's the same."

"It's whiter."

"It's blacker."

"He's pissed on me."

The bullies ran out of the toilets laughing and roaring. Any other boys there ran out too, leaving Ajibola and me. He was crying and frantically trying to adjust his clothing to hide the damp patch on the front of his shorts. I didn't say anything...I didn't know what to say. I reached into my pocket and gave him one of my Granda's white Irish linen handkerchiefs. I didn't know if I'd given it to him to dab his eyes or his pants, so I brushed past him, not wanting to witness any more.

*****

Then came the fights, the scheduled daily fights. There had been the occasional fights since I'd come to the school, always thin on premise. A stolen piece of bubblegum; a wrong look; a joke turned into an insult. The fights were held in one of the narrow entries close to the school. There were only two rules...the fight was to be stopped if somebody was bleeding badly, or if one of the participants gave up.

The fights with Ajibola were different...staged after school for Monday, Wednesday and Friday of each week. The big boys in the class chose his opponents, starting with themselves then working down a hierarchy towards those presumed puny.

Ajibola never gave up...so it was his bleeding which finished each fight. Even on his 'rest days' of Tuesday and Thursday his nose was a crimson smudge, dripping intermittently. Nobody intervened. Not those of us who attended each fight out of a strange sense of fascination; not our teachers, who never enquired as to his injuries, feigning ignorance and perfecting indifference; not his family, or so it seemed, their only visible action being to extend and fortify the broken glass turrets of their back-yard walls.

Then, on a Wednesday afternoon, it was my turn.

"Don't ye be letting the side down, we've all beaten him so far," boomed Billy.

"Do I have to fight?"

"What? You chickening out?"

"No. But there's been loads of fights, what's the point?"

"The point...the point is that he knows."

"Knows what? "

"Just that he knows."

Billy, as the biggest boy in the class was always the referee, even for his own fight. Oh, and I said there were only two rules...but he added three more, despite having ignored them in his fight with Ajibola. No elbows; no biting; no pulling hair.

Ajibola adopted a Queensberry Rules bared knuckled stance, arms thrust forward, fists clenched. I followed suit.

"Go on! Throw a punch."

"Get closer, you'll never hit him from there!"

"Stop dancing like Cassius Clay!"

"He's Muhammad Ali now."

"Who?"

"Clay."

"Nah. They're twins, my Da said so."

"Hit him! Not thin air."

There were no comments, supportive or derogatory, aimed at Ajibola.

I threw what I now know is referred to as a "haymaker" punch which Ajibola ducked easily as my right fist continued its trajectory, succeeding in clipping my own left cheek and ear.

"For God's sake my dinner's going to be ruined at this rate!"

"Get him to the ground and grapple."

"What's grapple?"

"Same as wrestle. Only you hug tighter."

I tried another flailing punch, missing of course, then lost my balance and fell to the ground. Ajibola pounced on top of me, and we twisted and turned, rolled and rumbled. I knew instantly that he was stronger than me as bodies interlocked. I'd never been as close to someone since being a baby. It seemed as if we were taking turns as to who was on top, but I was realizing that anytime I was on top it was only because he was letting me.

The spectators were getting even more restless.

"Do something!"

"Hit him! Don't kiss him!"

"You're not trying to make a baby!"

Then came a soft breathy whispering in my ear.

"Win, win. Please let me lose."

"Why?"

"Maybe they'll get bored and stop doing this.

Please help me."

This was the longest conversation I'd had with Ajibola despite us being school desk next-door neighbours for weeks. He loosened his grip; his body went limp. When he dropped his arms, I sat astride him and hit him in the face with my left elbow. Hard, then harder. Again, and again. His nose capitulated in time with his resolve.

"He's bleeding like a fountain, so the wee lad's won."

"But your man used his elbow, so he should be disqualified."

"Who's won then?"

"I'm the referee and my decision is, my decision is...a draw."

*****

At least that was the last fight they forced upon Ajibola. Maybe they'd got bored; maybe they thought his splattered face had put him in his place. However, there was no let up on tales of attacks, presumably by adults, on his family home. House windows broken; trash turfed into the front yard; excrement pushed through the letter box.

One Saturday, ahead of a Linfield home game, my grandfather and I called round at his brother's house, where Joey and his family lived also. This house was almost opposite Ajibola's. His father was on his knees, replacing what seemed to be a burst tyre on his car. Cars were rare at that time, perhaps ten cars parked in a street of about two hundred houses. An open top lorry trundled down the street, pulling up behind the car. The driver alighted his cab, barely acknowledged Ajibola's father, sat down on a low wall and started rolling cigarettes.

Ajibola and his father started loading the lorry with furniture and what were called "white goods", washing machine, tumble dryer, fridge. The mother did what she could to help, while managing the younger children who watched in complete confusion. The lorry driver stood up, fetched a bottle of brown lemonade from his cab. He downed several slugs, belched belligerently, then took his seat again.

Ajibola and his father failed time and again to load the lorry uniformly and safely. A sofa or chair would fall off as they tried to tie their belongings down with thick rope. Next time it was a dressing table which bounced off the truck, its mirror smashing on the pavement. Ajibola's mother burrowed among the stack of their belongings, retrieving a dustpan and brush, trying to clear up the mess. All the while the front passages of every house became filled with people watching in silence, as if choreographed and planned.

On the next attempt a wardrobe fell off, smashing two table lamps as it did so. One of the wardrobe doors detached itself, hitting the father on the head.

I nudged my cousin.

"Joey?"

"What?"

"Just this once?"

"Aye. This once – and any other flippin' once! The poor critters."

He grabbed my arm and we ran across the street …

Brian Kelly

Brian Kelly, aged 65, lives in Belfast, Northern Ireland, having returned to his home city after 32 years in the rural idyll of Teconnaught, County Down. While missing the camaraderie, televised horse racing and cheap pints of Clonmel in McMullan's bar, he is revelling in the new-found novelty of coffee shops, restaurants and arterial bus routes.

He has been married to Maria for 38 years, with 2 daughters, Alex (the Golden Child) and Catherine (the Platinum Child) - their phraseology, not his! His new best mate however is 9-month-old grandson Oliver, born to Alex.

He has returned to writing after 32 years working in the UK National Health Service and Queen's University Belfast as an IT Director and Corporate Project Manager. Brian has been fortunate to have been published since picking up his fountain pen and mastering two-fingered typing, with short story, poetry and non-fiction competitions submissions accepted in the UK, USA and Australia.

Night Song
By Jacqueline Bassan

Winter, 1979

I sat still, sheltering in place as the catchy chorus of the disco hit "Turn the Beat Around" rang out from the ceiling speakers, urging me to dance. Only this wasn't a disco. This was a nurses station, a rectangular archipelago where staff huddled to dole out care 24/7. Overhead fluorescents, not a sparkly disco mirror ball lit stacks of patient charts I had just piled neatly on metal trays. Steps away were some very sick kids.

I was a third-year medical student, eager to pursue my MD and work my way from gross anatomy (cadaver lab) to live patients. I looked past the glass-faced wall clock out the corner window at the silver December sky. Twilight time on the pediatric ward, and I was scared.

"It's quiet here now," said the cool and calm ward nurse with a wry smile. "We discharged a bunch of patients last night. We're down to three." She had an auburn perm, light freckles and a winter tan. Nerves of a pilot. A shiny diamond engagement ring. Her white teeth set off her starchy white jacket and skirt. I wore the same medical garb sans the ring. I was twenty-four and single. Noticing details of her appearance shielded me for a second or two.

The nurse swiveled her chair and pursed her lips

as she glanced at the lonely corridor that ran perpendicular from the station. "Any patients down the hall?" I asked.

The intern on call entered the station, chart in hand and answered my question.

"Yes. Her name's Aurora. Fifteen. She has a tumor in her belly the size of a grapefruit."

My heart sank. I'm not sure what I expected these patients to have. Kid's stuff? I'd been accepted to a med school affiliated with an emerging teaching hospital. The doctors who taught my classes had discovered cures or were still searching for them. A high bar was set. I picked up the hardcover *Nelson Pediatrics* off the desk and turned to "tumor, abdominal" in the index.

When I first saw Disney's *Sleeping Beauty*, I learned Princess Aurora's name meant dawn. I loved both names, Aurora and Dawn even before I heard "Dawn" the gorgeous Four Seasons record. Dawn was daybreak. Rebirth. Radiant colors. Frankie Valli's high notes, Bob Gaudio's brisk baritone, Buddy Saltzman's glittering drum rolls live up to the glory.

The elevator door whooshed open and a tech rolled out the portable ultrasound machine. I watched the creaking wheels stop outside her room just as the intern darted out of the stairwell. The intern emerged from Aurora's room a minute later. He swung his stethoscope casually around his neck, sidesaddle. As he approached, I closed the textbook.

I was on my own.

"An ultrasound measures the tumor," he said, as he looked straight at me. "The x-ray?"

"An x-ray could manifest dislodged ribs, depending on the tumor size," I answered. The intern nodded, made a checkmark on his clipboard. I was being graded, lest I forgot.

There was no NPO sign outside Aurora's door. No "Nothing by Mouth" alert pre-op. I hadn't seen a surgeon in spearmint scrubs zip by and scribble in Aurora's chart after marking incision borders on her belly with a Sharpie. I never heard the ping of monitors come from her direction. Good news. She was stable, unplugged, set to go home, or surgery was postponed a day.

"Ready to draw blood from 503? Just aim!" said the chief resident as he tossed his ballpoint javelin-style into the pencil holder. "Grab Lilah's chart." He appeared out of thin air. Did he seep through the drywall? I wasn't ready.

Can I practice on you? Second year of med school, we learned to use our stethoscopes by listening to each other's chests. Breasts were seen, chest hair was exposed. I didn't volunteer. Now in my third year, I knew this resident was a rising star and his demands got inflated on the climb. How could he expect me to perform my first blood draw on a child? "No veins" applied here. "Scut work" — venipunctures, starting IVs — were not my forte.

As I lifted 503's chart off the desk, I saw that

Aurora, in 510, had a visitor in the hall. A middle-aged male; I figured he was her father. He paced the corridor in his own world.

I wondered what I'd gotten myself into. History major, music minor. For fun I'd slip on a leotard and an LP and move to Leonard Bernstein's surging climax in *The Nutcracker's* "Waltz of the Flowers" where ballerinas speed up to allegro. I would dive into songs heart first, basking in their differing glows—the soul-searing "Love Hurts" by Nazareth vs. the Everly Brothers dreamy take on the same. Laura Nyro's clarion vocals on her own "Eli's Comin'" vs. Three Dog Night's scorcher. I started to write my own melodies on the piano. I was artsy not sciency. Yet I was drawn to the why's and how's of disease, wanting to make that proverbial difference.

"Lilah is seven. Type I diabetic. Admitted for ketoacidosis. Treatment?"

"Fluid replacement and electrolytes," was my response to the resident's grilling. "And insulin."

"Give her a bolus, per IV," he said to the nurse, who knew as much as he did. Just different titles.

We entered her room. Lilah was lying flat in her hospital bed. She looked tinier than her seven years. Fear flashed in her turquoise eyes. Her skin was beyond pale. See-through. We made eye contact. She sized me up. Finding veins was an art and I was no Picasso. They move, disappear. Kids flinch. I felt ashamed. Lilah needed help. I didn't want to do multiple sticks with the needle. The ethos of medical school was: Watch one. Do one. Teach one. I needed more time.

We weren't supposed to get emotionally attached to patients but when I looked at Lilah's face I melted. My grandma had been diabetic. I held the needle and tourniquet in my hand. My eyes became misty. I hoped she didn't see. I needed an infusion of the nurse's grit.

I returned to the station mission unaccomplished, as I informed staff. I felt a light tap on my shoulder. The girl with cystic fibrosis. Wearing a colorful hospital gown adorned with kittens and puppies. Her long brown hair tousled, uncombed. She wheezed like the whistle of a runaway train. She pulled her IV pole along as if it was a red Radio Flyer toy wagon.

"Hi, I'm Wendy. What's your name?" She came right up to me eye level, as I was sitting.

The nurse interjected. "This is our student doctor. She's here to learn."

"You want to be a doctor? How come?"

Wendy clearly liked to schmooze. And I was totally up for it.

"We have to drain her chest five times a day. You can watch the pulmonary nurse," added the nurse, glancing at her wristwatch. I was surprised the nurse said this in front of Wendy, but the little one took it in stride. Ward stories, or at least outcomes, were an open book.

She took Wendy's hand and walked her to her

room. When they were out of earshot, I asked the intern how she was. Would she grow, would she thrive? Breathe?

"We keep her going. She checks in every few weeks. But long term--" He gave a thumbs down.

"But by then there could be a cure, no?" I sounded like Rodgers and Hammerstein's "cockeyed optimist" Nurse Nellie from the musical *South Pacific*.

I went to the supply closet and changed to scrubs, grabbed a bonnet and gloves.

"If I sit up and lean forward, it helps clear my lungs," said Wendy after we drew her curtain.

"Good job," said the pulmonary nurse to our patient.

"Would you brush my hair?" asked Wendy, handing me her *Bionic Woman* hairbrush.

After the episode of self-doubt in Lilah's room, Wendy cheered me up. I stopped thinking about how I didn't belong. Her wheeze had stopped, and I held on to that glimmer.

"Good job, Wendy. You too," said the pulmonary nurse to me as we peeled off our gloves. I surprised myself that I was able to assist. Wendy was the first patient I'd helped.

An hour later, the ward was deathly quiet. Ten p.m. The disco music went silent. I heard a sneeze, a hint of life, an invitation from the lone corridor. I should see her, not just her chart.

Aurora's was the first room on the right. When I

passed her open door, I glanced inside. There she was. Her bed tilted up at 45 degrees. She faced straight ahead at the TV, which was off. I only saw her profile. Her eyes were wide open. Aurora pulled her sheet closer to her neck so her feet stuck out. She pointed her toes, one foot at a time. Slowly, using all her strength. Elegantly. I imagined her rising out of bed in her ballet shoes, en pointe. Holding out her arms in a ring in first position, as she did plié and relevé. I pictured a few jetés in the space by her bare end table. At fifteen, she was about ten years younger than me.

I nearly walked right into him, Aurora's father, in the hall. He smiled warmly. His tired face softened, easing the creases on his forehead. Aurora was still doing toe extensions in bed, controlling every muscle with precision.

"My daughter's a dancer. She's good, isn't she?"

"She's very good. Ballet or Modern?"

"Both. She's so creative," said Aurora's father.

"I took Modern in high school, too." Dad shook my hand. He entered her room; I went back to the station. Dance was my second language. Aurora and I had something in common.

At 3 a.m. the nurse said I could leave. I took the elevator down to B level, strode the bowels of the hospital to the dorms. I walked the echo-chamber of the old residence, its marble floors rock-hard on my arches. I longed for wall-to-wall carpet, a shag rug, anything to cushion the starkness of my surroundings. Inside my on-call room, the small sink inside the closet was a welcome sight. I splashed cold water, made suds with the free sample bar of Camay. The water tasted rusty on my mouth but the cold felt good. I found my AM-FM radio and tuned to Disco Saturday Night, still pumping in these wee hours. I kicked off my flats and danced to the beat. My shoulders, trapezius region, relaxed. Flashing red lights of ambulances docking at the ER beamed up to my window like strobes, casting blood shadows on the Venetian blinds.

I tossed in my cot, my pager propped up on the pillow. We slept with our clothes on, just in case. At 4:30 a.m. I went back to the fifth floor. Aurora's room was abuzz with visitors. Major surgery would be grueling for a teenager. I eyed the basket of cuddly stuffed animals below the station desk. Which one? A velvety grey shark, the teddy bear with movable legs were favorites.

I checked the chalkboard. Nothing under her name.

"Aurora's tumor is inoperable. Too large. Messing around in there would risk damage to vital organs. Liver, spleen. Aorta." The intern was standing behind me, reading my mind.

"So what's the next step?" I asked.

"Palliative care."

"She only has months?"

"Days. Maybe today."

So that was why there were no shrill pings, no

frosty blue blinking lights. She wasn't being monitored because monitors meant hope.

Why hadn't anyone told me before? Did they think as a history major, I couldn't handle the idea that a teen was about to die? As a newbie, was I only sent to rooms of patients who would make it through spring? I wanted to meet each patient, not just view their biopsy slides or lab results. Was I cut out for this?

The first time I did a leap in my bare feet in dance class I felt like I was flying. Is that how she'd felt, too?

Patient rounds were about to start for the day shift. I piled the charts neatly on the metal trays. Was it too late to bring her a cuddly bear? That wasn't a question for the intern. It was a question for the ages. And what would I say? "Hi, I love the name Aurora. It means dawn." Because it was true.

As more loved ones encircled her, the lights came up in that dim hall. "Turn the Beat Around" came on again from the ceiling speakers. It wasn't my place, or the time. I picked up the mournful tone of the chorus I hadn't heard before. Singer Vicky Sue Robinson's syncopated minor notes cast a spell of gloom. Disco had schmaltz, rhythm, a wild abandon, a tinge of sorrow. The Bee Gees "Night Fever," Sylvester's "You Make Me Feel Mighty Real," The Three Degrees' "When Will I See You Again," and Harold Melvin's "The Love I Lost" became the soundtrack of my first night on call. Discotheques would disappear in a decade but on the fifth floor the music was all around us. Without intending to, disco's unwavering pulse witnessed the triumphs and tragedy of the wards.

I took my usual jaunt through the bowels of the hospital complex. When I got to the dorm, I didn't stop at the elevator bank. Instead, I rode the revolving brass doors onto the street. I'd been indoors for days. I had on my thin starched medical jacket, A-line skirt, opaque stockings, T-strap flats. A layer of ashy wet snow had been swept to the curb. I heard the early stirrings of the city. Buses applying their brakes. The grinding of a push-cart, its steamy paprika-garlic scent of hot dogs wafting toward me. I stood in place on the sidewalk. Before long, I was greeted and embraced by the first rays of light in the sky that were her namesake.

I didn't cry for Aurora. Not until years later when I could no longer hold back, when other grief brought this one home. But I knew I'd never forget her.

Jacqueline Bassan

Jacqueline Bassan was born in Manhattan, raised in Brooklyn. Music, a theme in her "Night Song," is her passion. She made her stage debut at five singing Lerner and Loewe's "I Could Have Danced All Night" in the Catskill Mountains. She went on to play the Scarecrow in her 3rd grade class production of The Wizard of Oz. She began piano lessons at a young age. At Midwood High, she sang and wrote lyrics for the victorious sophomore and senior Sing. At 17, she took music coursework at Brandeis with a noted Scott Joplin/Bach scholar. Jacqueline graduated from Cornell, BA in history. During her 3rd year of med school, she wrote lyrics for and performed in the medical student show. She wrote a musical based on her own European history research. Her play had staged readings in NYC and LA.

Her current writing is focused on American popular song.

Mother of Two
By Luanne Castle

Her doctor told Jeannie the best thing she could do was to get pregnant again as soon as possible. While he was talking, Jeannie was reminded of when she was seventeen and her puppy got hit by a car. Her mother brought another puppy home from the animal shelter that very day.

Jeannie didn't think she'd go back to that doctor anymore. He also told her to get dressed every day and fix her hair, as if that was going to make her feel any better. Jeannie washed her sweat suit out every other night while wearing the flannel nightgown with the holes under the arms, so she could wear the same clothes the next day. She'd been wearing these for four months now, ever since that day at the grocery store.

###

She hoped the baby would sleep for another half hour or so. Ryan was playing in his sand box out behind the house, and she was thoroughly engrossed in watching *Young Mister Lincoln* on the Morning Movie while she sorted clean whites on the couch.

It had taken her a while, but eventually Jeannie had recognized a very young Henry Fonda's face beneath all the makeup he had on. She'd loved Fonda ever since *On Golden Pond*; it didn't matter if he was dead, there were always old movies on television, and that made him as real to Jeannie as if he were still alive. Fonda was the perfect person to play the lead in a movie like this. Jeannie thought it was very heroic and romantic. A man was accused of murder and Fonda-Lincoln was defending him. No, no. She had put a pair of Ryan's socks in the pile with the carefully rolled-up balls of Dennis' navy-blue dress socks. Dennis only wore navy socks to work; they looked best with the navy blazer he wore over his jeans. Dennis was on the road most of the time, selling electronic equipment to music studios. Dennis had found from three years' experience that a blazer and jeans allowed him to fit in with the casual people in the music business, as well as the occasional suit he had to deal with.

Jeannie had to be careful with Dennis' clothes. If she grabbed the wrong items when she packed for him Sunday evenings, he would be stuck with nothing to wear in Dallas or Nashville or Cleveland. She smiled at the thought of him trying to squeeze a four-year-old's sock on his big toes.

The trial scene in the movie was really getting exciting. The mother of the accused murderer refused to testify against one son to save another. As it turned out, neither son was guilty, but she would have been willing to let them both be executed rather than save one son at the expense of the other. Jeannie was struck with the nobility of the woman. She wiped tears out of the inside corners of her eyes and dried her fingers on her jeans.

Suddenly Jeannie realized she hadn't checked on Ryan in over twenty minutes. She ran to the kitchen window and looked out into the backyard. The sandbox was empty except for a yellow cement mixer and a faded red plastic pail. Just as a lump started into Jeannie's throat, she saw Ryan sitting under the tall Christmas tree, counting pinecones on the ground. She could be silly, she knew. Sometimes she worried so needlessly over the children. Although she acted neurotic when Ryan was a baby, she had thought the second time around she'd be better, more experienced and mature. But no, after the first stormy weeks were over and Samantha had penetrated into every little cell of Jeannie's heart, the anxiety over her was there just as looming and horrible as with Ryan.

Jeannie lifted the window sash. "Come on in now, honey. I want you to get washed up."

Ryan lifted his head and made an agonized grimace. "Not *yet*, Mommy. I'm very busy. I have to count all these codes."

"Pinecones, not codes. Come now, Ryan."

"No!" Ryan's stubbornness was always just under the surface of their relationship.

"We're going to the grocery store," Jeannie said enticingly.

"Oh, okay. I'll come now." Ryan smiled his most winning grin. As he walked into the kitchen, he said, "Can I pick out something?"

"We'll see. You wash your face and hands, and don't forget to use soap. Did you remember to empty the sand from your shoes? Well, go out and do it now before it gets all over. I'm going to get the baby up and I'll bring you down a clean shirt."

"Okay, mommy, you will see. I will clean up very good. Then I will *pick* something at the grocery store."

Jeannie opened the baby's door slowly, so Samantha wouldn't be alarmed. The warm yeasty smell of the baby had permeated the air of the little bedroom. Samantha lay on her back with her face turned toward the crib mirror, making faces at herself and laughing.

"You little peanut!" Jeannie exclaimed softly as she picked her daughter up. "You are such a pretty-witty little Sammi Sue baby."

To take off Samantha's diaper, Jeannie had to pull her tiny feet out of the stretch terry suit. Samantha stuck the toes of one foot in Jeannie's mouth. Jeannie nibbled them. "You have toes made of raw dough," she said; they had that consistency and fragrance. "I'm going to eat these up!" She gnawed at the toes of the other foot.

Jeannie put Samantha in a pink bib overall and matching shirt. She tried to smooth the blonde down on Samantha's head with her fingers, but the tufts didn't want to lay flat. "How is anybody supposed to know you're a little girl with that bald head?" She laughed and then answered herself, "Oh, they'll know because you're such a pretty-witty baby." Jeannie arranged a pink stretch headband with a bow on the side around Samantha's head, just to be sure.

Ryan walked into the nursery, holding his hands out in front of himself. "Are these clean enough, Mommy?"

"Let me give them the smell test." Jeannie sniffed Ryan's fingers. "Yes, I smell soap. You must have done a good job."

After Jeannie got Samantha locked securely into her car seat and Ryan into his seat belt, she went back into the house to get her purse and the diaper bag. She looked through it just to make sure she had at least two diapers, a pacifier, some baby wipes, and a belt to strap Samantha into the grocery cart, just in case the cart she got didn't have one. Okay, all set, she said out loud.

The parking lot of the supermarket was wedged between two major roads that angled across each other, and the railroad tracks cut across the point of the triangular lot where the two multi-laned roads intersected. Jeannie had to wait for a train to pass before she could pull into the nearly empty parking lot. Samantha started to cry from sitting confined for so long without moving.

When Jeannie parked the car and leaned in to take Samantha out of her car seat, she smelled dirty diaper. "Oh, great. Thanks a lot, Samantha. Why didn't you go at home?" Samantha smiled broadly at her mother.

"'Cause she didn't have to go before, Mommy," Ryan said.

"Hand me the diaper bag; I'm going to have to change her here on the car seat."

"Oh, yuk." Ryan squeezed his nose with his hand. "Let me out of the car first. Pugh! Peeee-ugh!"

By the time Jeannie was a third of the way down her shopping list, she knew the day was deteriorating fast. "I should have waited to go tomorrow," Jeannie mumbled to herself. Ryan ignored her and Samantha just looked at her.

"Mommy, mommy! Buy this!" Ryan called periodically. Half the time, Jeannie said no. The other half of the time, Jeannie silently took what Ryan handed to her and put it in the cart. Sometimes his choices were already on her list; he knew what he was used to eating, after all.

Samantha reached out once when Jeannie was studying prices on the grape jellies and knocked a jar of organic peanut butter on the floor. Jeannie quickly pushed her cart toward the next aisle, dragging Ryan along by the upper arm as he tried to crunch the glass shards under his feet.

Finally, an hour and a half after Jeannie had changed Samantha's diaper in the parking lot, they were done shopping. The groceries were paid for and bagged. Jeannie pushed the cart outside with one hand, holding Ryan's hand with the other.

"Mommy, did we forget the batteries for Daddy?" Ryan asked and, then when he saw the aggravated look Jeannie gave him, said "Uh oh! You forgot!"

Jeannie pushed the cart toward the outside wall of the building. It wasn't easy to move, it was so loaded down with groceries. The sidewalk next to the wall wasn't level but tilted downward to the glass window of the store. When Jeannie got it onto that little incline, the heavy cart rolled into the glass window and bumped against it. Jeannie flinched, but the glass was very thick.

She turned to her son. "Ryan, I want you to stand right here and hold onto the cart with all your might. Mommy is going to go back in and get the batteries. See the cash register and the lady working there? The batteries are right there. I won't go anywhere else, and I'll be able to see you from where I am. You take good care of your baby sister. Okay?"

Ryan's eyes got very big and round. "Okay, Mommy."

Jeannie went to the express lane with the batteries. Ryan was standing there, clinging to the grocery cart; she could see both children through the glass panes of the store. Samantha had only learned to sit up a few weeks ago and she was starting to sag a little. The woman in front of Jeannie handed the cashier a carton of eggs. "I want half a carton, please."

The cashier sighed. "They don't come that way, ma'am."

"But they've let me before. Just cut the carton in

half. That's what they do."

"I can't do that." The cashier looked to her left and her right, nervously.

"They've done it before. Ask someone else. Ask the manager," the customer persisted.

Hurry up! Jeannie screeched in her mind, I've got little kids waiting for me outside. She should never have left them out there, she knew. Oh, why didn't she bring them in to begin with? Now there were five people behind her in line. If she got out of line, she'd lose more time. And Samantha was getting so tired.

Jeannie glanced over at the children again. The cart was gone. For a moment, Jeannie didn't move. She looked again. No, the cart still wasn't there. This time Jeannie moved fast.

People seemed to stay in her way on purpose. They reminded her of sinister robots. The electronic doors moved *so* slowly. When she got outside, she looked about her wildly. The grocery cart with Samantha in it was sitting on the railroad tracks. Ryan was running a little way off, on the busy street, dodging cars that couldn't see him because of his size, as though he was trying to get to the baby in the cart, but the cars wouldn't let him. Jeannie heard the train at the same moment and screamed. There was nobody around to hear her.

She was only one person and couldn't get to both children at the same time. And she had no time to think about it. Jeannie ran as fast as she could through the parking lot to save one of her children.

Jeannie felt herself screaming as she ran. The sound was flooding out of her as if it pumped her body up to run faster and faster. She grabbed Ryan in front of a car and squeezed him to her, covering both their eyes so they couldn't see. The car saw her just in time and swerved out of the way. The end of the car's squeal coincided with the whistle, bell, and terrifying screech of the train. Jeannie started to run with Ryan in her arms, but she knew she wouldn't make it in time. Even as she ran, Jeannie wondered what she could do with Ryan if she did beat the train.

Within six weeks, Dennis had seen that Jeannie wasn't just going to snap out of her depression. He asked to take a leave of absence from his job, but they said no, so he'd quit and taken another job. It was less pay, but he could be home at five every day. Then he would do the errands for Jeannie. He dressed Ryan every morning himself and drove the boy to Jeannie's mother's house for the day.

Dennis was very kind to her, and Jeannie appreciated that. But he wasn't very eager for her to get pregnant again. He told her she shouldn't do it just because the doctor said so, but they should wait and talk about it more. He said they could talk when Jeannie was feeling better. But Jeannie knew it was because he blamed her for killing the baby. By choosing Ryan over Samantha, Jeannie had as good as driven that train over the grocery cart herself.

Luanne Castle

Luanne Castle grew up in Kalamazoo, Michigan, lived for years in California, and now resides in Phoenix, Arizona, next to a wash that wildlife use as a thoroughfare, with her husband and five cats. Her children and first grandchild live close enough that Luanne operates "Grandma Daycare" for the baby. Luanne received an MFA in poetry and fiction from Western Michigan University and a PhD in English from the University of California, Riverside. She has published four award-winning poetry collections. Luanne Castle's Pushcart, Best Small Fictions, and Best of the Net-nominated poetry and prose have appeared in *Copper Nickel, TAB, Verse Daily, Saranac Review, Bending Genres, The Ekphrastic Review, One Art, Sheila Na Gig, Feral Poetry, MacQueen's Quinterly, Does it Have Pockets, South 85, Roi Fainéant, River Teeth, The Dribble Drabble Review, Flash Boulevard,* and many other journals and anthologies. Her memoir, *Scrap: Salvaging a Family,* will be published in 2026 by ELJ Editions.

How I'll Miss Paris
By J Craig Dix

The best days of summer were gone along with the annoying buzz of passport Parisians. It was now November and only the true people filled the streets, heads down with hands in pockets. A waiter suddenly appeared from the busy café hurrying to the only customer daring enough to brave the frosty morning and deposited a ritual steaming cup in front of him.

Gaspard loved his city. Frantic and lovely, carefree or dark she was an energy that was always with him. Doing up the top button of his coat he sipped at the espresso. As the wind dusted the square, he thought of how today he finally had the luxury of being sentimental. From the café the owner stopped to glance at the solitary man, a customer he'd known for years who seemed lost in the moment. Why was he staring at a scene he'd shared for so long?

Gaspard noticed the familiar face ambling toward him and automatically glanced at his watch. Reynard looked much the same as when they'd first met before the war. A scuffed suede coat and wool cap wearing the shuffle of an indistinguishable man with his newspaper. Where he emerged from was difficult to say, but most importantly he was not expected.

"Bonjour Monsieur Gaspard." Nodding at an empty seat he asked, "May I?"

"Yes of course. I wasn't expecting…"

"My apologies monsieur. Something important has come up and I…"

Reynard's voice trailed off as he searched the other's face for a reaction but saw that Gaspard was focused on a small bird in a nearby tree. The old man shifted in his seat and began again. "And I do apologize monsieur. It was a request on short notice immediately requiring your expertise."

"You know I need time. Adequate preparation is why I'm here enjoying this coffee. The answer is no. It's that simple."

"But it is a gift."

"What part of no…"

"This is the easiest money you will ever make. First level recruit easy."

Gaspard tried to contain his irritation. "Why me if it's so goddam easy?"

"As I said, it's a gift. What man doesn't need a little more? Be fair to yourself and at least listen." Gaspard emptied the last of his cup and replaced it gently in the saucer. Reynard spoke while reaching into his pocket. "Clara Volte – age 28."

"A woman? That's a change."

A small photo appeared on the table. "Austrian. Most of the war she spent at school in Switzerland."

"A Nazi?"

"Not important."

"What else do you know about her?"

"What else would you need to know?"

Gaspard's eyes darkened. "Details. Details are always important. Any idea why she's on the table?"

"Politics I suppose. Somebody pisses off somebody else. You know. What's important is she arrives at Gare de Lyon in an hour to stay at La Belle Amande until tomorrow evening. Then she returns to Switzerland. You must confront her before that happens."

Gaspard paused for a moment then said, "It has always intrigued me how you use the word 'confront' for what it is I do."

"Would you prefer I say 'kill' or 'murder' monsieur?"

"Just an observation."

Reynard studied his hands as if they held a secret. "I was raised a good Catholic and the way I can live with myself is pretending you 'confront' your contacts. It is a trick I use to sleep at night." Pushing the photo closer he said, "So you see this is not something requiring your usual preparation. Can I count on you?"

Gaspard stared at the photo. "She looks about seventeen," he said quietly considering the offer as he ran his finger around its edge. "Very well."

Reynard tapped the newspaper twice and pushed it toward Gaspard. "The usual fee. I must go."

"I'm surprised,' said Gaspard casually. "You of all people know that someone who appears then leaves in haste draws attention. And I know how you hate attention." Reynard adjusted his cap as he flashed a broken smile. "Stay for one cigarette," said Gaspard. "A civil length of time."

Reynard popped a half-finished rollie in his mouth. Checking his pockets he said, "I don't have any…" but Gaspard was already reaching toward him with a lighter.

"Merci." Taking a long thoughtful drag Reynard asked, "But is it true?"

"What's that?"

"They say you are leaving Paris."

Cupping his hands Gaspard blew into them then rubbed the heat into his fingertips. "Where did you hear that?"

"People talk."

Gaspard sipped at the empty cup. "People are always talking. And unfortunately, when they run out of truth, they keep on talking."

Elbows on the table Reynard leaned in closer. "And that you are leaving the business."

"Really?"

"I'm not sure Les Directeurs believe in retirement."

"Sometimes I consider the benefits of a change. A quiet place to enjoy the rest of my days. Perhaps get married. They say Spain is where people go for privacy...and a simpler life."

"Yes. Very simple."

"No one could be expected to carry on this life of secrets forever. Everything has an end point. And you know, the saddest part would be not seeing Paris again."

"And les Directeurs?"

"I don't think they would expect a goodbye. After all I'm only thinking about it."

"You would be missed," said Reynard.

"Don't you ever consider a life beyond work?"

"Without my work I would have no life."

Gaspard scooped up the newspaper as he pushed back his chair. "It's such a shame." Reynard looked puzzled. "How the war destroyed the Paris we knew. I could name a dozen of the old haunts still buried under the rubble."

Reynard dropped his cigarette to the pavement and ground it under his shoe. "Things change. Even good wine sours when left too long."

***

As Gaspard slammed the taxi door he looked up at the clock tower rising above the Gare de Lyon. Fifteen minutes early, that should be about right. He had a reverence for the station where he'd arrived before the war. Paris had seemed like a good place to be successful although at what wasn't clear. The station had a classic sense of strength and style, two things he admired. In spite of reviewing what little he knew about Clara during the cab ride he couldn't shake his frustration that this job didn't fit into a proven formula that had served well enough to keep him alive. 'Confronting' someone was a process, and the process took time and planning to walk away clean. Without that this job needed to be as easy as Reynard had promised. How could Reynard not understand the importance of details?

Weaving through the crowd he stopped at the news stand to search for a magazine he could appear to be reading while awaiting the Swiss train. Too many were glossy publications detailing the coronation of the new English Queen. Articles like "Death of a King—A Woman in Charge" made him grit his teeth. To him the monarchy was an anachronism, nothing more than a circus act. Along the wall was a rack of sports themed weeklies where he spotted a colorful boating journal. Dropping a handful of change he continued along the platform. With each step he wound the magazine tighter and tighter trying to re-shape his trusted plan for Clara but his mind kept drifting to later that night. He wished he'd never accepted this job but not taking it might have aroused suspicion.

Positioning himself in a spot busy enough to disappear he flipped through the magazine wondering why he'd never been on the water. Page after page of magnificent wooden boats cutting through the waves on cloudless days. He pictured himself and Lily free at last.

When the Swiss train arrived the first off was a large group of teenage boys in matching team jackets with school crests. Close behind appeared to be their coach, a round surly little man with a cigarette hanging dangerously from his lip as he shouted instructions and pointed the way out. Most of the cars had emptied by the time a skinny young girl who looked to have been dressed by her mother stepped awkwardly from the train. *Oh Reynard,* thought Gaspard, *this is more than a gift.* Clutching a small leather valise to her chest she stood fixed to the platform head snapping back and forth before falling in with the crowd heading for the exit. More like a tourist than a target. Gaspard took three quick steps and followed. He watched the tiny young woman being knocked off course by the other travelers. She was invisible to them. How could someone this ordinary be of interest to Les Directeurs? Gaspard began to slow his pace and at the exit stopped to watch Clara hail a taxi. He knew he should be in the cab behind her preparing himself to finish this last job but by now it was obvious to him he'd given up on everything except their final meeting. After all he knew where she was staying and if she spent the rest of the afternoon shopping and sightseeing it wouldn't matter in the end. He'd done this so many times before. Besides there was an important call he needed to make. He let it ring four times and was about to hang up when he heard her voice.

"Oui, allo?" She said it slightly out of breath, and he could feel his need for her.

"Bonjour my darling Lily."

"Ah ma douce, Henri."

"Have you packed yet?"

"All morning I've been trying to squeeze in a few more things. You are très méchant to have me leave so many of my beautiful clothes. How will I survive with only one case?"

"We'll go shopping the moment we arrive. You found the train tickets?"

"On the bureau with the flowers. Such a sly one keeping our destination to yourself all this time. You are a great one for secrets."

"I wanted to surprise you. I've rented a place in Lisbon for six months. From there we can go anywhere we choose. Beginning at 9:40 this evening I promise there'll be no more mystery."

"Are you sure about this Henri? You're always saying how much you love Paris."

"The Paris I loved is gone. It's time to make new memories with you. One last thing my darling, I have some business to attend to but will meet you at the station by 9:30."

8:45.

From the shadowy doorway Gaspard's binoculars had a clear view of Clara who'd been kind enough to sit by the restaurant window. After an hour of watching her slowly pick at her plate it was clear she had nothing planned after dinner.

8:47.

Gaspard stamped his feet hoping it would relieve toes aching with cold while she finished her coffee and pored through brochures on the Eiffel tower. Truly a tourist. Clara finally emerged into the chill November night a silhouette against the window, her breath circling in frosty clouds as she pulled on her gloves. Turning up her collar she strode quickly toward a neighborhood still in ruins. Gaspard gave her a half block head start then checked his watch again.

8:49.

She vanished and re-appeared in the pools of light from the streetlamps before suddenly making a quick turn into a derelict building. Hurrying to catch up he found himself plunged into darkness. As his eyes adjusted, he strained to hear any sound confirming Clara was even in the room. There was only the echo of water dripping and the acrid smell of something foul nearby. He stood in what once was a small office now filled with stone and broken furniture. To his right a staircase led to what remained of a second floor.

"Excuse me Madame," began Gaspard. "My name is Inspector Filion of Le Sûreté. May I speak with you for a moment? First my apologies for the late hour and this less than friendly location but I was out for a walk and spotted you. I understand you arrived today by train and wanted to ask if you'd seen a man we are looking for. I have a photo of him."

No answer. Perhaps she isn't even here.

Pulling out a flashlight he slowly scanned the

room.

"I assure you it will only take a minute or two." The glassy eyes of a huge rat lit up for a second before it raced away. "I'm sure you'll agree this building is in a dangerous condition and no place for a conversation. I myself am a bit worried about these crumbling walls. Perhaps we could step out onto the street where I could show you my identification."

It was so quiet. She must have escaped out a back way. "BANG."

The flashlight exploded in his hand and the room went black as he staggered backwards against something wet. Blood streaming along his arm he stumbled toward the stairs. With each creaking step he swore at himself for taking this job. At the top step cold blue moonlight pierced the roof as he looked for a place to hide. He tried flexing his hand and the pain told him it was useless.

In the silence there was time to run through the disaster this assignment had become. He hadn't expected she'd have a gun. That was his fault. And it was no coincidence she was such a good shot. He'd been set up by les Directeurs. If they knew he was leaving it must have been that bastard Reynard. Why had he been so casual about facts with him? Didn't matter now. As long as they didn't know about Lily. Even if he couldn't she needed to get on that train. His instinct had been to go upstairs instead of out to the street and now he was trapped. But he knew this needed to end here not at the railway station. Clara would have to make the first move. Finish the job or be next on the list of les Directeurs.

There was too much silence. When a car horn blared outside and someone swore he was relieved, otherwise there was nothing. What was she waiting for? Even if he heard her on the stairs, he wasn't sure about the aim of his left hand.

Too much waiting. Being on the receiving end was something new. Something he'd managed to avoid. A nearby bell began to ring nine 'o clock. She'd planned it very well.

As the last chime faded, he imagined her on the stairs tucked out of sight. His position wasn't well protected but hopefully he'd get one clear shot. Gaspard had never been a religious man but found himself staring at the light breaking through the roof and wondered if he'd already given up.

And then he saw it. A small puff of breath floated from the stairs over into the light.

It made him think what he would do if he were the one on the stairs. All he would know for sure was that his target was wounded, but how badly? It would be better for her to think he was in worse condition than he was. So he fired wide of the stairs like a desperate man. She rose just high enough to take aim and he heard a bullet fly past his ear. Screaming as though hit he counted to ten then fired again in her direction. Immediately she stood up for the kill shot and Gaspard squeezed off two quick rounds, the second one piercing her chest. She tumbled backwards out of sight and for a minute he could hear her labored breathing. Slowly he approached the top of the stairs gun trained on where she'd fallen. Clara was sprawled across the staircase still holding her weapon.

"It's over," he said aloud.

***

Before the taxi came to a stop outside the station Gaspard had already paid and was stepping out onto the pavement. He hadn't expected his legs to feel like rubber and had to grab the car door to steady himself.

"You okay?" asked the driver.

"Too much wine," he replied.

"Ah oui," replied the driver and sped away.

***

Gaspard looked up at the clock tower. Five minutes. Hand bleeding into a coat pocket he moved as best he could onto the platform. A handful of people wandered the space, smoking and checking their watches while ignoring the old man and his broom sweeping away the day's debris. But none of them were Lily.

Farther down the platform he saw a woman pacing a broad circle in front of a shiny blue locomotive. That would be Lily. As he moved awkwardly toward her she recognized him and ran to his side. She threw her arms around him as he put a single arm around her waist.

"Hello you," he said quietly.

"You're finally here. I didn't think you'd make it."

"I made a promise."

Stepping back Lily noticed his hand tucked in the pocket. "What's the matter with your other arm?"

"It's my hand. I had an accident." He held it out sheepishly in front of her.

"Oh Henri." Lily took a handkerchief from her purse and began to wrap it. "You need a doctor."

"It's not as bad as it looks. I'm sure there's a First Aid kit on the train."

"You're not going to tell me how it happened are you?"

"It's not important." When she scowled at him he said, "I had a disagreement that's all."

"I knew you wouldn't say." Fussing with the lapels of his coat she smiled and said, "We should go. We need to be onboard by the second signal."

A horn blew over the P.A.

"Goodbye Paris," said Gaspard as he looked deep into her eyes.

Lily smiled and put her arms around him. "Yes darling."

As the second horn sounded he felt the blade enter between his ribs, high up on the left side. The pain began as a shout but trailed off into the echo of the horn.

"Let me help you," said Lily quietly as she guided him to a bench. He followed her voice like a puppy, as if she still loved him and it had been someone else who'd done the deed. Gaspard was confused. He looked at Lily. It was the same face.

"Les Directeurs were very annoyed you hadn't spoken to them about leaving. When I told them you thought your career was over, they agreed." Gaspard felt himself drifting away.

"Henri. You need to listen. This is important. Les Directeurs wanted you to understand two things; retirement is the luxury of those of no consequence and most importantly…"

Lily leaned in close. He could feel her breath on his face as she whispered.

"There are no secrets."

J Craig Dix

Craig has always had a love of entertaining people. It's taken the form of amateur stage work and song writing, to a radio play produced by The Canadian Broadcasting Corporation as the winner of the "Young Writers of Manitoba" contest. While a member of "The Scribblers" a group of writers/friends in Halifax his short story "The Scent of Hollyhocks" was published by the Canadian Authors Association.

Formerly a Museum Conservator, he now enjoys spending time crafting stories sparked by dialogue that may make them feel like short plays or TV programs. Most of his works are based in the past where interactions are more important than electronics.

Craig has one lovely daughter Lindsay and lives quietly in Halifax, Nova Scotia with his incredibly patient wife Susan.

Lean Away from the Night
By Deac Etherington

It was December in New England. I sat in the back row of the college auditorium waiting for them to announce the winner. That year's Writer in Residence, a journalist who lost a piece of his foot doing something heroic in Kabul before writing a best-selling memoir about how heroic he'd been, was the final judge. After his speech about chasing stars or something it seemed he was staring straight at me with an amused expression. This was probably just my imagination, him singling me out. Unless of course I had won. I almost waved back.

And the winner of this year's Fiction Prize…

My chest tightened. For someone beginning the last semester of college with dreams of becoming a writer, the Fiction Prize was validation. I had selected a pair of destroyed jeans and a Baja hoodie for the podium. I wanted a Laurel Canyon vibe. But I looked like someone who should be out stalking whaling vessels with spray paint and a kayak. I pushed my fingers through my hair one last time, wishing I'd gotten it cut, and rose from my seat. It would be a long walk to the podium. Especially since it was starting from the back row in the dark.

… Marjorie Marie Wolcott, for her story – 'Jinks the Talking Cat'.

Somewhere in the sea of heads between me and the stage there was a squeal of delight. I was mostly standing, then, caught between two realities – Marjorie's and mine. So I had a clear view of her leaping out of her seat and trotting to the podium while everyone clapped. I clapped, too, but mostly like a primate in a cage mimicking spectators because it has no idea what else to do. I tried to make the fact that I had left my seat appear intentional by continuing to the exit. Then I was outside in the cold striding toward the college bar under a cloud of self-doubt and doom.

———

I ordered a pitcher. My intention was to drink it all as quickly as possible. I leaned back against the bar with my glass and took in the room. The place was smokey and warm. The swell of voices mixing with *Fancy Like* by Walker Hayes. Jackets were draped over chairs, the light low, matches flaring – a windowless space, a sense of baser instincts drifting through the air like the curling eddies of cigarette smoke. College nights like these were liberating and risky. The girl with long dark hair and brown eyes was a risk. There was no question about that. She was sitting at a booth with two other girls who wore matching berets. For me it was like spotting a splash of color on a rain slick street. And I stepped straight into the traffic.

"Excuse me," I said, stopping their conversation. "I was just wondering if maybe you'd like to get married later, assuming you're not too busy."

They widened their eyes at each other, then looked up at me like I was either a tedious slug or tragic amusement or both. The girl with dark brown hair leaned forward and cradled her head in her hand.

"You'll have to be more specific."

"I do?"

"Well, there are three of us here. Your question did not specify a target. Perhaps you could re-frame your query to avoid confusion."

There was an awkward silence.

Then all three started laughing.

"Relax," she said. "Sit down."

She slid over on the bench seat to make a space. I took a deep breath, set my pitcher next to theirs, and settled next to her. Shoulders grazing.

"The thing is," I said. "After the ceremony we can probably get the Nutmeg Room at the Waterford Holiday Inn for our honeymoon. Comes with candles and complimentary Chianti. Magical. And your friends are invited to the reception. There's a Barry Manilow cover band in the lounge most nights."

"That's possibly the most compelling proposal I've ever heard."

"I was practicing over by the bar."

"Of course, marriage is a big step."

"I've always thought so."

"Especially when it's the very first step."

"Is that a yes?"

"Not exactly."

"That's close enough. I'm Preston Taylor."

"Let me guess. Your father hangs his whale belts next to your mother's Nantucket purse collection in the Hamptons."

"You've met my parents?"

She smiled.

"I'm Summer."

"Summer?"

"You know, the season everyone waits for?"

"That makes sense."

"These are my suitemates, Mia and Nina."

"Hello."

"Be careful – they're biters."

Summer's suitemates leaned forward, as if synched.

"I'll bet his family has seasonal residences."

"Like ospreys."

"Or the Kushner's."

"Wherever there's a critical mass of blue blazers."

"With gold thread pocket crests."

"Hey, whoever you are, is the family car electric?"

"*Guys…*" said Summer.

"But just look at him," said Nina. "So excited."

"Like a scene from that old show, *Happy Days*."

"Joanie and Chachi."

"Except not really."

"No, not at all."

"More like Potsie and Leather Tuscadero."

"Because he's not *cute*, exactly."

"No. He's more pubescent than cute."

"A pubescentness laced with charisma."

"Wait. Is that even a word?"

"Charisma?"

"Pubescentness."

"It is now. At least for our purposes."

"We're all from San Francisco," interrupted Summer. "Nina and Mia have been like this since the eighth grade at the Katherine Delmar Burke School – conjoined, you might say. No one really knows why. Even they don't know. Also, they're like those sharks that eat seals. One minute everything is calm and tranquil then WHAMO. Floating pieces of flesh everywhere. We get along because I don't mind all the blood in the water."

I stare at the snake tattoo clinching Nina's throat.

"I see you're admiring my python," she said.

"Why did you pick that?"

"No reason at all. Like, literally."

"We're nihilists," said Mia.

"The point is there is no point."

"Takes all the stress out of life."

"And guesswork."

"Except not really."

"No. Not at all."

"And when we're done with this Norman Rockwell scene at this leafy little college, we're going to be exotic dancers in the Tenderloin."

"Exotic entertainers, more precisely."

"Though our dances do entertain."

"Because we celebrate gender variables."

"Every last one of them."

"Which is saying something, these days."

"Are they making that up?" I asked.

"They never make things up."

"We're existential anomalies."

"Random energy. Like asteroids."

"Capable of obliterating planets."

"Or not."

"Everything comes down to trajectory, sooner or later. Ever notice that?"

"Wait," I said. "You realize that if the point is there is no point, then there actually is a point?"

They both looked at me. Stunned.

"You know," said Mia. "He's onto something there."

"He certainly is. Perhaps we got ahead of ourselves."

"Don't let them intimidate you," said Summer.

"Actually, I find them kind of interesting."

"See?" said Nina. "Like the Pyramids."

"Or the John Birch Society," said Mia.

"And now we really should be going," said Nina. "You didn't come over here to talk to *us*, after all." Then, as if on cue, they both slid off the bench seat. "It was nice meeting you, whatever you said your name was. You're not at all what we expected to come walking out of the winter night in this bland little place. Connecticut is so...*pale*."

"Pale and pretty."

"Well, he is pretty."

"Maybe pretty isn't the right word."

"No. Not at all."

"He could be the priest who was money before he found God," said Mia. "Handing out clean needles and condoms beneath bridges behind the Pope's back."

"*Exactly.*"

"Try not shaving for a week, whoever you are."

"And re-consider your hair. Like, seriously."

"That's important."

"*Very* important."

"Good night, ladies," said Summer.

"We shall all certainly hope so."

Then her roommates linked arms and sauntered out of the bar. I stayed on the bench seat next to Summer. She had a quiet voice that was slightly melodic and her body was a blend of perfect proportion and excess. Despite the smoky air I was picking up traces of her perfume. Already it seemed less an accessory than a part of her.

"Refill?" I said, reaching for my pitcher. "After all, we still have a wedding to plan."

"Ah, about the wedding?"

"Yes?"

"Afraid I have bad news."

"No –"

"We may have to put the wedding on hold."

"Why? Our engagement was going so well."

"Currently I'm involved with an older man."

I could tell from her voice she wasn't kidding.

"Seriously?"

"Older *and* married. It's a total cliché."

"How much older?"

"Enough to create a scandal on top of a scandal." She exhaled a plume of smoke. "Cringy, right? See now what you strolled over to play with?"

"Don't you feel bad for the wife?"

"Not especially."

"Why not?"

"The woods are full of wolves."

"What does that mean?"

"It's her fault for marrying one."

"That's one way to look at it."

"That's the only way."

She picked up her beer glass.

"Tell me your major," she said.

"Why?"

"I find it revealing."

"American Literature."

"Whatever for?"

"I am going to be a writer."

"Oh... I don't think so."

"What do you mean?"

"Because you would have told me that's what you are already. Not what you're becoming. Real writers have this anguished sense of predestination.

It's all very tedious."

"You have experience with writers?"

"You could say that. Listen, if you're interested in me it had better be as a science experiment. It would be a mistake to get attached."

"I've made mistakes before."

"Not like me you haven't."

"I don't care."

She narrowed her eyes.

"All right. Don't say I didn't warn you. We're hosting a queer acapella night in the basement of Rainbow House this Saturday. Nina and Mia will be in New York protesting something in Washington Square Park mostly because they like angry crowds. So I have no one to go with. You could come if you want. And not just because we need people."

"Well then," I said, smiling. "It's a date."

II

Rainbow House was a converted farmhouse on the edge of campus that attracted minorities of any category. At one point someone had hung a big pride fist above the front door. Eventually the colors faded, which only emphasized that the larger point was inclusion. Now it was just a fist – everyone's fist, at Rainbow House. I sat across from Summer at a tiny table in the basement. The table was decorated with a checkered cloth and a Chianti bottle holding a candle. The acapella group was called *Odds'n Ends*. They had a lot of enthusiasm but not much of an audience which only made them louder.

Summer wore yoga pants and a navy surplus shirt. Something was dinging. I saw that a tiny bell was attached to a strand of beads woven in her hair. A sad little monastic sound. Something you'd expect to hear contemplating prayer flags in Tibet. Summer believed in Mayan calendar prophecies, chi, and the concentric nature of reincarnation. She was convinced she'd already been a seamstress in 17th century China and a Bengali tiger named Lulie. Now and then Lulie's spirit revisited her, she said, because the beast's death lacked resolution. She was also pretty sure she had been the extramarital muse of the 19th century American industrialist who consolidated the railroads and built Grand Central Station, but she could not say for certain beyond her current day fascination with muttonchops. She called the little dinging bell a temporal bridge to her past selves.

"You like acapella?" she asked.

"Actually, no. I kind of hate it."

"Then why did you come?"

"To see you."

"What if I asked you to a cock fight?"

"They have those here?"

Pretty soon it became clear that *Odds'n Ends* were not going to fill the basement. To encourage those already seated to stay they began handing out free shots after each song. Then the free shots ran out. But not the songs. I leaned toward Summer.

"You know the thing about acapella? If you stay too long once people begin to leave the singers start focusing directly on you. Like mariachis. They kind of have no choice. Then you have no choice but to sit there while strangers sing in your face."

"Well, when you put it that way."

"Trapped in a basement with mariachis. Think about it."

"Fine. We'll go to my room. There's some Rosé, I think."

———

We climbed the basement stairs to a sprawling living room with random furniture arranged around the fieldstone fireplace. *Black Prophetic Fire,* by Cornel West, displayed on the mantle. Everything smelling like fusty couch cushions and wood smoke. I followed her to the end of a long hallway on the ground floor. A picture of Gertrude Stein was taped to her door. The kind where the eyes followed you. It was terrifying. The door opened to a common area where I glanced into the room the Nihilists shared. The beds had been pushed together and there was a layer of clothes on the floor. Nothing on the walls except a Confederate flag with Elvis Presley's face in the center. Why that was there, I couldn't imagine. Which was probably the point. Summer's room was smaller. It smelled like scented candles. A double-hung window overlooked the parking lot. Branches in the glow of the streetlights cast transient shadows against the glass. The mattress was on the floor. It was covered in a quilt decorated with little blue rocket ships.

"Take off your shoes," she said.

"Okay."

She picked up a brass bowl. Lit some incense. Then I noticed the big rock in the corner. Looked like it came from someone's stone wall.

"There's a rock in your room."

"I know. I'm borrowing it."

"What for?"

"To remind myself of things we never notice."

"Seriously? I never notice rocks all the time."

"Maybe you should. The technical term for this particular rock is lithified north American field stone. It's at least 200 million years old. Imagine, just for a second, what this rock has co-existed with."

She was quiet on purpose.

I looked at the rock again.

"Wow."

"I know. And now it's here."

"That's actually pretty cool."

"See?" She opened her closet. Grabbed some things. "I'll be right back. Make yourself comfortable." She disappeared into the hallway and headed toward a communal bathroom. The floorboards creaking as she walked.

Things were unnaturally quiet, then. Like the waiting room of a doctor's office. I looked for the ideal place to be positioned for her return. There was nothing in the room but a desk, a chair, and a mattress. I decided on the mattress. Might project self-confidence. But I underestimated the drop and flailed on the floor. In the struggle that followed, I saw my socks didn't match. I rolled back onto my feet and drifted over to the incense burning in the brass bowl by the closet. Smelled like pine needles. Then I found myself contemplating the rock. 200 million years… The door opened again. Summer had changed into a white terrycloth robe. She seemed to be wearing nothing else. My heart banged with adrenalin.

"Miss me?" she said.

"I'm a virgin."

She closed the door.

"Shut up."

I looked at the mattress.

"Technically, that is."

"Shut *up* I said."

"Also, my socks don't match. I'm pretty sure one is for tennis. And I don't even play tennis. But I'm more embarrassed by the other thing at the moment. Not that I expected it to come up or anything. I just figured I should say something. You know…just in case."

"Well. Aren't you the surprising Puritan?"

"It's not exactly intentional."

She stood there in the thick white robe.

"Okay. First of all, don't be embarrassed. Everyone is a virgin until they're not. It's no big deal." A car pulled into the parking lot outside her window. Two doors slammed. A girl started laughing. A gust of wind swayed the shadows of branches against the glass. "Also," she said, "there's no pre-set schedule for this sort of thing. I mean, just because you're a college senior… Well, anyway, there's no pre-set schedule. It happens when it happens. Don't worry about it."

"I only wish I had some say in the matter."

"Okay," she said. "Then what about now?"

"That's, well…now, you said?"

"Unless you'd rather not."

"I think the status quo is the problem."

"Then that's simple enough, isn't it?"

"You'd certainly think so."

"Okay. First thing, you need to relax."

"Maybe it would help if I took off these socks."

"Good idea. Why don't we start there."

I slid off my socks and tossed them toward the rock.

"The next thing," she said, "if you don't mind my advice…"

"No, I'd appreciate any thoughts you might have."

"The next thing is you need to stop focusing on what's about to happen. You need to focus on what's happening. There's a big difference."

"That's kind of difficult."

"Have you ever heard of Allan Watts?"

"Who?"

"Allan Watts. Author of *The Way of Zen*."

"I'm not familiar with that."

"It's about focusing on the moment."

"Oh."

"You really need to read that book."

"Tonight?"

Summer walked over to a plastic record player. The kind you got when you were fifteen and resurrected after the return of vinyl. *Anonymous Club*, by Courtney Barnett, started to play. She put a bandana over the desk lamp and turned off the overhead light. Someone outside was trying to break a beer bottle with a lacrosse stick. Whack-whack-*whack*. Clinking glass shards. Then she walked up to me and we embraced and I felt how our bodies fit together like this was something they were designed to do and we kissed like that for a long time. The focus shifted to the mattress on the floor. Fortunately, this time, I anticipated the drop. We kissed some more on the rocket ship quilt. Then Summer's hands were on my hips until they weren't and her face was framed in wild dark brown hair and her breath slipped across her bottom lip in a way that you would remember and which was part of this new conversation. These things burnished into my psyche like silhouettes flash-burned into walls after an explosion… Then time stretched out the way time sometimes does. The searing seconds re-synched with heartbeats and the temporal truth of things re-emerged like cliffs through fog. Summer's breathing against my neck struck all the way to the center of my spine. Then she said,

"Don't worry about birth control."

“What?”

“I’m very in touch with my body.”

III

She dropped out ten days later. I had no idea why beyond some kind of crises in San Francisco. The Nihilists left, too. Whatever was going on they did not want to miss it for something as pedestrian as a college diploma. I was supposed to wait until she got in touch. But nothing happened. Her voice mail stayed full and she abandoned her social media accounts. Then my old Headmaster offered me a teaching internship with the potential for a full-time position after a year. The problem was I did not want to be a teacher. I wanted to be a writer. And now I had visions of San Francisco, the mythical west coast cradle of the Beats. I was convinced that Summer and I had crossed some kind of relationship threshold at Rainbow House. Something that time and distance would only clarify. In this way the promise of the west coast simmered as winter deepened.

Finally, the Nihilist’s called.

“Hello?” I answered.

“Good. You’re there.”

“Wait. Who is this?”

“Nina. With the python?”

“Yes. Of course.”

“Mia’s here, too.”

“Where’s Summer?”

“Ah, well, there it is.”

"What?"

"The reason for our call."

"Is she alright?"

"Listen. We don't usually do this sort of thing. That is, take an interest. But Summer's situation has taken a turn and we have no idea who else to call. And it certainly appears that we should be calling someone. Naturally, you came to mind, since all this involves you. Tangentially, at least. So I suppose all we really need to know now is how soon you can get here."

———

I left after my last final. My old Camero swaying on the highway as it came up to speed. Then the orderly glow of dashboard dials as entire states began to slide past. There was really no other way to make a trip like this. I crossed through yawning plains and wide western cities and odd beat little towns held over from the glory days of Route 66 which still existed here and there deep in the heart of things. I was in a hurry to see Summer. But I was in another kind of hurry, too. It was the sunlit acceleration across grand and tragic spaces unchanged in time but for the ways we've devised to cross them – the going, going, *gone* to the edge of a new ocean. In America you got to a place like this by car. The feel of rubber gripping asphalt, white walled whirling mile after mile, splattering explosions of rain, wipers clearing and clearing again the pocked glass that elongated the arch of on-coming headlights before flinging them neatly passed. By car you had all the accumulated sensations of moving fast through the day and fast through the night while you guided the wheel with the tips of your fingers.

A few days later I was cruising along the Embarcadero bright against the black water of San Francisco Bay. I was meeting them at a bar called Vesuvio next to City Lights Books. Not knowing what else to do, I parked at the Ferry Building. Dialed the Nihilists and left a message. I could have taken a cab the rest of the way but decided to walk instead. The singular rhythms of the city banging through me like an endless loop of table-thumping jazz… North beach was a meandering tangle of mismatched sidewalks and telephone poles with impossible wires and narrow alleys and buildings with steps to mysterious doorways and flowering window boxes and Italian restaurants with little tables attended by waiters with white shirts and neat little aprons then further along the neon portals to strip clubs with big men outside wearing black suits and past this the after dark buzzing of tattoo needles above shops displaying hookahs and jade and cinnabar and then the very dark bars with faceless forms bent over tables with glowing cigarette tips – *this*, the mad man-made San Francisco night.

Near Columbus Circle I stepped past some ageless soul spreading his blanket out on the concrete at the base of a building, smoothing the wrinkles, positioning the plastic bags filled with his belongings, folding a pair of pants for a pillow, then carefully lying down on his side. He appeared to be snuggling with the granite. Just before stillness he turned a fully awake face toward me, a cropped tongue fluttering over grey teeth, and said – *Mustafa Kemal Ataturk was a secularist who dismantled sharia law in Turkey. What do you think about that, bucko?*

Vesuvio was crowded. I stood opposite the bar and scanned the first floor. I felt invisible and displaced like some ghost that had drifted out of Felinghetti's basement on the other side of Kerouac Alley.

"Goodness," said Nina. "You look like a pet abandoned at a rest stop."

I turned.

"Nina?"

"We got your message. Unless, of course, you expect someone else to be looking for you in here tonight." She was dressed like a flapper from the 1920s. Hair bobbed and dyed platinum silver beneath a silver beaded cloche hat. We walked up to the second floor where Mia was sitting at a table with her back to the wall. She was dressed the same way. Except her bobbed cut was jet black and her eyeliner had an Egyptian vibe. "Here he is," said Nina. "Told you."

"Wow. It's him all right. What loyalty."

"That's not it, exactly."

"No. Not at all."

"He's more like one of those pigeons that keeps

coming back."

I grabbed a chair and sat down. On impulse, from having been compared to a pigeon, I reached across the table for Mia's shot glass and downed it. Then I banged the glass against the table with a satisfying *whack*. Made both of them jump. I turned my attention to Nina's martini. But she slid it out of range.

"So aggressive," said Mia.

"Like a bullfighter."

"Or a steely-eyed sea-captain in a storm."

"Well, there definitely is a storm."

"And his eyes are just so...well, *steely*."

Nina crossed her legs and began licking a lemon wedge. Both peering at me beneath the brims of their flapper hats. Then they gave me the address of an attic apartment near Chinatown. It was a bit of a walk but not really, they said, like everything else in San Francisco. That's where I'd find Summer. I had to be sure to use the fire escape when I got there. They didn't tell me anything more.

———

Back on the street I felt the chill that comes with the confluence of city and sea and began walking. Gradually the neighborhood changed. There was odd evidence of domestication in the upper stories of buildings on the outer edges of Chinatown. Balconies with pots and bags of things and little clothes lines with jeans and old lady underwear and strings of herbs. And just inside the windows the dull yellow light of lives casting shadows and running out of time.

The address they gave me led to a building high on a corner. Street level there was a murky new age book shop that also sold bongs, sex lotions, and North Beach baseball caps. Windows with dark green trim and tragic bits of curtain marked the upper floors. The fire escape was in an alley in back. A little path cleared through rusty garden equipment and garbage cans along with an ancient tricycle with streamers. I worked my way up the metal stairs past flowerpots, laundry lines, the occasional litter box. I didn't realize why you would access an apartment this way. Then I did. It's how you got in if you were squatting.

A door at the top had been wedged open. Beyond it a foyer with exposed lathing and garbage piled in the corners. Old magazines. Used needles. Empty cans of Sterno. Someone's shirt. The foyer led to another door decorated with that same picture of Gertrude Stein from Summer's suite at Rainbow House. I started knocking. Then knocked some more.

It was the heroic journalist from college who opened the door.

He stood there in stained chinos with a fat little notebook straining the pocket of his shirt. His ice blue eyes settled on mine intently. It was one of those moments that slips out of sync like the stretched-out seconds in a car crash when the dying die – that limbo when truth gets rearranged personally and forever. A breath or two later, the world starts moving again. But it is no longer the same world.

"Can I help you?" he said.

"I'm here to see Summer."

He tilted his head.

"And exactly who are you?"

"You really don't know?"

"Any reason I should?"

I remembered the auditorium.

"No. I guess there isn't."

"Then we're done talking."

He started to close the door.

"Wait," she said. "Who is it?"

"Just one of your strays."

She drifted into the doorway in a sundress with miss-matched slippers. One had a goffer face with a pink tongue and eyes that wobbled. She looked at me as if surfacing from under water.

"Preston? From that college?"

"Surprise."

"What are you doing here?"

"College ended."

"But how did you find me?"

"The Nihilists."

"Of course. They love a good drama."

"So I guess this is the married guy?"

"Goodness. Not any more."

"What does that mean?"

"It's a long story."

"Well, I came a long way."

"I for one admire his moxie," said the Journalist. "Trailed you like a damn spaniel. I think this gesture of his has a certain…charisma." He looked at me and winked. Then he reached for his peacoat. "I'm going out for some air. I'll likely be gone a while." He moved past me into the hall. Plaster cracking beneath his shoes. Then there was the descending clang of his footfall down the fire escape. I turned back to Summer.

"What is this place?

"Temporary."

She turned away from the door and went inside. I followed. There was a mattress on a metal frame with wadded blankets. A claw foot bathtub in the corner with a make-shift laundry line. Oil lamps on grape crates foraged from dumpsters behind supermarkets. There was one window. A tall double-hung above the alley. The lights of the Bay Bridge glimmered through gaps in the fog.

"You never called after you went away."

"Well, that would have been awkward."

"Why?"

"He finally left his sad shopping-bag wife. Of course she's taking absolutely everything. But he says the urgency of austerity is good for the creative process. That's why we're here." She walked over to the window overlooking the alley. Raised it. The cool San Francisco night drifting in and pooling around us. She climbed onto the sill and leaned against the frame with her legs drawn up tight against her chest.

In this way she balanced between the world of the attic and an airy descent into oblivion. "He hates it when I smoke. So I do it in the window." She lit a cigarette. Her face in profile flashing bright before returning to shadow. "You just have to remember to lean away from the night."

———

I walked back to the Embarcadero. A ship's horn bellowed in the bay. The sound disembodied. Lost. Tendrils of fog curling around the edges of buildings veiling the predawn glow of city windows behind which the final dramas of the night were playing out. All things I would be leaving behind, after all. But my journey from Rainbow House to the edge of the world changed everything. I would accept that teaching job. I would follow where it led as my future unfolded on another coast. And I would continue to be a refugee from the back row of award assemblies. I had learned that a writer did not need awards. A writer needed a story. And now, as Summer's attic window receded into the vast canvass of the San Francisco night, I was quite certain I had mine.

Deac Etherington

Deac Etherington is a former high school English Teacher and Headmaster. He holds degrees from Connecticut College and Wesleyan University and lives with his wife in southern Arizona where you can drive all the way to the Sea of Cortez when you want to change the view. Deac was a finalist for the **2017 *Arcturus* Award for Fiction, Chicago Review of Books**; winner of the 2018 Flash Fiction Contest for *Light and Dark Magazine*; winner of the 2018 Fiction Contest for *Prime Number Magazine*; winner of the 2019 **Hemingway Shorts Contest**; winner of the 2020 Fiction Contest for *The Briar Cliff Review*; Finalist for the 2023 Sense of Place and Home Contest for *Dreamers Magazine.* His work has also appeared in *Projected Letters Magazine* and *The Baltimore Review.* Deac is currently at work on a novel. Find him on **Facebook**.

Almost Intact
By Cat Funk

Alpha. Tigr did not know the word. He embodied its meaning. He ruled his immense territory absolutely. All his creatures knew and feared. A tall fence surrounded the village within. It wouldn't keep him out if he chose to hunt its streets, but he respected boundaries, his own and theirs. He dealt with disrespect personally. He did not forgive.

Tigr ate what he slew and made the dying brief. The line of hunters he shadowed was unaware of him and would remain so unless he willed it. The wind at their backs carried their scent toward their intended prey. Fools. Their quarry would disappear before the stalking men knew of their existence. The lowest forest dwellers could detect scent many times better than humans.

Tigr eyed the last two in their line. He didn't like people, but as a last resort, they were better than an empty stomach. They were responsible for the dwindling supply of game. The territory had difficulty supporting them, and after many years, Tigr was losing patience. But all creatures need to eat, and he respected the pact. They didn't steal his kill, and he didn't make them his. For now.

His mother demonstrated their tacit agreement over a decade ago when he was still a cub. Her mother showed it to her, and so it had been for centuries. The First People respected the code, but those who came after often did not. Those could be considered prey.

These hunters were of those who came after. He didn't know yet if they respected the alliance. He hoped not. He wanted the thrill of the chase, the smell of fear, the taste of blood. Still, he remained cautious. Tigr rarely made mistakes.

***

Vasily led the hunt along a trail caught in the no man's land between late winter and early spring. What light they had was beginning to fail. Night and its dangers fell early this time of year. Dark lowering storm clouds threatened at their backs. They were well out of cell phone range. Cell service was unreliable, often hoped for, and never depended on.

Their path was a ribbon of treachery. The middle appeared solid but was deep, squelching mud imprisoned by the fickle icy edges. The villagers dubbed it east country tiger shit. It clung to their boots in clumps that grew, weighed them down, and sucked joy from the dregs of day.

Thighs burning, lungs heaving, Ilya trudged in his brothers' footsteps along the relentless track. In front was the eldest, Vasily, followed by the next three in descending birth order, and last was the youngest, Ilya, the baby despite his nine winters. Behind Ilya was their father, Petrov, who kept a stern and watchful eye on his sons. It was Ilya's first hunt, and while the boy was willing, he was easily distracted. Conversation was absent. They used gestures to communicate when necessary. Survival was a war they were already losing. Death was a bird of prey hovering before she struck.

Ilya was always hungry these days. Eggs and goat milk were perfectly acceptable sources of protein. It was more than some in their village had. But there was never enough, and watered milk fell far short after so many weeks. He also liked the pickled cabbage his mother made, but there was less of it than there used to be. Even the coarse, flavorful rye bread she baked tasted more like clay than he remembered.

Daniil, a boy he used to play with, had taken to his bed too weak for childish hijinks. Ilya used to bring him portions of his meager meals, part of his boiled egg or pickled cabbage. But his friend slipped away in his sleep two nights ago. He would never see Daniil again, and his heart ached at the thought.

So, instead of returning home to avoid encroaching darkness and the oncoming tempest, the family of hunters continued hoping to find game. A life-giving deer or boar would be ideal, but anything would be welcome, anything at all.

Vasily changed course eventually. They were at the top of a lengthy loop. It meant they were heading home. Encouraged, Ilya stiffened his resolve and pushed his heavy, mud-encrusted boots to keep pace.

***

Tigr also changed course. He no longer stalked the brothers from behind but alongside. His massive paws, unhindered by east country tiger shit, left prints in the snow the size of a man's hand.

***

The pantry was a narrow, windowless room added to the outside of the kitchen years after Petrov built the cabin. Halene finished punching down the bread dough and separated it into loaves. She covered them with clean cloths and placed them on shelves for their last rising and bent, finally giving in to the low, rising ache. A groan pushed its way past her lips. Her hands fisted. Nails dug into palms, and her knuckles were white on the wooden counter.

An hour ago, she'd taken a call on the black rotary house phone from Anya, the other midwife in the village. An unholy mix of shame and apprehension swirled through Halene's being. She was keeping this baby, but maybe she shouldn't. She would never judge another woman for ending a pregnancy, but she couldn't bring herself to do it. It was the whole meaning behind the word "choice," and this choice was agonizing.

For the first time, Halene denied the apprentice's request for help. She was far too ashamed to say why. Anya had solid skills and instincts despite her youth, but Halene's denial broke an unwritten contract. Anya was the only other midwife, and she was worried about a laboring mother's health and that of her baby.

It meant help would not be coming for Halene, either. "Sometimes you can know too much," she thought. There were dangers inherent with multiple pregnancies, dangers in unattended births. A doctor rotated through several villages, and it wasn't their turn for his visit today or even this month.

***

There was crashing in the brush off to the side of the trail. The men halted, lifting six loaded rifles to their shoulders. An animal bugled in distress. "Niet!" Petrov barked, his voice fierce despite its hushed pitch. Instinct brought instant obedience. Silence. Six men held their breath. Ilya's blood thudded a drumbeat in his ears. Tigr's breath huffed audibly, a harsh, discordant rhythm in the stillness. He was close, so close. Something heavy dragged over snow and forest debris. And then...then a sight the brothers never thought to see.

Deliberately, back humping with effort, Tigr dragged his kill across the path in front of the line of hunters. Ilya's mouth dropped in an O of astonishment. To see a tiger in the wild was a gift – a dream or nightmare. Deepening dusk gave the advantage to Tigr. His eyes saw much better in low light than the humans'.

Despite his hard work and heavy clothes, menace chilled Ilya to his core. The little hairs on his arms stood on end. He wanted to run, to scream, to cower. He held.

Tigr dropped his hindquarters in the middle of the path, the limp neck of the stag dangled from firmly clamped jaws. Taunting, two eyes full of challenge and predation met twelve eyes brimming with awe and fear. Petrov, the patriarch, reached around and lowered the gun Ilya didn't realize he was still holding up.

Ilya had never seen a tiger before, but he'd seen a few black bears. This animal, an Amur tiger, the biggest of them all, made those bears trivial.

Tigr dropped the neck of his stag. His eyes never left the line of hunters as he placed his body between his kill and the men. His ownership and challenge were palpable. Instinct demanded the chase.

***

Ilya's terror craved release. He wanted escape. If he ran, he would die. He desperately wanted to run. The pincer grip of his Papa's clenched hand on his shoulder held him.

With a sharp gesture of his head, Petrov redirected his sons. As one, they followed, stepping backward. They moved at an oblique angle off the trail away from Tigr, not in simple reverse.

Eyes intent, Tigr paced them slowly, instinct at war with the pact.

Resolute, they held their pace. Following Vasily's lead, Ilya flung his hands out high and wide – shouted. Ilya's voice was high-pitched fear. Vasily, Petrov sounded angry and aggressive. The others joined in, false bravado in every cacophonous note.

Tigr lowered to a crouch. His haunches shifted. He could cover most of the intervening distance in a single bound. He was a coiled spring, primed. His kill. His territory. Daring the humans to break and run, he lusted after the pursuit.

Each hunter was terrifyingly aware of their status change to hunted. They maintained their pace and increased the distance by increments. Time slowed.

***

Halene knew it was foolish, but she wanted the contractions to stop. She wanted the baby to go away. The thought of caring for yet another hungry mouth made her stomach knot. It was a sensation that had nothing to do with her labour.

She had a muscular build with broad shoulders and hips made even wider by the bearing of five children. She considered the men in her home to be ignorant, but even she was surprised by how easily she hid this pregnancy. No, she never showed much while she was carrying. By the third one, her body had adapted, so she showed not at all with the last two. Yes, she dressed to hide it with extra clothes, aprons, sweaters, and such, but even so. No one, not a single soul, knew she was expecting another baby – including Petrov. She reflected on the irony of sex in the dark. A part of her knew it was unreasonable to be angry her efforts at concealment were so successful. So, what.

Hiding her pregnancy from the rest of the world made it feel less tangible. It was easier to pretend it wasn't happening. Denial made the last months less anxious. At her heart, she was sure no one would be pleased. She wasn't thrilled herself. At least another boy would eventually help with the logging. But the investment in his growth and training was hardly worth the effort. But a girl – well, a girl would be problematic.

Another low groan originating from deep within crawled its way from her soul up her throat. She felt pressure in her pelvis. She supported herself with her elbows in the corner of the counter in the narrow room. "Oohaah." The baby was coming fast. Fast labour came with its own dangers, many of which could take her life.

***

Tigr watched, disappointed they did not run. When they were nearly out of sight, he backed to a bush and marked his territory. Regal disdain was evident in each movement. He would let them live for now. Out of sight, the humans maintained their backward gait but dropped their arms and quieted. Several minutes later, to Ilya's relief, they turned and walked briskly, still at an oblique angle from Tigr, in a direct line toward the village. Ilya desperately wanted to be far, far away, but held his pace to his brothers'. Stark fear twisted sharply in his belly. They were hours away from home. Each hunter hoped, fervently prayed, Tigr was too busy with his meal to care about them.

Tigr cared very much.

No one spoke. They were all alive, all filled with wonder and dread. How long would they remain alive if they were competing directly with Tigr? Ilya's belly let out a growl of protest. It earned him angry, anxious glances. How long could they last without a productive hunt? Resources were short. They could not afford to make the long journey from the village to the nearest town large enough to purchase food.

Any time spent now on that journey took away from their livelihood, logging. Every year, beginning in early spring, when the ground grew too sloppy for the heavy equipment, they had to stop for a few weeks, often a month or more. When the ground was that mushy, no one and nothing travelled. Snow and ice-covered gravel roads became muddy bogs before drying up for summer. There was an anxious hurry to accomplish as much as possible while they were able, including transporting product and laying in supplies.

Mother Russia ignored those in her far east except when she wanted something: logs, a secure eastern seaboard, or tiger parts. They preferred it that way. No one in the village wished to have Moscow's cold, assessing gaze turned toward them. Feed the beast. Don't do anything unexpected. Survive.

Ilya almost groaned aloud with relief when they began to pass more familiar landmarks. But his stomach descended to his heavy boots with disappointment. They had not seen any other deer or wild pig at all. Their only sighting was a thin winter hare that quickly disappeared deep into the thorny underbrush.

Their hardship would intensify with an empty-handed return. Mama would not say anything. She knew they were doing their best, but she would look. Her eyes, dark with concern, would play across her family, weighing.

His discouragement outweighed his relief as he trudged on. The brothers were now less alert, believing that Tigr was satisfied elsewhere. They just wanted home. Heads pivoted less often atop tired shoulders. More pairs of eyes focused on the ground instead of their surroundings, and they were less attuned to the dark, enveloping forest.

***

Halene didn't need the feel of the baby's head between her thighs to know it was there. Its angry protests loudly heralded its birth, the rest of the baby still encased by the moist warmth of her body. She snatched a towel from the counter, caught her newest child neatly with her next contraction, and began to dry her.

What was she going to do? She named her Marya, the noisy little rebel. She was smaller than her brothers. A few minutes later, the placenta slid out in a rush of blood, too much blood.

Her legs buckled. Clutching Marya to her breast, she slid to the floor. It was hard to think. She was lightheaded. If she lost consciousness, she was more likely to die. Marya began to suckle enthusiastically. Halene began to massage her loose belly. Contractions tightened it painfully. Against her will, her eyes closed, and her head fell back against the wooden floor.

***

Tigr cached his kill and continued to shadow the hunters. He could stash it safely in dense underbrush and return to the frozen carcass later. Prey was not plentiful enough to take for granted. For now, he continued stalking out of sight parallel to the humans. The wind from the approaching storm was now in their favour. He still wanted the chase.

He stepped on a branch. It was damp. He had to put the full force of his weight on it to make it crack. The sound carried as intended. Now, they would hurry. Now, he would pounce.

***

Light and colours swirled as she came back to herself. Marya was fussing, bobbing her nose against her breast. Halene changed her to the other side and let her own head drop back to the hard floor. If she didn't stop the bleeding, they could both die before the men came home. She felt her belly again. Firm. Good. Okay.

She allowed herself to rest for a few minutes before leveraging herself up to a sitting position. The day was still young, though a storm churned in the distance. Halene grimaced as she anticipated the arrival home of her men, hours away. More than one storm brewed. Well. Things needed doing. She might as well do them.

***

Only Vasily and Petrov were ready when the buck bounded across their path. The bright pop of gunfire cracked through the forest. One vaulting stride later, he collapsed. Two heaving breaths after that, his life was gone. Ilya hadn't even raised his gun.

The humans rushed to the animal. It was Vasily's perfect heart shot. Petrov directed his sons to quickly clean it while he tramped a circle around them in ever-widening arcs, alert, gun at the ready, eyes roving.

He shook his head firmly in the negative when Ilya made to scoop up the organs to take home with them. They left the organs in a steaming pile with the head as an offering for Tigr. It had the added benefit of lightening the load. The two oldest brothers hung the buck between them, and they picked up their pace. They were not far from home now and heartened by their success.

Their trail ran parallel to that of the deer for a few paces. A broken stick lay in the mud, – a single pawprint three times the size of Ilya's hand across it. Ilya didn't dare ask out loud, but did Tigr drive the buck toward the line of hunters? The thought did funny things to his stomach and drove him to keep up.

***

Tigr watched the hunters prepare the buck from his vantage point inside a copse of bushes. When they were out of sight, he moved soundlessly into the trampled clearing and paused, scenting the air. They were gone and moving away. No one else would dare disturb him. He stepped daintily toward the remains. After one last look around him, he lowered his muzzle and began to eat the offering. They fully respected the code. The hunters could leave with their lives.

***

The men eventually arrived back at the cottage; dark having settled much earlier. Warm lamplight glowed in the windows of home. The rising wind rocked an oil lamp hung hopefully on the eves of the shed near its door. They had electricity, but it was less reliable than oil in stormy weather. Still silent with deep reverence and gratitude, they hung their prize in the shed, survival assured for the near future.

By the time the sound of boots stomping off mud and snow on the back steps rattled through the house, Halene had fed the animals in the barn. The cats enjoyed the placenta, while the goats, chickens, and pigs enjoyed their feed. The sow had a litter of nineteen piglets earlier in the season and just weaned them last week.

As a measure of her hope, desperately needing the success of her hunters, she splurged, and a piglet flavoured the thick stew staying warm on the stove. The rest of the evening meal was on the table, including freshly baked bread without the clay extender. A pie, made with a careful measure of their precious sugar and a few of the last apples, spongey and wrinkled but still good, waited on the sideboard.

Even if the hunt were successful, preparing the carcass would take time, and its flavour would improve with hanging anyway. Her men would want to eat immediately on their return and, after such a day, would need more than boiled eggs and watered milk.

They had abundant wood, and the stove was pumping out heat, a fresh stack of split oven-sized logs lay beside it. The house was nearly spotless, the faint fresh stain of blood on the pantry floor the only reminder her appointment with death was for another day. Marya slept, silent, a slightly larger lump within the bulk of Halene's shawl. A fine sheen of perspiration on her brow made her homely face glow.

Her men burst through the door with an eruption of noise. Hours of tension held in check exploded like thunder with their last steps into safety. Petrov followed his sons up the back stairs with the extinguished lamp. Vasily and Ilya shouldered through the entrance together, only fitting because of Ilya's smaller size. "Did you see that?!" enthused Ilya. "Those paw prints were bigger than my hand! Bigger even than your hand! They were huge! The biggest tiger ever!"

At the mention of the tiger, Halene's pulse quickened. It didn't slow until each member of her brood was inside, and she counted heads, looked for injuries.

Vasily ruffled his little brother's hair, an act calculated to irritate. "That's because you're no bigger than a bug."

It worked. "Ya? Well, you're an annoying mosquito." He ducked his head from under Vasily's hand and countered with a child-sized fist, easily caught and held.

"Bug."

"Mosquito."

"We got a big stag!"

"I've never seen a tiger display his kill like that."

"He was challenging us, no doubt."

"He told us we were hunting on his turf."

"He was huge!"

"We're so lucky we got away with our deer!"

"Not so much luck."

"Ya, Tigr sent it across our path."

"You think so?"

"Why?"

"Holy mother!"

"Peace offering?"

"Pact?"

"One predator to another?"

"Maybe all. Don't get cocky."

"We're not."

"Why would you say that?"

"Tigr is incredible!"

"If we have a pact, it will only last while there is enough game for us all – and while we honor it."

"What do you mean?"

"Of course, we honor it."

"Who would challenge Tigr?"

"Eventually, some idiot may try to kill him for parts."

"But then we will all be fair game to him, to his cubs."

"His mates, too."

"Just so."

The silence began thoughtful and lasted while chairs scraped, and buttocks settled. Arms reached for fresh bread and pickled cabbage. Steaming bowls of stew changed hands as the brothers passed them down the table. Mouths worked.

The ash wood ladle was smooth from prolonged use and stained dark along its lower half from the juices of countless stews. Halene's long-dead grandfather made it for her as part of his wedding gift when she married Petrov decades ago. The wood was brittle with age and use.

Relief flooded Halene at the successful hunt. Her loved ones were safe. Everyone around her table was healthy, not a small feat. Carefully, she ladled the hot stew into seven bowls and tapped it on the edge of the pot to remove excess. Male conversation swirled around the table again. Marya woke and began to nuzzle to soothe herself.

Halene refused to raise her voice. "My day was also eventful." She may as well have been a chair. "I'm healthy, as is Marya." Perhaps a footstool. The brothers enthused about the hunt. A dull axe would receive more notice.

Her patience gone, she smashed the ladle onto the table in front of her husband. The precious, well-used handle splintered and broke. Its loss nearly saw the end of her control.

Petrov finally met her furious gaze, startled and angry. Marya made mewling noises as she searched for comfort.

"Did you let one of the barn cats inside?" Vasily questioned Ilya. His voice was loud in the sudden stillness.

Belatedly, Ilya looked at his mother. Petrov opened his mouth to chastise his wife.

"Don't," she said with a sharp silencing gesture, the short, splintered handle of the spoon held in her hand like a weapon.

Petrov's face became thunderous. He pushed back his chair as Halene dug inside her shawl. The boys rarely saw conflict between their parents. Even Vasily watched in awe, eyes wide.

Halene produced her wrapped bundle the moment before Petrov stood. She thrust her into his arms. Challenge warred with fury on her face. "Her name is Marya. She's yours." The urge to call her husband an ignorant fool was strong. Mindful of her first five children, she held back the rant she longed to unleash.

"How did this happen?"

Perhaps she should have delivered it after all. "The usual way." There was no trace of humor in her reply.

His features softened as he pushed the wrappings away from Marya's face to see her better. She turned her head and lifted her upper lip, instinctively attempting to nurse. "Ah, daughter. We are already spread so thin." After a few moments, he handed her over to Ilya, sitting beside him. "We will all have to work extra hard to care for her," he stated. The unnecessary announcement brought uneasiness to the table.

Ilya saw his doubt reflected in his brothers' eyes. He lowered his gaze to his new sister's face. How could this little lump of humanity cause so much consternation? She had no say in her arrival. When Marya began to squirm, he passed her along. He observed his brothers' indifference as they passed her around the table. Something indefinable shifted.

Halene gathered hands full of the detritus of the meal and turned to collect the pie and clean dishes to serve it on. The black landline rang. The conversation around the table quieted as she answered. It was the young midwife. Her patient today was the same age as Anya. She was weeping and angry. "They died. They both died. It was horrible! Why couldn't you have at least come? Why?"

"Tell me what happened."

"The umbilical cord was barely the length of my hand. It ripped the placenta out while the baby was descending through the birth canal. They both bled out. They died, and I couldn't save them." The last, she cried out on a wail. Deep, searing guilt assailed Halene. It was the consequence of a broken pact. It didn't matter that until today, it was religiously intact.

"Such a rare condition. There was little you could have done differently and little I could have done had I been there." Halene hoped the words meant more to Anya than they did to her. She knew the truth of them, yet sorrow overwhelmed her soul...and guilt, deep, unreasonable guilt.

The midwife's young patient needed an ultrasound and a cesarian section. Neither were available in the village, even had a doctor been present. The nearest clinic to offer such facilities was hours away over rugged terrain.

The scraping of chairs alerted her, and she turned back. The boys were heading out the door. Her sons did not make eye contact. She knew where they were going. But not tonight. It shouldn't be tonight.

Furious, she met Petrov's eyes. Her pain was more than physical. "You would dare."

He dropped his gaze but continued out the back door behind his sons. His arm was draped across Ilya's shoulders, guiding the boy before him. Ilya's chest swelled with pride. It was the first time he was allowed to join the men in their evening social at the pub.

Alcoholism was the scourge of Petrov's family. It was a tradition for the men to gather in the pub in the evening. The hunt, the success, the tiger sighting were all worthy reasons to gather. Babies happened all the time.

Halene resettled Marya inside her shawl, snug and warm against her body. She threw one of Petrov's old rain slickers over her head as the first raindrops fell. She stepped into a worn pair of rubber boots and into the yard to inspect the venison hanging in the shed.

The storm broke over the village. Rain pounded down in sheets. Lightning flashed, and thunder crashed instantly.

Cat Funk

Cat Funk has been inflicting her stories on friends and relations since elementary school. She hasn't found the rule book yet but believes that when she does there will be a sternly worded paragraph about serving cats if that is actually your name. She enjoys living the cliché with her two spoiled felines and harbors a secret dream of becoming a hermit someday.

The Shadow Girl
By Amy Lauer Goldin

The small girl with the carefully arranged blond curls twirls in her red coat, white gloves and black patent leather shoes. Her mother sits on the bench and lights a cigarette as they wait for the bus. Everything shiny new, and ready for display.

She is mildly confused about all the fuss. It is not her birthday. Not yet Christmas, despite the nip in the air. Her mother's voice is telling her not to touch her hair. Don't scuff your shoes. Be still and stand up straight. The crosstown bus wheezes to a stop at their corner and the girl and her mother get on. She feels shy on the bus; overdressed and too colorful. Everyone else is in drab work clothes. There are men in caps and overalls, and women in cheap car coats, some with aprons peeking out from below, wearing sensible worn-down shoes. She catches curious glances aimed at her from some of the bored passengers. An elderly woman smiles in a kindly manner, her tired brown face momentarily brightening.

The smoke from her mother's cigarette wafts down to her, mixing with scented drugstore soap and hairspray. Sometimes when she lies in bed at night waiting for her mother to come home from work, she can close her eyes and conjure that smell.

When she hears the high heels clicking up the stairs, she knows the scent will be making its entrance momentarily, with a fragrant good night kiss to follow. Soap, smoke and hairspray. It is a comforting blend.

She wonders where they are going. She hasn't been told. Her instructions were to be a good girl, best behavior, no monkeyshines. She looks out the window at the traffic, the stores, the lights. There are still Kennedy posters in a few of the darkened shop windows. They look like the round metal button her mother wore on her coat for months. She thinks back to the night she and her mother and aunt Bonnie huddled around their small television, watching the grainy black and white footage of the handsome young Irishman and his beautiful wife being showered with confetti. Her mother and aunt had cried with happiness, as if a family member had been elected President.

Thanksgiving has just passed, and the Christmas displays are popping up here and there. She recognizes Rudolph in a store window pointing a hoof toward washing machines. This strikes her as funny and she starts to giggle, then catches herself. Best behavior!

The bus stops at the next corner and she is being led off in the firm grip of her mother's hand. The night air is fresh and bracing after the warm crowded bus. Once on the sidewalk they stop. Her mother looks around carefully to get her bearings, and off they go, high heels and Mary Janes creating an echo on the darkening streets. They walk along for two blocks, past a hardware store and a barber shop, both closed for the evening. She takes note of the colorful barber pole. It is the same kind as the one in the shop next to their apartment building. She wonders if this is some sacred talisman that all barbers share, like the statues of the Blessed Mother on the many lawns in the neighborhood near her school.

Soon they are standing in front of a diner. The hamburger smell wafting in the cool night air makes her mouth water, and the booths are bright red and white shiny fake leather. It looks like a party to which she has not been invited. She imagines herself drinking a coke from one of those big coca cola fountain glasses and eating hot salty French fries with ketchup. She longs to go into the diner but knows instinctively to keep this request to herself.

Her mother taps a nervous toe against the cement and smooths a gloved hand over her lacquered French twist. The girl can tell they are waiting, but she doesn't know what they are waiting for.

After a few chilly minutes she feels a sudden tension transfer from her mother's hand to her own gloved hand. Her grip tightens abruptly, and she is again being reminded to be on best behavior, stand up straight, smile.

There is a man walking towards them. She can feel the electric charge of adrenaline flow through the gloves from her mother's firm hand to her small one. Her mother is smiling. Her smile looks rehearsed, like one of those Hollywood movie star smiles in the magazines. This is confusing. She is constantly being warned about strange men, yet this man is walking right up to them. She has never seen her mother speak to a man on the street before, with the exception of the neighborhood shopkeepers, the mailman, and occasionally the priests at church. Her mother laughs nervously and exchanges some quiet conversation with the man. He is tall, and her mother must tilt her face up to speak to him. The girl has never noticed her mother's face from this angle before. It looks oddly distorted and is disconcerting. She is accustomed to the way that face looks when it is tilted down towards her. Her mother's voice sounds different too. There is no firmness in it. No fatigue. It is slightly breathy, with a forced casual tone. They discuss the bus trip. No, no trouble finding the place. There is no mention of the hours of preparation, hairdressing, outfit selection. After this confusing and awkward small talk, her mother says, "Well then, shall we go in?" Her heart leaps at the prospect of going into the diner to eat. She is already picturing herself sliding into the long, cushiony booth and swinging her shiny shoes under the table. But no. Now there is some hurried discussion in hushed tones. Not as light and friendly as before. She catches bits and pieces. "…Can't be seen together, I work near here." Her mother's face hardens and looks like fine china that could crack and break into pieces at any minute. She looks like she is trying hard not to cry. This is a look the girl is familiar with, and it makes her anxious. Now her stomach feels tight and uneasy. She wants to yank her mother's hand and run away from this man. Why are they even talking to him? Her mother knows men are dangerous. She says so all the time.

The girl has to pee now and feels fidgety. She is having a hard time standing up straight, but her mother is in enough distress already. She mustn't add to it.

At last, their strained conversation dwindles to an awkward end. The long silence that follows seems to intensify the increasing chill of the night air. The man taps a cigarette out of a pack and lights it with a nonchalant flip of his zippo lighter. The two adults look away from each other, gazing toward separate distant horizons. Finally, the man fumbles in his finely tailored overcoat and extends his arm. In his hand is an envelope. Her mother squares her shoulders, and with as much dignity as she can muster, reaches for it, accepting it with two gloved fingers as if it were something foul and dead. She drops it into her pocketbook without looking at it.

Finally, the tall man looks down at the girl, as if noticing her for the first time. There is a bright streetlight behind him, and she is standing in his shadow. She doesn't want to look up into his face. She doesn't want to know or remember what he looks like. Suddenly everything seems distorted, as if she were viewing this scene through a funhouse mirror. The careful composure she has maintained all afternoon, evidently for this moment, is gone. Her face is a mask of anxiety. She is afraid she will wet her pants in front of this unwelcome stranger, in this unfamiliar part of town, in her new outfit, in front of her mother. She clutches her mother's hand tighter. The electricity is gone, but the steadfast firmness is there. She clings to it.

The man leans down a bit and says her name. How does he know her name? It terrifies her that this stranger knows her name and seems to have some sort of sway over her mother. She wants to run, to scream at him to not say her name, never say it again! She wants him to leave them alone. Instead, she manages a shaky "Hello."

He tells her what a pretty girl she is. Says she looks like her mother. She knows she should say thank you but says nothing. Her mother has always told her that good looks are an accident and can be a curse. He notes that she is tall for her age. Her mother turns her face away again, looking toward that elusive urban horizon.

He tells her to be a good girl. Her face grows hot. She wants to tell him she IS a good girl; everyone says so, but again she remains silent, only nodding her head slightly in the affirmative. Her heart is pounding, like when she runs up the three flights of stairs to the small apartment they share with Aunt

Bonnie. She longs to be back in the soft comfort of a home filled with only women. She is frantic for this whole evening to be over. She wants fervently for this to have never happened. She feels as if something has been broken and can't be fixed, and that somehow it is her fault.

He reaches for her free hand. Before she can pull it away his large hand with the thick gold ring presses something into it. She looks and sees it is a five-dollar bill. He tells her to buy something pretty with it. Her mother abruptly says it is time to go. He says her name again, then goodbye. He looks at her mother again and seems to want to speak but says nothing. Her mother's eyes look hard and glittery, and especially blue under the harsh streetlight.

The girl is relieved when the man finally turns and walks down the street. He casually flicks his glowing cigarette butt into the gutter, slides his hands into his pockets, and disappears around a corner.

Her mother looks down and asks if she is cold. In an unsteady voice she replies that she is alright but needs to use the lady's room. Her mother tenderly runs her gloved hand down the small, flushed cheek. Suddenly everything comes back into focus. The traffic sounds emerge, the chill of the night air cools their faces and they walk toward the bright lights of the diner together.

Amy Lauer Goldin

Amy Lauer Goldin is a writer living in St Augustine Florida. Her prose works include short stories and an upcoming novel. She is an active member of Ancient City poets and has been featured multiple times in their literary journal, AC PAPA, and the poetry anthology Florida Bards. She has authored several plays, which have been featured in the Five & Dime Festival in Jacksonville, A Classic Theatre and at Flagler College and other theatrical venues in and around St Augustine.

He Called it a What?
By Geoffrey K. Graves

As this will demonstrate, a 1960's eighth grade biology class was far more rudimentary than what is taught today. Mr. Peters (not his real name) was our biology teacher at the Wilhelmina C. Peabody Junior High School (not its real name) in Santa Sabinas (ditto), California (real). In the biology lab section of the class, students outfitted with goggles, protective bibs and scalpels, performed the dissection of dead earthworms and frogs. I have no idea how my worm met his maker because he was dead when I got him. I am no worm murderer, and I could not have asked him how he expired even if I could have resuscitated him for the obvious reason: I don't speak worm. The point is, those were dangerous times to be an earthworm. From what I heard on a recent National Public Radio show, these educational dissection procedures still survive in schools today. Pity the lowly earthworm, mourn the doomed frog.

Once we students mastered the worm postmortem, we were ready for the more challenging frog autopsy. I have no idea what future value there was for me in performing those procedures. Except for a few weirdos, most of us really didn't want to dissect anything. Where was PETA, or PETW, when you needed them? In my whole life I have yet to perform another autopsy on anything and I seriously doubt the need will ever arise. Insofar as I know, there wasn't then and isn't now an overwhelming demand for coroners of non-mammalian creatures, and even if there were I doubt it would pay much.

But the worm and frog dismemberings were of minor importance to us kids because we had been tipped off by older brothers, sisters and friends about a far more intriguing lecture to come that was the highlight of eighth-grade biology. From day one, each of us was only waiting for what we called revelation day when two diagrams would be unmasked, and those diagrams were there right above the chalk board, taunting us the entire semester, curled up in spring-loaded tension waiting behind Mr. Peters. Would he ever get on with it? Two charts, side-by-side. Sometimes it was hard to pay attention knowing he was, evidently, saving the best for last.

Mr. Peters was a soft-spoken man who always wore a crisp white lab coat. Grade 'A' testosterone must have run in his family because he had one of the thickest five o'clock shadows I've ever seen, his dark stubble a blue-black. Whenever he lectured, Peters held a wooden pointer with a black rubber tip on the end. He seldom let it out of his grasp, holding it tightly like an adult security blanket. Sometimes he would scribble away on the chalkboard, pointer tucked under arm, and other times he presented slides on the overhead projector, directing our attention to pertinent information on screen, but always the pointer was there.

As days in the class turned into weeks and months, we were all wondering what in the world he was waiting for. Finally, a week before final exam, time was up, and we knew he had to unroll those two charts. Revelation day had arrived. The entire class was giddy, wound up as tight as the charts and barely able to contain ourselves. As junior high schoolers, hormonally speaking we were at our pubescent fever pitch.

It soon became apparent why Peters had been stalling. He was as nervous about the lesson as we were. He took forever, over-embroidering explanations he'd already said until he slowly, finally unrolled chart number one: an illustration of the female anatomy. On the left side of her body, the woman was shown with skin on, naked. On the right, her innards were displayed.

Peters' mouth went dry. He sipped a glass of water, then with trusty pointer in hand, he started at the top of the female figure telling us things we already knew, nasal passages, tear ducts, larynx and so on. He finally got down to the breasts and, speaking evenly in a slow emotionless monotone, he said, "These are the breasts." Sip water. "There are two of them. One on the left. One on the right. Side-by-side. As you can see." Sip, sip. "There are glands in the breasts capable of producing milk to feed an infant. And this is the areola which surrounds the nipple which expresses that milk I just mentioned."

"Mr. Peters, I have a question about the nipples," piped up one brave youth. "Does one of the nipples express chocolate milk and one vanilla because my brother told me that was true."

Peters took a breath, narrowed his eyes a bit trying to figure out if Robin was being serious or having him on, then he remembered something. He said, "No, Mr. Graham, that is not true, and your brother should have known better because he asked that same question three years ago in this very class which I suspect you know. Now, then...."

Emboldened by Robin's question, John Kulish weighed in next. "Mr. Peters, two questions. First, is the milk from the nipple the same as cow milk?"

"No, Mr. Kulish, it is chemically different. What's your other question?"

"What's the purpose of the aerola?"

"The purpose of the areola is…well, I really don't know. Perhaps you can research that and do an extra-credit report for us. Now, class, please hold your questions until I have finished. Where was I, the arm tits? Pits! I meant pits, darn it!"

Tittering from the class took a while to die down. "You were starting on the areolas," Debbie Utley, one of the sharper students, said, guiding Peters back on track.

"Thank you, Deborah. Yes, we were on the areolas," Peters said, starting up again though clearly flustered. "There are two areolas. One per breast.

There are two nipples. One per areola." Peters worked his tongue in his mouth in search of any saliva. His parched lips were as dry as his mouth. He kept sipping and swallowing and taking slow deep breaths, but it was no good. As he got more nervous, we kids were getting more nervous, the tension in the air thickening.

Peters moved his pointer down to the pubic region, and with quivering voice said, "This, here, is the pubis area." He swallowed hard, as though a piece of the school cafeteria's dry roast beef was stuck in his throat. He loosened his black tie. Same black tie every day. "And this is the va-, va-, va- ...gina."

I thought Peters was going to pass out. He hadn't even unrolled the male chart, but sweat was dripping down his blue-black sideburns. This is no exaggeration. In that short time, the man was sweating profusely, and his pointer was shaking like he'd developed a palsy. He could barely keep his black tip on the chart.

He finished with the woman and rolled up that chart with a whap, then slowly drew down the male chart and began again from the top. Hair, scalp, eyebrows, eyeballs, brain, cerebral cortex, etcetera. After dawdling several minutes more, he arrived at the male privates, pointer shaking like crazy with each wobble of the pointer producing a whap-whap noise. It was too much for him and he turned, grabbed his water glass and took too big a gulp, coughed, spraying it all over the chart. He pretended to accidently drop his pointer, took a long moment to bend over, breathe, and regroup. As he came back up Peters let his lab coat arm surreptitiously wipe the chart with a swipe that completely missed. He continued lecturing as the water rolled down in rivulets, puddling on the floor. He fanned his face with his pointer-free hand.

"Whew. Warm day," he smiled weakly and moved over to the thermostat where he turned on the AC full blast.

This may sound like some cock-and-bull story, but none of it is invention. Any kid who was in that class talked about it for years. I'm still talking about it, and I'm old. This guy was freaking out. He steadied his pointer with both hands and placed the rubber tip on the man's pouch and said like a metallic-voiced robot, "This is the scro-tum. And inside the scro-tum," he pointed at the gonads, "are the testicles," which he pronounced tess-tee-culz. "There are two of them. There's one on the right side. One on the left side. These tess-tee-culz are what produce see-men, a liquid filled with spermatozoa which, once, uh, planted, seek out the egg in the female that eventually grows into a baby."

"Question about the planting," Robin Graham tried.

"Can it, Graham!" Peters exploded, whipping out a handkerchief from his lab coat pocket to blot his glistening forehead and the beads of moisture that had formed on his stubbled upper lip. His perspiration had now created two large rings under his lab coat armpits.

Every kid in the room was about to lose it. I caught a glimpse of the girl to my right whose face was red. She was peeking at me at the same time and we both gave each other a look that said, "Can you believe this guy?" We clamped our hands over our mouths because we were ready to lose it. If nervousness was a disease, our class had caught the contagion. The whole room was throbbing with suppressed energy like Poe's telltale heart as Peters' pointer moved ever closer to the you-know-what.

He finally got up the gumption and placed the black tip on the illustrated man's member, and it was like Peters had been hit with a 220-volt live wire, the vibrating pointer producing an even louder flap-flap-flap sound like a playing card against a bicycle's spokes. The moment had at last arrived. Revelation Day. The entire room was holding its collective breath."

Then, Mr. Peters said something I will never forget, and this is what he said: "And this..." (lick dry lips) "...is the man's pennis."

That is not a typo. Pennis. Not penis. Pennis. And our biology teacher didn't know how to say it. Every kid in the class was ready to hear penis, but Peters said pennis. Rhymes with tennis. Pennis.

One thing that was good about the "pennis" pronunciation was that it kind of deflated the nervousness out of us kids. Imagine one big thought bubble floating over the classroom that said, "Huh?!" We were all stumped.

By the time you're in the eighth grade, you've pretty much got down the names of the private parts of the male and female anatomy. Children say they have to pee-pee, not pen-pen. Peters' pronunciation had us all looking at each other, perplexed. Did I hear that right? I mean, this guy's the biology teacher and if anybody should know how to say it correctly, he'd be the guy, right? Hm, maybe I've had it wrong all along."

Well, Peters had timed it perfectly because the bell rang right after the "pennis" had been described. He yanked that chart so hard it fell onto the floor where some spring in it tried to roll itself back up and class was dismissed.

There were some interesting conversations outside the room afterward, and there were some interesting conversations around dinner tables that night. Here's how it went at my house:

————

ME - Hey, pops, you know what you told me my thingy is called?

My father shot a look over at my mother and said slowly....

POPS - ...Yeeessssss.

ME - Are you sure it's called that?

POPS - Yes. Why do you ask?

ME - Well, Mister Peters gave us the biology

lecture today about male and female anatomy, and when he got to the middle of the man chart, he put his pointer on the dick and he called it a pennis.

POPS - A what? And don't use the dick term in front of your mother and sister.

ME - He called it a pennis.

POPS - Pennis?

ME – Yep, pennis.

POPS - He's nuts.

ME - No, he called them tess-tee-culz.

POPS - No, I mean he is looney toons. It is called penis. Not pennis.

ME - You sure?

POPS - I am sure.

ME - But he is a biology teacher. How do you know your parents didn't tell you wrong and you passed on bad info to me?

POPS - Lookit. Peters doesn't know his nuts from his hat. I know it is a penis. My parents called it a penis. Your mom knows it is a penis. Her parents told her it is a penis. Right?

MOM - Yes.

POPS - It is a penis. Penis penis penis. Hear me? Everybody's called it that since time immemorial, since Adam and Eve. Everybody but Peters. If you want to call it a pennis, go ahead, but everybody you say it to except Peters is going to laugh you out of the building.

ME – Okay. Is a vagina called a vagina?

POPS - Yep. Now, take your little pennis and go

do the dishes.

ME - Okay. That was pretty funny, Pops.

POPS - Right. Dishes.

As I cleared the table, my father said to my mother, "That school needs a new biology teacher. Pennis!"

Geoffrey K. Graves

Geoffrey K. Graves' work has been recognized and/or published internationally: 2023/24 Pushcart Prize Nominee (US); Longlisted Disquiet Prize 2024 (Portugal); TulipTree Publishing 2024 & 2020 (US); Witcraft 2023 (Australia); Finalist 2021 Bellingham Review's Tobias Wolff Award for Fiction (US); First Honorable Mention (2nd place winner) 2022 Periscope Literary/Word Press (UK); Shortlisted 2021 Bath Flash Fiction Award (Ireland); Writer's Digest (US) - #1-Notable Short Story 2020, #2-First Prize Short-Short Story 2020, #3-Honorable Mention Short Story Humor category 2023; Winner Micro-Fiction 2020 Grindstone Literary Anthology (UK); Finalist 2019 Cutthroat Barry Lopez Nonfiction Award (US); and elsewhere. He lives in Palm Springs, California, with his wife, a backyard full of goldfinches, rabbits, hummingbirds, and an occasional coyote with mandatory roadrunner. He worked in the script department at CBS, Television City, Hollywood. He has a BA and MA from CSU, Fullerton. His first publication was the co-authored satirical novel "Seven Days to Disaster," published by Major Books in 1976 about a secret agent on a budget who drove a Nash Metropolitan. He now writes fiction and non-fiction serious and humorous short stories, and has a humorous collection he's shopping around.

The Hindenbug
By Kevin L Hostbjor

CHAPTER 1
The Edge of the Great Wood

After a brief flight, I joined a small swarm of soldiers gathering at the western edge of the Great Wood. My sudden arrival at the Exercise Grounds caught their attention and they began grousing.

"Why send us here?" Enf'n asked. "The sky is beautiful, and we lose time from protecting the farmer ants while they gather their pieces of leaves. The colony needs those leaves to survive."

Other ants echoed her griping. "Yes. Alf'y. Why every day?"

Enf'n called out again. "Why march to this bleached stretch of sand? We abandoned it long ago." She arched her mandible high, clicking it together seven times.

She is older than the others.

Stepping up on a smooth protruding rock at the center of the exercise area, I loomed several ant heights over the soldiers. "Why? Don't you remember the stories?" My six legs spun around allowing my dark compound eyes to sweep the entire swarm. "Our colony left the Great Field after the attack. Thirty-two moon cycles ago, our mortal enemies caught us unprepared. They killed many of our ancestors." I spread my mandible and shook my head. "Never again."

To stress my point, I fluttered my wings. "Most of you only claim a few cycles of the moon. I first witnessed the brightness of the round moon eleven cycles ago and hope to see another eleven. Maybe twelve."

In response to Enf'n, I raised my head and clicked my mandible together eleven times in rapid succession. "You must prepare. You must practice. You must protect our Queen."

Enf'n spoke again. "Why fear the Reds? Am I not bigger than them? And what does a drone like you know about fighting?"

For the first time, I noticed her larger than normal soldier body. I credited this to her age. Until this new assignment, I never associated with females.

Looking into the eyes of the gathered soldiers, I gestured to Enf'n. "Yes. Enf'n is bigger than a Red, but unaware. Reds move with a wild fury unlike anything imaginable."

I spun around again.

"Remember the stories. They circle and attack you in numbers. They bite off your legs."

Many voices murmured.

"Once limited in movement, they bite you in half or bite off your head."

Gasps filled the swarm.

"They take your body parts back to feed their larvae."

More gasps. One ant collapsed. Enf'n stood motionless, her eyes following my movement. Stepping down from the rock, she moved to face me. Lowering her mandible, she bumped my head. For some reason, my wings fluttered again.

She acknowledged. "For six black legs … and survival."

With a shake to clear my head, I launched into the air and began searching the area. Seeing no signs of danger, I landed on a tree branch and watched.

Enf'n scrambled up on the rock and bellowed. "Begin! Take turns surrounding one another and practice your attack. If surrounded, practice defense."

After their exercises concluded, the soldier ants marched single file back to the nest and took up their guard duties, protecting the workers, our Queen, and her eggs.

CHAPTER 2

The Darks of Their Eyes

Two days later, the morning broke with a red sky. From a distance, I watched Enf'n lead a swarm of 100 soldiers to the exercise field. None of the rookies claimed over four moons.

A slight breeze followed them.

It grew.

The attack occurred after they began to exercise. Not from the field. The Reds entered the Great Wood on both sides, merged and attacked from the forest … from the direction of safety.

From my perch in the tree, I saw Enf'n scurry to the talking rock. She called the alarm and ordered her soldiers to take position. They faced their enemy and steadied themselves for battle. Reds began a horrific attack, five or six of them surrounding any outlier soldier and removing her head.

For every Red removed from the fight, three black soldiers fell. Outnumbered, six to one, Enf'n realized the futility of a mandible-to-mandible fight.

She shouted orders. "Retreat. Follow me!" She tried to rally her swarm hoping to escape into the Great Field, through its tall grasses.

As she turned, thousands of Reds poured out of the grass, and I realized the name of the exercise field needed to be changed to a killing ground.

I heard Enf'n bellow. "Save the nest. Take as many Red heads as possible. Fight to save the Queen." She stepped off the rock and began tearing into the enemy.

One by one, her young soldiers fell to overwhelming odds. Backing into her former position on the rock, her mandible chattered and clicked like a maniac. "Death to all Reds".

After seeing her decapitate a dozen of their fellow comrades, the Reds hesitated. Regaining their courage, they hoped to intimidate their black enemy. They circled and closed.

Enf'n stood firm and began stomping her feet in a six-legged pattern called the death dance.

Ignoring her threats, three Reds started to sneak

up from behind her, two of them pressing the first one. Seeing their brave comrade, the Red army began to surge forward.

As the Red behind Enf'n maneuvered to clip her back leg, it noticed my shadow and looked up. I swooped down and removed its head. Its body parts rolled into the other two Reds. They tumbled. For the moment, all Red ants hesitated while analyzing their new threat.

I fluttered up and grabbed Enf'n with my six legs and carried her aloft. Many Reds screamed some guttural language. Ignoring their savage words, I raised my rear and pooped hoping the splatters of my descending scent soiled several of them enough for them to kill each other in their bloodthirsty confusion.

"Let me go. Take me back." Enf'n roared. "If I must die, I wish to die with my swarm." Pulled tight into my thorax, I felt a quiver from her back as she struggled to get loose.

I shook her with my legs. "Enf'n. Die if you must, but only while protecting your nest and your Queen. Not those last few soldiers remaining in the field." As I flew her into the Wood, water gushed from the skies.

Other drones noticed my returning flight. After I explained what happened, they flew around passing the word. "The Reds attacked. The Reds attacked."

I settled on a short rise above our nest entrance. "Enf'n. You fought the Reds. You saw how they fight. Any other black ant who ever fought a Red is dozens of moons gone. We only know stories. Some call them myths. Teach the soldiers. Prepare them."

Once again, she lowered her mandible and bumped my head. I began an uncontrolled flutter.

With our heads still together, I felt her body quiver again. "You honor me Alf'y. No other drone has ever done this. No other drone ever moved me like this."

CHAPTER 3
All Quiet on the Western Front

At first light, Enf'n exited the nest and called to the nearest ant. "Gather our soldiers. We must prepare." A scurry ensued. Before long, soldier ants covered the entire area around the nest.

I watched her from an overhanging branch.

Enf'n approached one soldier. They lowered their mandibles and bumped heads. She turned to another soldier and repeated the action as the first ant did the same. One head bump after another continued. From my elevated perch, the movement of head bumps acted like a ripple in a pond, expanding until every soldier ant bumped another.

Every soldier now understood how to fight a Red.

Enf'n called out to the amassed army. "Death to the Reds. Long live the Queen." She clicked her mandible seven times.

She is Amazing.

I lifted from my branch and hurried to the

western edge of the Wood.

The army swarmed as one to the Killing Grounds. They marched with stealth, no battle cries, no clicking mandibles. They marched in seven columns, seven soldiers abreast. They marched until the field came into view and then scurried into the trees and bushes and shrubs and tufts of grass and weeds until the entire army vanished.

Only an occasional drone flying from one branch to another gave evidence of movement beyond the breeze teasing the tall grasses. Only the fluttering of their wings breeched the silence.

Enf'n moved out into the Killing Grounds and mounted the talking rock and clicked her mandible. Six soldiers moved from behind a small log and positioned themselves before her.

She scooted down to meet them and started to march toward the Great Field at the end of the world. Three soldiers moved to either side, marching in line. They approached the tall grass and entered its maze of tufts and folds. The second ant on her left side screamed as the lead soldier lost her head between one blade of grass and the next.

"Ambush!" Enf'n shouted. "Back to the Wood." The remaining six soldiers turned to scurry back to our awaiting army. The former lead soldier on the right, now the last in line, lost one leg and another. Then she lost her head.

I watched Enf'n clear the grass and rush to the talking rock. She turned to discover only three of her brave soldiers remained. "To the Wood." She raised her head to see me perched on my usual shrub. "Now!"

As Enf'n darted into the Wood, the Red army poured through the grass. A dozen drones took flight from their various locations and called from above. "Attack."

Our army flooded from the trees and a melee of clashing mandibles ensued.

Suddenly, all fighting stopped when a loud crack of thunder tried to deafen our hearing. Then another. The ground shook. I looked up to see only a few white clouds in the blue sky.

I flew down next to Enf'n, perched on a log to survey and direct the battle. Her six legs stomped the death dance. I nudged her. "What is happening?"

From our left, a giant creature with two gray legs stomped through the stunned armies. In its wake, many of our brave soldiers lay smushed and hundreds of Reds with them. The talking rock protruded from the bottom of a huge depression.

"How does a creature move on two legs?" I asked.

Enf'n shook her head.

The ants, still startled by what happened, saw another giant rush by. Then several others followed. Each of them left smushed Red ants, flattened grass, and large depressions in the earth.

Some of the giants used their two upper appendages for carrying long sticks. They lifted them high in the air. Another loud crack of thunder struck. Smoke belched from the stick.

I turned to Enf'n. "We must leave this field. Let the giants kill our enemy."

Several distant thunder cracks broke our thoughts. Something whizzed by and struck the tree above us with a whack. I flew up to investigate and landed in an indentation in the bark. Venturing in, I found a smooth black object at the back. It stunk.

Moving back to the entrance I looked beyond the Killing Grounds. From this height I observed giants on both sides of the Great Field with thunder sticks. They charged each other. Blue legs stomped a two-legged death dance with gray legs. In every dance, one or the other fell.

I fluttered down to Enf'n. "I went higher into the tree than ever before. I discovered something amazing."

"What?"

"The Great Field is not the end of the world. There is another Wood on the other side."

CHAPTER 4

Shaken Not Stirred

I flew above the army as they marched back to our nest. With so few soldiers lost, their mandibles click clacked with triumph. The rhythm of victory proceeded us, and the entire nest waited for our arrival with excitement. I landed next to Enf'n as she approached the nest entrance. Several worker ants moved forward to greet us.

"The Queen wishes to see you."

I clicked to Enf'n. "Go. I'm sure she wants to congratulate you on your victory."

She shook her head. "You know very well; the victory falls at the feet of the two-legged giants."

"Still." I wriggled my mandible.

Four of the workers rushed to my side. "You too, drone."

"Me?"

Their mandibles clicked. I counted eleven clicks.

"I've never seen the Queen before. I don't know what to say."

Enf'n stomped a foot and wriggled her abdomen and again, I heard a slight quiver. "You say nothing. Let me talk."

The workers led us into the nest. Others followed and many stayed by my side. As we moved, a thought frightened me. My wings fluttered. "What if she wants to eat me or feed me to her larvae."

Enf'n stopped and turned. "What part of say nothing confused you?"

I clicked a nervous clack.

***

Deep into the nest, we trekked. I know my life began deep down, during my pupae stage, but the memory of those early days is lost. I fluttered.

Enf'n noticed and quivered with a humorous giggle. "Your confusion is normal. Only the Queen's worker attendants know how to find her. Scents in these tunnels confuse everyone else. It is for her safety and the safety of her eggs."

"You don't seem confused."

She clacked her mandible. "I know."

We entered another chamber and my thorax jumped.

A voice unknown to me spoke. "Hello daughter."

I looked at the Queen and back to Enf'n.

Enf'n bowed her head. "Hello Mother. My Queen."

"Why is this drone here? Is he for lunch?" She gurgled a deep rumble.

Enf'n raised her head and moved it side to side. "No Mother. I desire him for my first mate."

The Queen clacked her massive jaws. Several worker attendants moved forward. "So, you intend to take my place?"

Confused, I tried to understand. Enf'n is the Queen's daughter? Only a Princess takes a first mate. Princesses fly. In my sensory confusion, I lost control and my wings fluttered.

Dozens of workers surrounded me displaying no intention of letting me get closer to the Queen.

"No Mother. I intend to leave your nest and extend the colony to a new location."

"Bah!" She shook her head. "I know when your older sister maimed you as a child by clipping one of your wings, her jealous actions warranted a death sentence. But kill my own daughter. No." She shook her head. "Banishment became her punishment. I removed your second wing to keep you balanced and functional."

The Queen gazed at her daughter. "Founding a new colony is difficult without wings."

"Alf'y, my drone, has wings."

"Your drone has a name? Oh my. This is serious." The Queen tipped her head and her jaws clacked again. "Is there any way to convince you this is nonsense?"

"No Mother."

"Then hear my words. Take your drone and six others, giving you seven. Take 49 of the outer nest workers, 147 soldiers, and 77 farmers. No more, no less. Travel west across the Great Field."

I flinched. The Queen's head turned.

"Yes drone, I know it's not the end of the world. I ventured across the Great Field, after leaving my mother's nest, many moon cycles ago." She sighed. "My first mate and I established a nest there." She considered me again. "Thank you for your part in vanquishing the Red devils."

I raised my head, and my mandible began to open.

"Do not speak!" The words echoed through the chamber.

My sensory confusion manifested itself and I wondered if the echo came from the Queen or Enf'n. No matter. I kept my mouth shut and lowered my head.

"Daughter."

Enf'n turned from scowling at me and back to

her mother.

So, her voice kept me silent.

"Go into the Greater Wood on the far side of the grassy field. Travel until you find a stream. You must find a way across. Continue until the ground gets moist. Look for the Great Tree. It's the largest tree in the world and has roots rising into the sky and branches blocking the light from above. Beneath one of those roots is your destination. During your journey, food is available on the dark side of trees and logs. Make use of the sustenance."

The Queen's mandible quivered. "Ask to see the Great Queen. My Mother. Call her the Hindenbug. She has great knowledge. Her insight is your only hope."

Enf'n quivered. "The Hindenbug?"

"Yes. Now come bump heads with me."

CHAPTER 5

Crime Scene Do Not Cross

It took hours for my head to clear after leaving the Queen's chamber. I began to understand things for the first time. The quivering I felt while carrying Enf'n came from the stubs of her wings. It explains the trembling when we bumped heads. It also accounts for why my wings flutter when she wriggles her abdomen.

She is not a soldier, she is a Princess, and my wings serve her.

Our selected and volunteer ants grouped together outside the nest. Enf'n, my Princess, addressed them. "Is everyone ready?" Many clicks and clacks answered amidst bobbing heads and stomping feet. She called out. "March!"

280 ants followed Enf'n toward the Great Field. The army formed into seven squads, each with 40 ants, comprising 21 soldiers, eleven farmers, and seven workers. One drone fluttered above each squad. With no Red army to fear, the army marched together, mandibles clacking. The six drones and I watched out for danger and carried messages.

The squads passed the Killing Grounds depression, three to one side, four to the other. No one wanted to step across the crushed bodies of our fellow colony members.

During our march through the tall grasses, I expected to find bodies of the fallen two-legged grays and blues. Instead, we encountered parallel scoured canyons to traverse. Something monstrous injured the earth. Curious, I flew higher and followed the trail, ending at a frightening sight. I discovered rows of enormous anthills. Dozens of them. They dwarfed our nest. If these hills belong to the Red colony, our journey is doomed. There is room for millions of Red devil villains.

Hoping for a path to sneak by unnoticed, I flew higher to see which direction their nest entrances faced, to our dark side or the sunny side of the hills.

My search revealed no evidence of nest entrances, only planted sticks. The giants used these mounds to grow their thunder sticks. Each hill contained one vertical stick with two branches growing side by side near the top. With haste, I flew back and reported to my Princess.

Later, when the sun scorched the earth, we rested in the shadow of a huge fallen tree. It had a cavernous, empty belly. Something carved out everything from the inner tree, leaving only its bark, but I found its surface hard and smooth. No fungus.

Strange.

Above the cavern, at both ends of the tree, grew two huge round ugly flowers. Dark and stiff brown blooms indicated they died long ago. The wind breezed by, and one squeaked and turned.

Hours after departing the shade, the Greater Wood came into view. With renewed enthusiasm, my Princess led the army into the Wood, leaving the Great Field behind.

As if she knew its location, Enf'n took us behind a fallen tree. The separated bark on this tree revealed its center. Fungus and mildew spread along both sides of the void. The army moved in to feast and recuperate.

CHAPTER 6
You Shall Not Pass

Early the next morning, we left the shelter of the void, invigorated, and rejuvenated. We marched until I heard strange sounds. The numerous trees in the Wood concealed the sun, but I estimated hours until midday based on our marching time. I flew ahead to investigate.

I remembered the Queen telling us to march to a stream. I saw flickers of light, reflecting on water, where the sun managed to gain entry through the tree canopy. Feeling brave, I flew closer.

Water in a stream moves from one direction to another. This water remained still. An occasional ripple flickered with light, giving me a brief recollection of watching the army heads bumping together in an ever-expanding circle.

"Oh dear."

I flew back to my Princess and reported my discovery. We marched to the edge of the water. Enf'n shook her head and her mandible clicked. "This is not a stream." She clicked several times again, musing. "I name you the Great Lake."

She turned to me and the other drones. "Fly around the Great Lake and search for a path across."

With two drones, I flew to the left, while four others investigated to the right. In little time, I discovered an end to the Lake. A jumble of sticks, small logs, branches, mud, and leaves edged the Lake. The barrier prevented the Lake from spreading. I directed the other two drones to explore further, as I examined the barrier hoping to find a safe path across.

Determining the barrier easy to traverse, I started to return when movement caught my attention. An enormous furry creature splashed out of the water and headed for the Wood near my Princess. It ran on four legs, trailing a huge appendage.

"What sort of monster is this?"

It thrashed in the brush for several minutes and returned half carrying and half dragging a tree branch. Making fast work of removing the leaves, it trudged back into the Lake. In its wake, one of our squads lay smushed where its appendage heaved across them.

I flew to the Queen and found her directing the remaining squads to shelter in a depression near the base of a large tree. After a few minutes the other five drones returned. Further to the left, the two drones found a cliff where water trickled below. At the bottom, they discovered a path, estimating three days downhill travel to a safe crossing.

I shook my head. "Then three days back up the other side."

The other drones gave worse news. The Great Lake extended a long distance in the other direction and narrowed further away. When they found a crossable path, a long pink snake shot out from the mouth of a gross green monster. It grabbed one of the drones. Then its bulbous mouth belched.

One of the other drones reported seeing several green monsters. He lost count. The route is too dangerous.

I moved to the front. "My Princess. I found a path at the edge of the Great Lake. The furry monster built a barrier. It is a short distance across."

"What about the monster? You saw it destroy an entire squad." She looked back to the Lake. "One drone lost … an entire squad destroyed. We must ensure a safe crossing without losing more."

"Yes. My Princess. However, six squads remain. It is a good number." I pranced on my six legs.

Enf'n lowered her mandible and bumped my head. My wings fluttered.

***

While foraging through our temporary shelter, we heard the splash of water again. The furry monster returned to the banks of the Great Lake moving in our direction. Its determined gait meant only one thing. The creature intended to destroy us. It took three steps with its mammoth legs and a mandible from some other monstrous creature clasped on its leg. The beast howled in pain and flopped back and forth.

I turned to Enf'n, relieved she found this shelter. If we remained by the Lake, the creature's floundering left no room for our survival.

The manic flopping of the beast slowed to a stop.

"My Princess. The beast is dead. We should take this opportunity and cross the barrier."

"What if the great monster from the earth comes up again? One bite from its mandible and I lose my entire swarm. What if the behemoth has friends? No. We wait. We watch. If safe, we leave when morning comes."

***

The morning arrived and the earth moved. Another giant two-leg stomped by. This one walked on dark brown legs. It lowered to the ground. The way its leg bent made me wince. My legs don't bend like this.

Ouch.

I watched its upper appendage twist and pull until the jaws behind the massive mandible pulled from the earth. The giant stood. The great mandible, furry beast, and something connecting them all dangled from its side. It turned and moved away.

"My Princess. Our way is clear."

"Agreed." She called to the rousing army. "March!" Turning back to me, her back quivered. "Show us the way, Alf'y."

At times, I walked with my Princess. At other times, I flew to the next twig, leaf, mud pile, or branch and showed them the way. On the far side of the Great Lake, squad mandibles click clacked as we marched on in search of the Great Tree.

CHAPTER 7

I Have a Bad Feeling About This

Our six surviving squads entered an area of Wood where dampness clung to leaves. The ground darkened. Even the air felt laden with moisture.

I landed next to Enf'n. "My Princess. I think it's going to rain. We need to find shelter."

She shook her head. "This is the moist ground my Queen Mother told me about. The Great Tree is close." She clacked her mandible. "Take the drones aloft and search. The Great Tree's roots grow into the sky."

I directed the drones to fly together in a line with

a short distance between. Late afternoon, we found it. The tree rose to great heights. At its base, several roots rippled outward, up, and down. Once again, I imagined ripples in a pond. I signaled the other drones. "To the Princess."

***

The drones and I advanced toward the Great Tree on the ground, marching with our respective squads. Enf'n directed us away from several root bridges and around others.

She knows the way.

In the distance one large root reached high into the sky. When we approached, a swarm of black army ants surrounded us.

The squads and I began to circle the Princess and take up defensive positions. Facing imminent death, I fluttered my wings and clacked my mandible.

"HOLD!"

I never heard Enf'n call out with such force and authority before. She turned to her defenders. "Back in formation. This embarrassment stops now."

Confused, as usual, I moved with the squads and reformed into six marching squads. Most of them shivered in place.

The largest drone I ever saw stepped forward to greet my Princess. "What is this? Give me reason not to order my army to decimate yours."

"I am Princess Enf'n. My Queen Mother, Cal'n, sent me to see the Great Queen, her mother.

The drone stepped back three paces. His mandible opened and closed without clicking. With a flurry, he bowed his head and fluttered his wings.

After several awkward seconds, he raised his head again. "I apologize for this misunderstanding, Princess. Please allow my soldiers to escort you to our nest entrance. There, the Great Queen's attendant workers can escort you to her chambers." He launched into the air.

The great army in front of us parted and several soldiers beckoned for us to follow. They led us to the entrance and Enf'n directed the six squads to associate with occupants of the Great Queen's nest. "Tell them our story."

The Queen's attendants called for Enf'n to follow them. She turned to me and quivered. "With me."

Several worker attendants moved to prevent me from entering. My Princess spoke again, clicking her mandible six times. "He is with me. I won't tell you twice."

Once again, I followed my Princess into the depths of a nest and experienced the now familiar sensory confusion stemming from the Queen's defenses. We entered the Great Queen's chamber.

"Who is here?" The Great Queen mumbled. "My old eyes fail me."

I wondered about her shriveled body and withered balding skin, most of her hair gray and brittle.

"Great Queen. It's Princess Enf'n. My Queen Mother, Cal'n, sent me to see you and ask to see the Hindenbug."

"Cal'n, you say?" The Great Queen jiggled with laughter. "Only Cal'n ever dared call me the Hindenbug. My favorite daughter."

The Great Queen tried to shift her head. Several attendants moved to assist her. "Come closer child. I wish to tell you a story." The Great Queen lowered her mandible and the two bumped heads. Their antenna entwined.

As I watched, they rubbed antennas and kept their heads together for several minutes. When the Queen raised her head again, her antenna drooped. Enf'n moved a few steps back.

The old Queen turned to her attendants. "It is done. Pass the word. Great Queen Enf'n is here to help our nest flourish once again." She turned back to Enf'n. "My Queen, everything here is yours." She swung her head toward me. "Take your first mate now. Save your colony."

"How? New Queens mate with their first drone in the air. After mating, the male dies and falls to the ground. Then the new Queen finds a nest and lays her eggs."

"Silly girl. This is your nest now. There is no need to fly." Then the old Queen dropped her head and died. Attendants began to remove her body from the chamber.

Enf'n called me to her side. In my sensory confusion I dreamed of flying high into the sky. There I met Enf'n, My Queen, and we coupled. When finished, I fell from the sky and landed in a field of tall grass.

I opened my eyes. My Queen bumped my head and clipped my wings. Attendants gathered and carried them deep into the nest. Other workers picked me up. As they began to move me away, I glanced back and uttered my last words.

"For six black legs … and survival."

My Queen's back quivered.

END

Kevin L Hostbjor

Kevin L Hostbjor grew up on the west coast (best coast) and after a long stint in the United States Navy, landed in the Pacific Northwest. A graduate of the University of Washington with a Bachelor of Science in Metallurgical Engineering and City University with a Master of Science in Project Management, Kevin settled into a gratifying career as a Project Manager Professional (PMP), concluding with the Army Corps of Engineers.

His self-published novel, *The Musher Man*, is a serial-killer thriller, set in the late 1960's Montana. It brings a Jack the Ripper character into a Jack London wilderness environment. Currently, he is in the process of editing his second novel, *The 4th Cohort*. Set in the 80's, imagine Ayn Rand adapting *Ender's Game* by Orson Scott Card into *The Abyss* underwater environment.

Kevin lives in Spokane Valley, WA with his wife, Terri, and whippets Loki and Brewer.

It's Called SPAM
By CM Kelly

"Back in the day …."I realize that such an opening leads one to some preconceived conclusion about what will follow, so my challenge is to shake up your preconceived thought with a light, maybe funny, and somewhat educational story.

In the late 1960s, we moved from a 3-bedroom apartment in Scranton, PA to a farmhouse built in the 1800s on a dirt road, just a few miles outside of town. For some unknown reason living on a paved versus dirt road was a differentiator in one's social standing. I never knew why, but in those years, it made sense. Apparently, in the 1950s or thereabouts, the farmhouse was converted into a hunting cabin or club, thus it had the modern conveniences of electricity and indoor plumbing. When we moved in, the house underwent a major renovation — or more of an overhaul. New roof, windows, wiring, plumbing, floors, furnace, well, septic system, the works.

With the farmhouse came a few acres of land, more than enough room to allow the nine of us space to play kickball, baseball, and football. At one point our dad put up a crude basketball court made from a pair of four-by-fours and a piece of plywood. The combo grass-dirt court was easy on falls but made dribbling quite a challenge. The house and the land came complete with a list of never-ending chores, ranging from cutting grass to painting fences, trimming trees and bushes to hand digging the basement, the latter being a story itself.

With open fields on all sides, a small creek in the backyard, two ponds just a stones throw away, and tall pine trees in the front yard, this old farmhouse was the idyllic place to raise a family of nine children. With great pride, our mother declared, "We live on Windrift Acres." I recall how proudly she put up a hand-painted sign on the corner pine tree stating so.

I don't know if it was my dad's or mom's idea, but right after we bought the farmhouse, we constructed a 20x15 foot family room addition with tall windows overlooking the creek and ponds and a fireplace at one end. The room, of course was trimmed in 1960s wood paneling, providing our Irish clan of 11 much-needed elbow room. I can safely say that this room was pretty much built with child labor. There would be many projects at this homestead that didn't just build muscles, but also character. Since the kitchen was rather small, the family room became the focal point of the household because it contained the one TV we owned.

In Archie Bunker fashion, my father had his favorite chair right in front of the TV (for Gen X and Millennials, think of Sheldon's spot from the *Big Bang Theory*). This family room brought us together for the nightly, post-dinner tradition of watching TV shows. Of course, living in a remote area meant we were lucky to get one TV station, so our viewing choices weren't just limited; they didn't exist. My father initiated the original channel surfing by having one of us 6 boys climb up on the roof and turn the antenna until a station was found.

To complete the setting, we were a family of modest financial means, strong in character and honesty but always light with the dollars. So, on to the main topic: "It's called SPAM." Although the family room was the center of activity, we had all our meals in the kitchen. For such a large family, I don't know how my mom got by with just a basic stove with one oven and a refrigerator the size you'd find today in a garage. No microwave or dishwasher, just a well-used two-slice toaster. Due to the size of the kitchen and because of our financial condition, the kitchen table was a picnic table we moved from the porch, the old wooden kind you would find in a park. My mother hated it. The kitchen door was the main entrance to the house, and the picnic table was the first thing any visitor would see, a telltale sign of our economic standing.

With nine children, mealtime at our house looked more like a cafeteria than a homey Norman Rockwell painting. Breakfast was a procession of children running through the process of taking showers, brushing their teeth, checking the dryer for clean clothes, and finding lost shoes, or coats. Most of us would wolf down a bowl of cereal while others would grab a few pieces of toast; of course, they had to have cinnamon sugar on top.-We were essentially on our own while our mom was busy making the batches of peanut butter and jelly sandwiches for our lunches. The process was loosely choreographed to get the *troops* to the front gate before the school bus arrived. Only on Sunday did breakfast differ. . Because we were all headed to the same Mass, it was the only time we had Mom and Dad join us for breakfast. Mom would cook Dad his eggs and bacon while the rest of us did the cereal/toast routine. Once in a great while, Mom would make scrambled eggs for the children, a treat generally reserved for holidays or birthdays.

Lunches were the standard peanut butter and jelly sandwiches, sometimes just peanut butter or just jelly, but never cold cuts with cheese. I don't recall anything else in the brown paper bags we took to school for 12 years, but we might have the occasional cupcake or celery sticks. When we got older and attended high school, we were allowed to buy a cafeteria lunch once per week. What a treat that was. I don't remember the price of the cafeteria food, but I do recall a milk carton costing six cents and an ice cream sandwich a dime.

Dinners were less confusing than breakfast. During the week and on Saturdays, most of the nine were either at a sporting event, Scouts, or catechism classes. Thus, the "school night" seating around the picnic table was rarely maxed out. Those of us getting home after 6:00 p.m. were usually faced with dried-out, overcooked leftovers. Sunday was more traditional, with the whole household sitting down for a chicken dinner with vegetables and mashed potatoes. Of course, all dinners started with reciting Grace; we sat up straight, chewed with our mouths closed, spoke when spoken to, and asked to be excused from the table.

Mom did have her routine: Sunday was almost always a chicken dinner, Wednesday was spaghetti night, Friday was either pizza or a tuna noodle casserole (never meat on a Friday), and Saturday was hamburgers with oven-baked French-fries. As you can surmise, our mother did not do elaborate or detailed cooking; how could she with such a large crew and a two to three-hour serving window?

I remember some aspects of dinner at Windrift Acres that are noteworthy, like having scrambled eggs with cut-up hotdogs for dinner, opening can after can of apple sauce, and boiling potatoes in what resembled a five-gallon painter's bucket and the mountain of potato skins that came with it. One staple in almost every meal...a taste and image that still runs a cold shiver down my spine...was the yellow wax beans heaped on our plates.

We never had "fancy" meals growing up. Thanksgiving Day turkey and Christmas Day ham were once-a-year events, and those dinners, in many ways, did resemble a Norman Rockwell painting.

Funny side note: In the 1970s, with the skyrocketing prices of beef there was a nationwide beef embargo, well this didn't impact my family. The only red meat we had was the lowest-grade hamburger or something called a cube steak.

The one dinner I painfully remember was when Mom cooked up some pan-fried canned ham (i.e., SPAM) and mashed potatoes with those yellow beans. In the 1970s, canned hams were the "in thing." Mom convinced us, or at least me, that the canned ham was akin to a Christmas Day ham.

Years later, while in college, I had breakfast in a diner with a friend. I ordered fried ham and scrambled eggs special. With just one bite, I recognized the ham on my plate. I mentioned to my friend sitting in the booth with me that this restaurant served the expensive fried ham my mother served us at home. He immediately broke into a burst of deep, prolonged laughter and told me that the fried ham next to my eggs was fried SPAM. He explained what he thought SPAM was made of, which I won't repeat here.

A range of emotions went through me. First, I was embarrassed by my social standing for thinking that SPAM was an expensive ham. Yes, even at college I was still the green hick raised on a dirt road in the mountains of Pennsylvania.

The second, more powerful emotion was that my mom duped me, a concept I couldn't accept. While growing up, our mother repeatedly told us, "You're as good as any of those other children, no matter what they say, think, or wear." Whether we wore hand-me-down clothes, hitchhiked to and from events, drove in outdated-rusted cars, or had to get a paying job as soon as we got our driving learner's permit, our mother consistently drove into us, that people with money were no better than me, my brothers or sisters. She established a core value that character matters the most, not what you wear, what you drive, the size of your home, or how much money you have.

Getting over that emotional disappointment took a while, but in the end, I had to admit that Mom duped me. SPAM was not a fancy, expensive, imported ham. I've rationalized this memory by believing that my ever-optimistic mother was just making lemonade out of lemons.

CM Kelly

With two engineering degrees, CM Kelly's passion has always been focused on numbers, formulas, equations and algorithms. Raised as the fourth of nine children, in an abandoned farmhouse on a rural dirt road, the families household was rich in character, though light on finances. Hard work and laughter were constants. In many ways, it was akin to a "Waltons" setting with a touch of "Archie Bunker". His upbringing lit a flame in him: to advance, to achieve, to not be a burden to society and to "amount to something". He unapologetically pursued the American Dream.

Now retired, He enjoys writing about his life experiences; growing up in a large family, working in underground coal mines, pursuing business deals around the world, climbing the corporate ladder, and building billion-dollar projects. The travel stories are full of unique and quirky encounters. The coal mining stories reflect the challenges of working underground. A few of the stories capture the ups and downs of climbing the corporate ladder and run-ins with politicians, the likes of Manchin, and Blagojevich.

Never boring, sometimes surprising, and occasionally educational. If you enjoy Mike Rowe, ("Dirty Jobs"), you will like his short stories.

Best Beloved
By Bridgett Kendall

I was so sad when I woke up on Tuesday, March 3rd, 1959, the day the 654 trolley buses were to be retired. I grew up riding down and up Anerley Hill to school and back, listening to the swishes of the trolley poles on the overhead wires. In my child's head I was all grown up, waltzing like a proper lady in my turquoise taffeta ball gown.

On Tuesday morning I began to bleed heavily and the loud engine noise of the replacement 154 Routemaster bus that carried me to the hospital engulfed me in an omen of dread. I lost my six-month-old baby.

The following Sunday morning was miserable, cold, foggy and the day of the bus ride when I got off a stop too early. It was the most momentous thing that I've ever done.

~

Before my story unfolds, I'm going to emulate Gulliver, who starts his travels with a short but crucial period of his life before his voyage. During the war I was evacuated, living with Miss Spruce, who I recall only for the mole on her pointy right nostril, and her insistence on total obedience and quiet behaviour. There was one daily pleasure: we read together. Whether it suited my age-group or not

– four to eight – I was never bored. What child wouldn't indulge in make-believe on the island of Glubbdubdrib? There were *Gulliver's Travels* and *Robinson Crusoe*, but my favourite was Kipling's *Just So Stories*. The most special was The *Beginning of the Armadillos* – because I'd seen a real hedgehog and I believed that a hedgehog could have been transformed into the first armadillo.

But there was a singular magic charm in the book: *O My Best Beloved*. The author kept addressing this lucky girl. The words were music – you could dance to them, sing them as you dressed in the morning and when you were sent to bed without any tea because you'd walked mud into the house.

Under the blankets every night I repeated those precious words, and hoped that would make someone love me.

I feel sicker than ever today. We're leaving to catch the bus to Derek's parents' place for Sunday lunch. They say things like "heaven help our grandchild if he inherits your ginger hair," or "orphans have no idea." I'm a coward. I never argue. And today I'm dreading that the smell of blood coming from my overflowing womb will overpower the stink of animal blood that permeates the flat from their butcher's shop downstairs. Confiding any of this to Derek is out of the question.

~

I shiver at the horror and a ghastly intuition that the Routemaster motor will be unequal to Anerley

Hill's steepness; that it will stall and run backwards out of control and there'll be mangled metal and bodies littered all over.

I'm wearing the sorrows of a spring when a late frost has caused the premature death of the fruit blossoms and all their potential. Dirty yellow fog threatens to become a peasouper. Next second it lifts a little and the bright yellow blooms of a lone forsythia bush beckon me from the gloom to sun yellow brightness. I want to grab it and cling on to it, but it slips away like my baby from my womb; like a meteor smashing down right in front of me and separating me from the rest of the world.

The air tastes like sour milk. I gag and acid bile surges into my throat.

Where the hell is Derek? He only went to get the brolly. You look outside and it isn't raining. The fog deceives. When you go out this invisible rain soaks and freezes you. I'm left shivering on the pavement outside our flats, a block built on a site destroyed by a V1 flying bomb in 1944. I was hopeful when we rented a tiny flat but now my dreams of a happy home are annihilated like the lives and buildings that the bomb consumed. Underneath me are dead bodies lying buried where they fell. Nothing is how it seems.

Derek enjoys keeping me waiting, but if I ask what kept him he'll say he was doing me a favour, and I'm an ungrateful pig.

Just five minutes ago his eyes narrowed, and he

said, "Take off that dowdy headscarf and wear the beige hat with the feather. You know, I've a good mind to go on my own." He paused. I waited. "But then how would I explain your absence?"

"Just tell them the truth."

His cheeks flamed. "And spoil their day?"

Oh, if only he *would* go on his own, but he's committed to playing happy families so that the illusion of our perfect marriage is maintained. I know I still look pregnant, but how can I lie when they ask if the baby's still kicking or something?

Plus, today we're going to meet his brother Vernon's new baby Kevin. "You're not to mention your miscarriage," he said, "It'll ruin everything."

After my terrible ordeal – unbelievably only five days ago – I thought with unfounded optimism that he'd be sympathetic. No chance.

~

He'd been away in Halifax – he's a commercial traveller, or as Derek says, a travelling salesman – in his opinion by far the more fitting modern title for the profession, though it seems to me to be the same job. He likes to big himself up to impress me. Anyway, I couldn't get to a phone until Thursday, and then I could only leave a message with the hotel receptionist, and the message was please to come home a day early, but he claimed he didn't get the message and in any case he was meeting a potential new client who he couldn't have possibly cancelled because there was every possibility of him getting the most business ever. I wouldn't be complaining when he got his commission would I? In any case men didn't get involved in women's stuff. It wasn't natural.

~

It's probably only been a couple of minutes, but my tummy is cramping and the stupid hat is soaked. I can feel rain running under the collar of my mac. I must look dreadful in spite of Derek's instructions.

At last; he's here. So there are streaks running down my face powder are there? That's because, Derek darling, I caked on the powder in an effort to disguise the tiny blood vessels that have newly colonised my cheeks and nose. Now the rain has done a thorough job of ruining it.

Well, it'll match the hat and my lifeless red hair. My goodness – the hair. Fancy him making me go for a shampoo and set yesterday. My head was buzzing under the hood of the drier which was burning my scalp and I thought I was going to faint. Even worse was the mundane chat among the women and hairdressers. You know the sort of thing. The price of sausages; someone's bunions. All so remote to me in my fragile state. My hair wouldn't hold the waves anyway, so it turned out all for nothing.

At least he hands me the brolly. "Walk faster. If we miss the next bus we'll be late."

"I *am* hurrying." My womb contracted again. What an uncaring wife I am. Just think, I'm bleeding and bruised, I shy away from his family and I can't give them a grandchild or him a son.

~

I don't think I can ever forget what he said yesterday. At breakfast he reckoned his egg was too runny. Almost in one breath: "you're useless, can't even boil an egg properly, and your pastry – how many times have I told you my mother can show you the proper way? Yours is disgusting – turns to sand in my mouth." Then his sneering voice got slower and louder as if he was revving up an engine from freezing. "I can see why your womb doesn't function properly. It's as dry as your pastry and as barren. No wonder the baby was desperate to clear off." He shouted this last sentence, throat bubbles exploding when the words ran out, and he slammed out the door. I stood there feeling so shocked I couldn't move. At first I took it to heart. He was right. I'm completely useless. I'm only 22 and already withered like a thirsty flower. I felt dizzy and clutched the kitchen table for support.

A minute or so later, with actions born of habit, I started clearing the breakfast dishes, my head spinning and my hands clumsy. His uneaten egg slipped out of the eggcup onto the floor. You wouldn't believe how painful bending down to clear it up was. Just like the contractions I had before the miscarriage, the cramping was intense and made me stiffen until it passed, and then my whole body rebelled as if a giant screwdriver was turning me into a spiral of anger.

I began thumping the table with my fists, cutlery clattering and a plate smashing on the floor. I whacked the table-top until tears were pouring down my cheeks. That was my rock-bottom. Tuesday's pain and grief and Derek's jibes and bitterness heaped on top. I vowed that it was the last time I'd let him get to me.

~

We walk towards the bus stop, only five minutes, but I can't keep up. The midwife told me to bandage my breasts tightly to stop the milk from coming in. It's painful and isn't working. Periodically my breasts throb like hell until milk comes pouring out, soaking the bandages and my vest. I'm actually wearing two, but I'm petrified stains will leak through my clothes. And I can smell myself. To crown it all, I'm wearing two pads, just in case.

While I'm scuttling along behind Derek, praying that I can keep my body from embarrassing me, my head begins to seethe with anger. Why should I have to humour his precious family? Why have they picked on me to make their constant digs at? Vernon's wife doesn't have to put up with jibes. Maybe it really is all my own fault. Maybe I stick out because I don't understand how normal families work. I don't know.

~

My father died on the Normandy beaches and my mum's sadness never left her. When I came back from Miss Spruce's, mum leant more and more on me, and she became sadder and sadder. Home was a couple of rooms above a greengrocers with a shared toilet and one gas ring for cooking. Not that mum did much of that. She worked downstairs in the greengrocers but was always taking time off. Often, she'd still be in bed when I got back from school. She got worse and worse.

Eventually the doctors certified her as insane and locked her up in Bethlem Royal Hospital. In the end I think she really was insane. She died in 1951. At fifteen I went from looking after her, me and the rooms in Upper Norwood, to leaving school and moving into lodgings in Anerley and working in a newsagents.

~

I'm certain that Derek is deliberately walking as fast as possible so that I get left behind. I look at him from the back. I can just make him out. He's walking as though he's dead set on some important mission, yet his head keeps jerking to left and right, like he's on his guard against someone jumping him unseen in this murkiness. His brown suit trousers are too long, the turn-ups flap around on the wet pavement, and the belt of his brown gaberdine mac is pulled in so tightly that he looks like a man of two halves. Two men in one. What a strange invention. It must be the fog playing tricks.

And now overwhelming sadness sweeps through me. For a brief moment it's not sadness for the life that was snuffed out at the moment of birth, but for us, for Derek and me. I know now, nearly two years into the marriage that my longing to be someone's

Best Beloved needs more than just a new dress and magic words.

In front of me is a stranger who's walking with two left feet. Quite the opposite of his elegance and self-assurance when we met in the spring of 1955.

~

I can still see his legs kicking and flicking like springs to the rock 'n' roll beat. All of us wallflowers on the dance floor of the Orchid Ballroom envied any girl he chose to jive with. He was small and skinny and neat, and my friend Sylvia and I couldn't take our eyes off him. Derek, when we met at that dance the muscles in your face were so alive they sparkled. Eyes, mouth, cheeks, all glowed with life.

He told me that he picked me to dance because he loved my dress. It was a new multi-petticoated dress which I'd saved up for from the higher wages I earned in the typing pool. I'd taken evening classes so I could get a better job and now this sought-after man was mine. I couldn't wait to be seen and admired on the dance floor with him.

~

The fog has come down thick and Derek has disappeared from sight and I've lagged far behind. I've not seen or heard a single other person. They've too much sense to be out on such a foul day. Now I can hear muffled voices and here I am arriving at the bus stop, surprised at hearing Derek and his friend Douglas talking quietly, almost whispering. Douglas seems to say, "Shush now; later," before he looks at me and smiles in welcome. "Jean, how nice to bump into you. Are you all right?" Honestly, I don't know what to say. What's he doing here? There's an awkward silence. Derek turns his head away.

So I say, "Hello Douglas." There's a whirring and buzzing in my head. I take a step forward and put my hand on the nearest arm, which happens to be Douglas's. He grabs both my arms and I can feel him taking my weight. "She needs to sit down." he says, "Can you get to that wall?" He propels me over, and although it's too high to sit on, at least I can lean on it. "Thank you, I feel a bit better now." The fainting sensation is lessening, and I'm embarrassed and anxious. Derek hasn't moved. I hold my breath, but he's looking at Douglas, not at me. There's a soft expression on his face which I've never seen before. He's never looked at me like that. The shock of that look.

The roar of the bus comes from nowhere, the engine pitch gradually diminishing and then the idling engine whose fast rhythmical beat translates into my baby's heart in terrible distress. I try climbing aboard. I grab hold of the pole on the platform, but my strength is spent. Hands grab my waist and hoist me up. I realise it's Douglas helping. Derek ignores me.

My fuzzy head makes me lurch from seat to seat. My wits expiring fast due to the chain of minute physical decisions I've been forced to make, I half fall and half propel myself into a seat. My legs are left behind and my head and torso are stretched awkwardly on the window side. I stay like that. I've exhausted my physical and mental capacities.

Of course this all happens in a few seconds but it's so harrowing that every action, every word, every sensation is etched in my memory.

I expect Derek to follow but then I hear him calling after me. "Douglas and I are going to sit upstairs." For all I care at this moment they could be emigrating to Australia. I close my eyes. I start to wonder why Douglas was at the bus stop at the same time as us. His stop is several ahead of ours. Why did he come back to travel to the same place again? Still, what does it matter…?

"I'm sorry, I'll find my purse." The conductor. I didn't even spot him when I got on. He probably thinks I'm drunk. I scramble to sit upright.

"Where to miss?" He raises one eyebrow. I squirm.

"Crystal Palace please."

"The station or the top of the hill? Low Level or High Level?"

"High Level." We exchange coins and ticket. I lean my head on the window.

I want to blank out any thoughts, but the voice in my head won't shut up chewing over Derek's peculiar behaviour with Douglas. They're not what I'd call mates... all cigarettes, beer and dirty stories. Now I think about it, Douglas doesn't smoke and neither does Derek when they're together. When I get back from Croydon late on a Saturday afternoon, the usual weekend fug and stink of smoke has cleared.

Douglas was there when I needed him this afternoon. He's taller and bigger built than Derek. Yes, he's a nice man. Derek in his company is always nicer to me. Douglas has some influence that puzzles me. I wish I knew his secret.

He comes round most Saturday afternoons to play cards. As Derek says, the living room is too small for us all to do our own thing, so he gives me five shillings and I go into Croydon, look in the shops and have tea in Allders. When Sylvia was living here, I'd meet up with her and it was fun. Now Sylvia's moved with her new husband to run a guest house in Brighton. Derek still insists that I go out to have some nice time away from the house, so now I go to the big library to change my books and read all sorts of interesting things in the reference section. Every fortnight I change the money into a ten-shilling note at the Post Office and hide it inside the split lining of my handbag. I've saved up quite a bit. It'll come in useful one day.

~

Derek and Douglas met while posted in Cyprus during their National Service. When Derek returned home, he was highly strung and he took pleasure in nettling me. When I asked him what was wrong he got all on the defensive. "You wouldn't understand what it was like out there, always having to be on the alert." I hoped he'd settle down when we were married. I tried various tactics: sympathy, silence, arguing back. Nothing helped. He got worse.

Early last year he told me he had a Scottish friend who'd moved to a new motor mechanic's job near here. Douglas rented a bedsit further along the Croydon Road towards Elmers End. Douglas is reserved, but always courteous. Derek started to urge me to go and enjoy myself on Saturday afternoons. At one point I even wondered whether he and Douglas were plotting some crime; fanciful I know, but what was I to think? Time went on and nothing changed and nothing untoward happened, so I accepted the gesture and nowadays I'm glad that Derek has a friend whose company he enjoys. Men sometimes prefer male only company and women sometimes prefer female only company. Perfectly natural.

~

With my glove I rub a peephole through the fogged-up window. I peer out at the rows of shops and businesses, and even though I can't really see them through the dismal rain, I feel a bond with the shabby buildings in their Sunday impotence.

Moving slowly past the observation hole I've rubbed in the glass, a small boy, all alone, waves at me. He holds his little hand upright and moves his fingers up and down, like kids do. I can see bright red hair peeping from under his grey cap. He's dressed for the weather in a gaberdine raincoat and wellington boots. The boy is mine. I'm convinced. His hair is the same red as mine. He drifts away out of sight.

Oh my baby, I'm sure I heard you cry; a teeny plea for life. I saw your hand, the tiniest thing you could ever imagine, the perfect wee fingers. I'm so sad and sorry that you're alone.

Why have we been stationary at the bus stop outside the Robin Hood pub for several minutes? Nobody has got on and there's nobody waiting. And I'm not aware that Douglas got off. Surely we're past his stop by now. I wonder briefly but I don't really care as long as Derek is occupied elsewhere. I turn to look at the conductor. He's sitting on one of the long benches reading the News of the World. The engine is idling. Maybe the bus is early, and they've decided to stay here for a while before turning onto Anerley Road. More likely the driver is as terrified as me of driving up Anerley Hill. Inside me a pressure cooker starts to heat up. The valve emits a low hiss and I start rubbing a bigger hole in the window glass. The hiss grows more urgent and my hand rubs ever-expanding circles.

Right now, nobody is looking, nobody is provoking me, nobody is prodding and poking. I want to re-live the birth and death of my baby. Other events have intervened and robbed me of the experience... my unique experience. I don't want to forget it. They call it a miscarriage, but I hate that word. Like you've just tripped up. So get up and carry on.

I asked the midwife whether my 24 weeks old baby would live. "Not a chance." She was curt. I asked what the baby would look like. "Imagine a goose egg with hairs." What? Why would anyone say that? Wouldn't you say something like a baby kitten maybe? Or, and I didn't know this till later when I saw the tiny hand dangling outside the towel the midwife had quickly wrapped it up in to take it – he? she? – away, perhaps a 24-week baby didn't grow limbs until later. But even so... a goose egg? I'd never seen one. Did my baby have a shell, (excuse my ignorance; nobody taught me)? I saw my perfectly formed baby protected by the shell and then at birth its tiny fingernails scratching and poking until it broke out. When I lived at Miss Spruce's I'd seen a scraggy newly hatched bird which had fallen out of its nest. Its skin was transparent, and I could actually see its miniature heart beating. And then it stopped. I remember being mesmerised by this event. But my birthing experience was as harrowing as a ride in a Routemaster is from a ride in a trolley bus.

~

The midwife was as strict as Miss Spruce.

"Your legs are in stirrups so that I can work at the business end without you in the way."

"Women have been suffering birth pains forever, and none of them made such a fuss as you."

"At this stage the sex of the foetus is immaterial."

She called it "the foetus" or "it", so I did as well, and it's only now that it occurs to me how horrible that is.

"You must stop trying for a baby Mrs Duffield. Your pelvis is too narrow. You're not the first woman who has to accept that she can't carry a baby to term."

"Don't be silly. Of course it didn't cry."

By far the worst part of all was the silence I carried in my arms when I walked out the hospital gates.

~

A tiny lady in a black coat and navy headscarf gets on the bus, the driver revs up the engine and we slowly pull away. The bus seems reluctant. I don't blame it not wanting to climb that hill. What a burden of responsibility. The lady comes and sits by me and that agitates me. The bus is almost empty, but I can't say anything, can I? She's even tinier than me, like an ancient child. Her coat is threadbare, by its skimpy fit probably a wartime model, and her scarf is frayed. Her worn face is pale, and her thin lips creased and colourless. The bus stops as the traffic lights turn to red.

I notice that, of its own volition, my hand is still keeping a porthole of clear window from fogging up. On this Sunday in a drab south London road life seems to be holding its breath.

The lights change and the bus rounds the corner, its engine whining its complaint.

I let out a long sigh. Then a hand grips my right

arm. Firmly, but not hard. I stare at it – a miniature hand encased in a black glove, shiny with use.

I feel warmth seeping through all the fabric layers to my skin, and the touch of tiny fingertips. The lady's face is set straight ahead. The motor settles a bit – not straining, not complaining. I take one of those long breaths that you haven't planned for. My chest is surprised but does its best to accommodate this unexpected volume of air, holding on to it for a bit too long until it expels it unevenly and noisily.

The lady speaks. I've never heard anything like it. Her voice is brittle as though forming words is alien to her.

"Listen to the chugging engine urging you to move on and away, on and away." Is this riddle for me? The lady must be strange in the head.

Whatever...a surge of hope floods through me. It takes me by surprise. Hope for what though? I shake the feeling off. It's ridiculous. I have no answer. Thank goodness, the odd lady is getting up and she's rung the bell for the bus to stop. I wonder if she lives in one of the big old houses that line this bottom part of Anerley Road. Surely not. Only rich people like doctors can afford them.

I turn to see where she goes, but she's invisible. She must have gone round the back of the bus. There's a lingering glow in my arm, and it's spreading like melting butter on toast up into my shoulder and my head, and soon I'm suffused with warmth.

What miraculous fingers. And it dawns on me that other fingers have played curious roles during this strange bus ride. My own hand drying a porthole on the bus window as if to keep the world's eye on me. Perhaps also it's so that I don't lose sight of the world. There were Douglas's unseen fingers ensuring that I was safe; the red-haired boy offering me a salutation like a familiar secret.

I'm transported to a gruesome flashback: my midwife's fingers with official scrubbed fingernails, tidying up what my body couldn't hold onto, like the lady in the fish and chip shop wrapping up a portion of fish and chips in a newspaper parcel.

Where did she put my baby? Is it dumped in a dustbin or burnt to cinders in an ash-pit? Or will a fireman find it, mangled, in the carnage of a Routemaster that couldn't cope with the steepness of Anerley Hill? Outside in the swirling fog a ghost-like figure trudges up the first slope. The bus labours alongside. I foresee that as the hill steepens more as it struggles to reach High Level, the gap when the engine will be between gears will be unsustainable and the bus will career backwards: somersault over and over and my blood will mingle with the wreckage …

… my fear grows wings and the answer to the riddle reveals itself. On and away, on and away. I leap to my feet and pull the bell just in time for the bus to stop at Low Level before the fateful final ascent. I lurk behind the bus hiding from Derek, cross over, and rush up the short road to Crystal Palace station. I take a train to Victoria, use the Ladies to clean and tidy myself, and board the train to Brighton and Sylvia's home. That's the beginning and end of my plan.

In the compartment a lone woman reads a magazine. I sit on the velvet upholstered seat in the opposite corner. What next?

Sleep.

I waken as the train is slowing down. I gaze, spellbound, at the pillow of mist which caresses the tops of the tree trunks and their still naked branches in the distance. I'm startled to hear a voice. "When a tree loses its leaves does it thinks it's dying? Then, does it know that it will live again?"

The other passenger has lowered her magazine and posed the second riddle of the day. From somewhere uncharted I unearth an answer. "Maybe life and death are simply times to travel through in different clothes."

"Of course," and the woman goes back to her magazine. My thoughts meander with tenuous links between them, mainly shadowy ideas about life and death. Nothing to grasp hold of; only that today has unearthed mysteries of the world that have never touched me before. And who am I to unravel them? Earlier I'd never question that Derek was the centre of my life. Who is he now? What is he looking for?

And isn't my baby like the trees? In different

clothes in different times? Nothing can change that. And so I fall in love with the most precious gift in the world. My own Best Beloved.

~

This old lady has learnt not to regret. Innocence and ignorance were normal then. I was alone, my baby alone, victims of the times. An alarmed and patient Sylvia cared for me until one day my delusions and hallucinations subsided and a longing to own my life surfaced. I recovered. Dear Sylvia saved me from the asylum. I became a librarian. I think – I hope – I fired many children's imaginations with storytelling. Doubtless a forgotten legacy but that's OK.

Did Derek and Douglas live happily ever after? Somehow I think not.

Bridgett Kendall

Born in Gloucestershire, England, from age five Bridgett became obsessed with playing the piano. A graduate of Trinity College of Music, London, she became a successful music teacher and accompanist, married musician David and raised three children. During this time she also completed an Arts Degree with the Open University. On retirement in 2006, a move to Burgundy, France, inspired new challenges, one of which is running a rural gîte. In 2013, in denial of her advancing years, and with an undiminished and irresistible creative urge, writing became Bridgett's new part-time career. Concentrating mostly on the short story form, her stories have been highly commended, short and long-listed in a number of competitions and published in online publications. She has also been short and long-listed in the short memoir genre. Her magpie imagination generates wildly diverse ideas about the human condition that lend themselves to expression through dark realism, dark humour or magic realism.

Some Things Cannot Be Fixed
By Neil McKinnon

Noburo lingered behind his grandfather and looked at the empty chair under the tree. His father would never sit there again. He quickened his pace, inhaled and pushed up his shoulders. The weight of his duty pressed, and he felt the loneliness of responsibility.

It was three years since Jiichan first took him to the river, three years since he started his collection. He was ten then and he remembered keeping his toes stiff so his man-size rubber boots wouldn't come off in the sticky gray mud.

The river was swollen from spring runoff and leafy poplars tumbled in the brown current. The old man touched Noburo's shoulder and they stopped to watch two geese nudge yellow balls of fluff into the swirling water.

Jiichan cleared his throat. "Look at the river, Nobu-chan. It never stops. It's like our family. We've been flowing in and out of the world longer than there's been water between these banks."

Sunlight broke from behind a cloud and for a moment the river sparkled. Noburo looked up but the sun blinded him so he couldn't see his grandfather's face.

"We work hard," Jiichan continued. "But there's

barely enough to feed each new mouth as it drifts into the world."

Noburo watched the baby geese float by in the dappled water.

"It's not your destiny to be rich, Nobu-chan, but you don't have to be poor. There's something more important than money. It's not free like the love a parent gives to a child. It can't be seen or touched and the government doesn't tax it. It's *respect* and it's paid only to those who earn it."

Jiichan took his hand and pulled him free of the mud. Noburo was confused. How could you earn something you couldn't see or touch? How could you not be poor without money?

He kicked at a stone and tripped by the side of the path. A mottled brown bird quacked and dove into the air, so close Noburo felt its wing brush his cheek. He landed inches from a nest containing seven greenish eggs. He picked one up and struggled to his feet. "Can I keep it, Ojiichan?" he asked.

"Yes," the old man answered, "but only one."

At home his mother showed him how to make a hole at each end of the egg and blow out the contents so only the shell was left. Then she patted his head. "Don't take too many, Nobu-chan. When you blow out an egg there is one less bird to fly."

The next day he found a picture of the bird in a book at school, a mallard duck. He began combing the bush and fields to find other specimens and soon he had a growing collection. Jiichan made a wooden box, stained it the color of red wine and inserted a glass top. He divided the interior into squares each large enough to hold a single egg. Noburo labeled every square and started a notebook with information on each species.

He felt the satisfaction that comes with learning. "Look at my collection, Papa," he said as he carried the box into the kitchen one evening after dinner.

"Don't be too proud, Noburo," his father answered. "Pride is a weakness that makes one think of the past instead of the future."

"Yes, Papa."

"Soon it will be your duty to work and there will be little time for bird's eggs," his father continued. "Put them away now."

He put the eggs under his bed, pushed aside dishes and sat at the table to do his homework. For an hour his mother watched him struggle with math. When he looked up, weary with misunderstanding, she smiled and said, "*Ganbatte*, Nobu-chan ... don't give up."

His father snorted. "Too much learning isn't good for a farm boy. It might give him ideas about working in the city when his duty is with his family."

Noburo's mother set her mouth in a straight line. She patted the back of his head and then cleared away the dishes.

His grandfather never spoke of respect again, but the lesson was repeated a hundred times: in the depth of a neighbor's bow, in the way his parents deferred to his grandparents and in the way Jiichan included him in every conversation. As he grew to fill the rubber boots, Noburo came to understand that giving respect was one way of earning it.

***

They were a footnote in the saga of war. When the bombs fell on Pearl Harbor and the government sent West Coast Japanese Canadians to camps, his father kept the family together by agreeing to work on an Alberta farm. Their own farm and possessions were left behind, never to be returned.

They hoed beets from sunup to sundown. Noburo slept in a basket at the edge of a field while his parents worked. In winter, the family shivered in an uninsulated shack while his father shoveled coal in a nearby mine. They slept on a bed with no mattress and learned not to linger in their makeshift outdoor toilet. Frugality became a habit. Eventually, long after the war, they put a payment down on a farm of their own.

Noburo's father was not young. A mortgage added to his burden of responsibility and caused him to stoop as he hurried from one chore to another. A small man with shoulders too high for his neck, he faced the world at an angle as if he expected to get hit and thought that, by living obliquely, the blow would glance off. His eyes, once wide, had narrowed in concert with the possibilities in his life and his face reflected the trauma of losing everything. Unfairness was the kindling with which he daily built a fire and, unlike his advice, he dwelt on the past. "We had a house, a farm and a fine life. They took it away. What good did it do us to work hard and obey the law? Everything is gone now ... except for the numbness in my soul."

Once, Noburo overheard his mother. "*Shikata ga nai* ... it can't be helped. Everything is behind us. It's time to forgive and move forward."

"Shikata ga nai is a pill for the timid," his father replied. "The amount of forgiveness in the world is limited and should be saved for those who truly deserve it."

Noburo's stomach constricted with the understanding that, once broken, some things cannot be fixed.

***

On his last day in grade five, he ran all the way from school. "I'm home. I passed to grade six!" he shouted as he flung himself through the screen door. He waited for his mother's familiar, "*Okairi*, you're back," but there was only silence. In the kitchen he found his father holding his hands over his eyes.

"What's the matter, Papa?"

"Sit down," his father said without moving his hands.

Noburo's heart raced. Why did his father not look at him? Where was his mother? He waited.

Finally, his father lowered his hands. "It's your mother, Nobu-chan. She has the cancer. The doctor says she will die." He stood and went outside.

Noburo sat until it was almost dark. He imagined his mother floating on the river. He remembered how she touched the back of his head when his father was angry and how she smiled when she helped with his homework even if he didn't understand it. A lump formed in his throat. He waited until it went away. Then he got up and went to the door.

A lone poplar stood in the yard. Its leaves were limp, weighted with dust. A whisper of dry air turned them so their sallow undersides flickered in the dim light. His father was standing beside the tree staring at the house. Noburo raised his hand, but his father's eyes looked through him. He lowered his arm and switched on the light.

Every week they drove to the hospital. At first they brought rice and miso soup, but she soon became too ill to eat. Noburo used his allowance to buy a newspaper and each week he read to her. She squeezed his hand and said it made her happy to find out what was happening in the world. When she could no longer speak, she reached out and touched his arm as he read.

He was flipping through the paper trying to decide what she would find interesting when her breath stopped. He watched carefully hoping that she would move. For a time, there was silence. Then he heard his father behind him. The sun disappeared from the window and shadows came into the room.

He lifted the newspaper and began to read aloud.

"Stop, Noburo," his father said. "It was time for her to go. She was very sick."

He quit reading, carefully placed the paper beside her outstretched hand and left the room.

His grandparents tried to fill the space after his mother died. "They want to help," his father explained. "But they are old so we must help them. They are our family and it is our duty. It will be your job to help Obaachan."

Helping his grandmother wasn't easy. She was frail and often overwhelmed by the requirements of living. Noburo took on most of the household duties. He washed clothes and cleaned the house. He heated bath water. He learned to make miso soup, okazu, and gohan — the food his grandparents loved.

When he was washing dishes and dreaming about playing baseball it seemed that doing his duty was a hard thing. Once Baachan silently moved behind him and patted the back of his head. He closed his eyes and the presence of his mother was so real, his body shook. Sometimes when he did his homework, he thought he heard her whisper, "Ganbatte, Nobu-chan." But when he looked up there was only her chair silent and empty as the eggs in his collection.

Though Jiichan's body was slow he still walked to the river. One day Noburo took the glass-covered box and followed. Seated on the grassy bank he described each bird that had provided an egg for his collection. Jiichan looked at him. "Ah so, Nobu-chan. You know a lot about birds, but these shells are not birds. Did you know a bird does not fly until it leaves the nest?"

***

On his twelfth birthday his father said, "You are old enough to help with the farm." They stood beside a small pen attached to the side of the ancient barn that, in winter, sheltered a few white-faced Herefords. The day was sunny and the cattle chewed silently in the shade of the building. "They are lazy and fat, Noburo. From today they are your responsibility."

Noburo looked at him with surprise.

"I won't be here forever," his father explained. "Soon, I will join my ancestors. You must look after the farm."

It was his duty. He hauled hay and water and crushed grain to feed during winter. In spring, he pulled calves from new mothers. He learned that animals deserve consideration as much as people. "Never run them," his father said. "They become skittish. Then they lose weight and every pound costs money. Be quiet with them and they will learn to accept and respect you."

The beets also took time. He stopped going to school and his teacher came to the farm. "The boy is a fine student, but he is absent too often," she told Noburo's father.

"He is a good boy," his father replied. "He

knows his duty."

Sometimes Noburo tossed in his bed, respect and duty writhing in his mind, coiled and twisted, so it was impossible to tell them apart. It was all confusing. You showed respect by doing your duty and you did your duty to gain respect. And there were many waiting for him to do his duty—his father, his grandparents, his teacher, even the animals—he also had a duty to the memory of his mother. When he dropped into a fitful sleep, he dreamt two snakes were trying to swallow him while his father watched. "Help me, Papa," he cried.

"You are a good boy," his father said before fading from the dream.

Once Noburo had acquired respect for cattle his father considered the farm successfully transferred to his son. He withdrew from work and spent his days seated on a chair under the poplar tree. One day the chair was empty when Noburo returned from hoeing beets. "Where's Papa?" he asked Jiichan.

Jiichan chose his words. "Your father tried to make the same journey as your mother, Noburo. He is in the hospital."

Late at night the light from the hall shone into the hospital room and made the skin on his father's face resemble waxed paper. His closed eyes were set deep in his skull. The only sound was his breath moving slow and irregular through the shadow of his open mouth.

Noburo had the feeling of tears, but his cheeks

stayed dry. He touched the hand curled like a talon on the blanket. His father opened his eyes. "You are a good boy," he said.

His father's body wasted, subtracting from itself and twisting with each transaction. Late one evening air refused to enter his throat. Noburo listened to the sudden silence of death. He waited for sadness, but none appeared. He felt loss but it wasn't for the spark that had left his father's body. It was a feeling that something had disappeared, and he couldn't remember what it was, like he was the victim of a robbery but didn't know what had been taken.

***

After the funeral he walked with Jiichan to the river. The murky water moved slow and placid below the bank. "Your father wanted to go," Jiichan said. "The world made him tired. It wasn't the loss of things. It was the loss of self-respect. His pride and self-esteem had floated away. He was like one of your eggs, Noburo ... a shell with nothing inside."

Noburo watched a mallard duck fly low over the brown water. He heard Jiichan's words, but the understanding would come later: a man who has had his self-respect stolen cannot pass love to his son...just a sense of duty. For now, standing on the riverbank, there was only the feeling that he was a very poor man indeed.

The End

Neil McKinnon

Neil McKinnon was raised on the Canadian prairies. He served in the Royal Canadian Navy and has been a businessman, archaeologist, university lecturer, and freelance writer. He has worked in China, Japan, Mexico, Canada, and the U.S. and holds a B.S. in math and BA and MA in archaeology.

Neil's articles have appeared in Canadian, Mexican and U.S. publications. His first book, Tuckahoe Slidebottle, was short-listed for the Stephen Leacock Medal for Humour and for the Alberta Book Award for short fiction. Neil's novel, *The Greatest Lover of Last Tuesday* came out in 2015 and his first nonfiction book, *A Ticket to the Grand Show*, was published in May. He has read/signed, conducted workshops and made presentations at more than 100 venues. He has also served on literary juries and edited/published academically.

He ran the Calgary Marathon in the same year that he collected his first pension cheque. He and his wife, Judy live near Vancouver and have been married for 59 years. They have produced two globe-trotting daughters and inherited two brilliant grandchildren

Special Delivery
By T. Dan Nelson

"Let's go to the creek."

"Okay."

"I'll see you in the alley."

"Okay."

Gary was just over seven years old. Bobby was about a year younger. They had to sneak away to the creek as it meant walking along Bennett's Corner. They weren't supposed to go near there. The curve in the road at Bennett's Corner was on a gravel road riddled with ruts, potholes, and washboards. It wasn't uncommon for fast-moving cars to lose control.

In preparation for their secret escape to the creek, Gary went to get a minnow bucket and a slingshot. Bobby went to get the net and the spear.

Although the net was a modified butterfly net, it worked great for catching all kinds of creek creatures. Every time they went to the creek, however, the net came back with new holes in it.

Bobby found that dental floss worked well to darn the holes. His mother mentioned how proud she was that he was using so much floss. She'd be disappointed to learn that rather than being used to keep Bobby's teeth clean, the copious amounts of floss were being consumed by frequent creek net repairs. At this point, the net was nearly halfway composed of dental floss.

Due to frequent repairs, the net was much shallower than it was originally, which happened to improve its performance as a creek net. Because Bobby had freshly repaired it earlier in the morning, the net was ready to go.

The spear was firmly rubber-banded to the handle of the net in two places. Bobby made the spear from a long straight stick he found in the back yard. He ground one end to a point by rubbing the stick at an angle against the pavement in the driveway. Gary came up with the idea to attach it to the net handle so they'd never leave it behind.

The spear was for fish that were too big or too quick to catch in the net. Though they hadn't yet speared anything, it wasn't from a lack of trying. They were confident that they soon would.

With net and spear in hand, Bobby just needed to sneak through the garage without being noticed. Then he'd meet Gary in the alley. After that, it was easy.

Last time they were at the creek, Gary and Bobby decided it was important to bring a slingshot because they saw a beaver. Or it might have been a muskrat. Regardless, despite their best efforts, they couldn't hit it with rocks. The spear didn't even come close. They needed a slingshot.

Gary's older brother Donny could punch holes through soda cans from clear across the driveway using his slingshot. So surely it could hit a beaver from across the creek. Since Donny wasn't using his slingshot that day, Gary quietly borrowed it.

On the way home from the creek last time, Gary and Bobby also discussed collecting the creatures they caught and keeping them. Gary's dad had a minnow bucket in the basement included among his fishing gear. Since his dad wasn't using his minnow bucket that day, Gary quietly borrowed it, too.

From the basement, Gary simply needed to go out the back door, which opened to the alley. When he did, he found Bobby waiting and ready to go.

Bobby had his Cub Scout canteen strapped across his chest, which reminded Gary to fill his own canteen and bring it along. Once Gary returned with his canteen, they were off.

Their favorite spot on the creek was just outside of town, about a mile from Main Street and a quarter mile past Bennett's Corner. The road leading there was asphalt for a few hundred feet after which it turned to gravel. It was mid-morning on a clear, hot, humid summer day. As usual, they stopped to rest about halfway to the creek near a long row of mailboxes.

They sat in the shade and drank water from their canteens. Knowing they'd refill their canteens at the creek, each drank most of his water.

Stacey Williams lived in the house just a hundred yards or so behind mailbox row. She was in the yard pulling weeds from a flower bed when the boys sat down.

Gary liked Stacey. About twice his age, she was his favorite babysitter. He'd tell you why if you asked him: "She's pretty and funny and she plays Go Fish and Hot Wheels and one time she brought Twinkies and she's not afraid of snakes."

Stacey waved to the boys and Gary waved back. With their canteens nearly empty, they got up and continued their journey.

Upon arrival at the creek, Gary half-filled the minnow bucket with water. Bobby started hunting crawdads using the net. Gary and Bobby figured out how crawdads commonly escaped danger. They scuttled backwards using their tails. They're very quick, too.

Gary and Bobby most commonly caught crawdads nestling under or near what they called "crawdaddy rocks." They discovered that when crawdaddy rocks were rolled upside down, crawdads scuttled away from them.

Crawdaddy rocks were roughly six to fourteen inches in diameter. Rocks any smaller didn't offer enough cover to a keeper crawdad; if any bigger, the rocks weren't easily rolled, and they were getting too wide for the span of the net. Though crawdaddy rocks were sometimes completely submerged, they were more commonly only partially submerged. Sometimes they only barely touched the water.

Before rolling a crawdaddy rock, it was important to position the net properly. The top of the net was brought to rest on the creek bottom just a few inches away from the rock. Regardless of whether the rock was to be rolled upstream or downstream, the open face of the net would be centered directly behind the rock when it rolled. So as the rock was rolled forward—away from the net— a crawdad scuttling backwards away from the rolling rock would land squarely in the net. Crawdads scuttling away from crawdaddy rocks didn't often escape Gary and Bobby's creek net.

Crawdads hanging out near rocks that were too big to roll were by no means safe from the net, either. Gary and Bobby developed an effective technique to deal with big rocks. They called it "scooping." If it was too big to roll, they would scoop the rock.

Scooping a rock meant running the top of the net along the creek bottom toward the rock until the net's leading edge was pinched between the rock and the creek bottom. Then the net was quickly pulled out of the water, with the leading edge of the net riding the face of the rock all the way out. That way, any creek creatures trapped in the net couldn't escape.

Although scooping big rocks wasn't as productive as rolling crawdaddy rocks, their biggest crawdads were caught scooping rocks. Sometimes they caught minnows that way, too.

It wasn't long before the minnow bucket had a dozen crawdads in it. Two of them were monsters. So, they started collecting other creek creatures to add to the bucket: minnows, chubs and—oh boy! — *tadpoles*! These creatures were easily netted once spotted.

Walking home after a few hours at the creek, Gary and Bobby had to stop frequently. The bucket was so heavy they had to take turns carrying it. As they walked, they were deciding what they should do with their bounty.

"If we take 'em home, our moms and dads will know we were at the creek," said Bobby.

"But we can't just dump the bucket because they'd all die out here without good homes," said Gary.

Upon arrival at the row of mailboxes, the solution to their problem became clear to Gary. All the mailboxes shared the same basic, classic design. They were metal with rounded tops and doors on the front that hinge at the bottom. These mailboxes would be perfect to protect the creatures from harm until people collected them along with their mail and took them in.

"Let's play mailman!" Gary said excitedly. He picked up a stick and poked it into the bucket. Once a crawdad had latched onto it with its pinchers, he pulled the stick out with the crawdad dangling from it. Gary placed the crawdad, stick included, into the first mailbox. Shutting the mailbox door, he declared, "Special delivery!"

"Special delivery!" cried Bobby gleefully, as he pulled out another crawdad and placed it into the next mailbox.

"Special delivery!" shouted Gary, delivering a chub into the next.

"Special delivery!" shouted Bobby, saluting as he shut a tadpole in the next.

And so on until the end of mailbox row, sixteen mailboxes in all. Although most mailboxes received only one creek creature, the last three mailboxes in the row were nearly filled with creatures.

Unknown to the boys, each creature would soon meet its demise, dry roasting in a little metal tomb. By the time most folks came home from work to check their mail, these creatures were not only dead, but oozing putrid fluids. Of course, the smell was less than pleasant.

Not witnessing the results of their delivery efforts, it never occurred to either Gary or Bobby that any harm would come to their beloved creatures once placed in the safety of the mailboxes.

It would be a couple of days before Gary and Bobby played mailman again. Upon opening the mailboxes, they were heartened to find that folks were taking the creatures in. A week or so after that, it would be mailman time again. So it went for the rest of the summer.

With each day playing mailman, they took their duties more seriously and they became more professional. By summer's end, they had learned to equally distribute the creatures among the mailboxes, so the last few mailboxes didn't get more than their fair share.

A standard delivery routine had also developed. Each delivery was accompanied by the announcement "Special delivery," followed by an identification of the creature or creatures being delivered. For example, "Special delivery: a crawdaddy for you!" or "Special delivery: a chub for you!" Or, "Special delivery: a crawdaddy, a chub, two minnows, and a worm for you!"

A light, crisp mailbox door slam was followed by a salute, a kick of the heels, and a nod signifying work well done.

Although Gary and Bobby weren't being sneaky about playing mailman, they successfully evaded detection due to their haphazard work schedule. Had they played mailman every day, or with any degree of regularity, they certainly would have been found out.

Unknown to Gary and Bobby, who thought everyone shared their love for creek creatures, the recipients of their deliveries were not in the least bit appreciative. In fact, the affected parties had assembled a task force to determine two specific things: one) who was perpetrating this evil, and two) what punishment was going to be handed down once the perpetrators were caught.

In the meantime, the task force decided to warn the perpetrators. Large signs were conspicuously posted on either side of mailbox row to deter the unwanted deliveries: "These mailboxes are exclusively for US Mail. DO NOT PLACE ANYTHING ELSE IN THESE MAILBOXES."

Gary and Bobby noticed the signs one day while playing mailman. However, neither of them could read. So, the mailman game continued unfettered.

The task force met informally in the evenings at the Williams home, the house nearest the crime scene. A sheriff's deputy was among the members of the task force. One evening, he announced to the group that he had discussed this situation with Sheriff Department personnel.

"It's a felony for unauthorized personnel to place anything in a mailbox," reported the deputy. "We can pursue charges of vandalism, too. We can also look into the possibility of domestic terrorism . . ."

After a few weeks went by, accompanied by two more visits from the mailbox terrorists, the task force decided to assemble on a Saturday morning. The objective of the meeting was to set up a mailbox watch. They planned to establish a schedule for surveilling mailbox row.

Task force members were asked to volunteer as necessary to ensure the mailboxes were under observation between nine o'clock in the morning and five o'clock in the evening, Monday through Saturday. They were determined to find these evil-doers and bring them to justice.

Hearing bits of several conversations being carried out in the living room, Stacey stood at the front picture window gazing outside. A montage of phrases rose above the din of the various conversations:

"... sonuvabitches are gonna fry ..."

"... all over my daughter's wedding invitation ..."

"... it's gotta be some hoodlums from out of town ..."

"... this has got to stop NOW ..."

"... felons in our midst ..."

"... prosecuted to the full extent of the law ..."

"... I can watch all day Tuesday ..."

"... that Johnson kid is always down at the creek ..."

As Stacey stood in the living room looking outside, she saw Gary and Bobby appear. They were approaching mailbox row. One was carrying fishing gear while the other was struggling to carry a minnow bucket.

Although she couldn't hear their delivery announcements, she could see the boys pulling things from the bucket and dutifully placing them into the mailboxes. "Was that a salute?" she wondered.

All conversations in the Williams home abruptly stopped when a high-pitched squeal erupted from Stacey as she discovered the identity of the mailbox terrorists. The squeal surprised even Stacey. She turned around to find herself at the center of attention.

"Rocky almost caught a squirrel!" she said, lying,

pointing through the window at the family dog to divert attention away from the boys at mailbox row.

"That dog wouldn't know what to do if he ever caught one," said Stacey's father, laughing. Others with squirrel-chasing dogs chuckled and agreed.

As the task force members returned to their conversations, Stacey quietly slipped outside to have a private chat with the boys.

T. Dan Nelson

Originally from the Midwest, Dan now lives in the mountains of Colorado's Front Range. Born and largely raised in Iowa, Dan earned an undergraduate and a graduate degree from the University of Iowa. There, Dan got his feet wet as a writer. HIs first poem was published in Earthwords–a creative writing magazine produced by the University of Iowa Undergraduate Writer's Workshop.

During a decades-long career in quality management, Dan did a lot of business writing. He (ghost) wrote thousands of tailored procedures for companies engaged in systemic quality improvement. He also authored a book about quality management and authored dozens of articles published all over the world in quality management industry rags. Dan also did some ghost writing for a company that created website content for mental health professionals.

More of a speaker and a creative thinker than he is a writer, Dan's writing currently focuses on how screwed up the world is, why it's that way, and what can be done to leave a better world to those who come. Occasionally, Dan comes up with something people actually want to read, like the short story published here.

Lesson in Pie
By J.R Reynolds

My grandmother and I are sitting at the Springfield Community Center watching people come to honor my grandfather with a Memorial Service. My grandmother suffers from Alzheimer's, so I'm not sure if she is aware of why we're here. She is simply enjoying an outing away from the Care Center where she lives.

The people who come to the Memorial were his friends. People who Grandfather did business with or helped during the years he'd lived in Springfield. There are people from the VFW where Grandfather was a member. Looking around the room I realize these people represent my grandfather's life.

As each person stands and tells their story I can't help but wonder what Grandfather would be thinking as he looked down on his friends. Knowing Grandfather, he's laughing.

When everyone has spoken, a man from the back of the room who I've never seen before slowly makes his way to the front of the room He stopped and looked around until his eyes came to rest on me.. He was dressed in hand-me-downs or else he had been sick because his clothes were obviously too large for him, but they were clean.

"My name is George Johnston," he said. "Peter

Harrison and I grew up together. He was a big brother to me and my best friend. He taught me to read, write, and throw a spit ball. From him I learned to dance and fight. I've never had a dad, but Peter Harrison was the type of person I wished to be like."

"Peter wasn't prone to bragging but if you wanted to get him started just ask about his wife or his grandson. He would go on for hours."

"I don't know if you were aware, Peter spent every Thanksgiving and Christmas morning cooking and preparing the holiday meal down at the Homeless Mission here in town. He did it for years and had become an institution down there."

"He found work for the people who came through the Mission. He saw the good in people and was willing to give them a chance. One of his favorite sayings was, "If it wasn't for the love of a good woman I might have ended up here myself." Mr. Johnston paused and then softly said, "Peter Harrison will be terribly missed." He turned and slowly walked to the back of the room.

I wasn't aware of this about my grandfather. He had always left the house early on Thanksgiving and Christmas morning, "to run errands," my grandmother would say. He was always home in time for dinner. To us it was normal.

This was a secret world about my grandfather, and I felt hurt, but there was a lot I didn't know about him. I asked him once where he was born and about his parents. He told me he had crawled out from under a rock, so that made him a first edition.

Suddenly here is a man who grew up with my grandfather and had been his best friend who was revealing many things previously unknown to me. I needed to talk to him. I saw him at the door putting on his overcoat, so I started in his direction but was stopped by people offering their condolences.

When I got free, Mr. Johnston was gone. I hurried outside and saw him near the bus stop. I rushed up to him and introduced myself to him. I told him of my ignorance about my grandfather's activities over the years.

He told me, "Your grandfather always played down the things he did at the Mission because praise embarrassed him. He'd say, "I'm doing what anyone would do." Unfortunately, there aren't many doing what your grandfather did."

I inquired about where he and my grandfather had grown up and he replied in Ashland. Then I asked about my grandfather's parents, he said he never knew them. He was evasive about who raised them. I asked several more leading questions without success. Finally, he said "When I was sixteen I followed your grandfather here to Springfield and he got me a job at the fruit packing company down by the tracks."

His bus was coming, so I asked how to contact him. I explained that I wanted to find out more about my grandfather. He said I could find him at the Mission.

I asked, "Do you need money, or work? Is there anything I can do to help you?" He smiled and said no.

As he boarded the bus he turned and said, "If you really want to do something for me, get me a BetterBilt pie."

"What was that?" I asked. "A butter built pie?"

"No, I would like a BetterBilt pie." He said and spelled it out for me, the driver then closed the door and Mr. Johnston was gone.

Over the next several weeks I canvassed the stores, inquiring at small Mom-n-Pop stores and the huge Super Stores. I asked the bakeries if they had ever heard of BetterBilt pies. The answer was always the same, no one had heard of such a thing. I'm beginning to wonder if Mr. Johnston was pulling my leg.

I still had to eat so I worked ten hours a day in the shop finishing orders for customers. I like working with wood and building cabinets from scratch. It felt like Grandfather was here watching over my shoulder. We've worked side by side for so long I still catch myself talking to him as I work. Sometimes I can almost hear his answers to my comments and questions. The question I don't hear an answer to is "what is a BetterBilt pie?" If people were to come into the shop, they'd think I've lost my mind. It's hard to be here by myself. The shop is so quiet and full of memories.

When I'm not at the shop, I'm at the Center with

grandmother or on my quest to find a BetterBilt pie. If I could find out about the pies maybe I could solve the mystery of my grandfather's early life.

It's funny how Alzheimer's affects people. Their memory will be clear, then a fog rolls across their mind and their memories fade. I'm a stranger to Grandmother most days when I visit, but she likes visitors. Sometimes she asks if I know her husband and comments that he visits her in the afternoons. It's sad, but she's in good health and seems happy. She likes to talk about the garden at her house and how proud she is of her son who is in the military.

This morning, I picked flowers from grandmothers' garden for her. She is having a good day and recognizes me right away. We put the flowers in a vase and decide to go for a walk since it's a beautiful day. The Center has a nice fenced in courtyard for residents and visitors.

"Grandmother," I asked, "Have you ever heard of BetterBilt pies?" She thought for a moment and said, "You should ask Grandfather about that, he can tell you more than I can." She paused and looked around then said, "It's nice out here, do you have a garden?"

I told her," I take care of your garden at home."

She looked confused and said "That's nice, I think it's lunchtime. I'll have lunch in my room today. Please bring my tray to me." I realized then that her memory had faded, and she thought I worked there.

After getting grandmother settled in her room I headed back to the shop. As I walked through the lobby one of the nurse's aides stopped me, "Excuse me, is Mrs. Harrison your grandmother?"

"Yes she is." I answered.

"I couldn't help overhearing you in the garden," she replied "When you asked your grandmother about the BetterBilt pies, and I realized that my grandmother has mentioned something about them while reminiscing about her childhood. If you'd like, I can ask her if she would talk with you."

"Yes, please do!" I exclaimed. "Does she live here at the Center?"

"No, she lives with my parents and I," she replied.

I gave her my business card, "Call anytime, if I'm not home leave a message."

At last, after weeks of searching I've found someone who knows about the pies! It definitely is a beautiful day as I head back to the cabinet shop.

I didn't expect to hear from the girl right away, so I was surprised to hear the phone ringing in the house when I came in that evening. "Hello?" I answered.

"Yes, is this Mrs. Harrisons' grandson?" a girl asked.

"Yes, I'm Dwight Harrison."

"My name is Lynda Robbins. I'm the girl from the Center this afternoon. I spoke with my grandmother, and she said she would be glad to talk with you."

"When would be a good time to meet with her?" I asked.

"I'm off work on Tuesday. If you would like to come at 11:30, I'll fix lunch for the three of us."

"Tuesday is fine with me, is there anything I should bring?"

"Just bring yourself, Grandmother and I will take care of the rest."

The weekend seems to crawl. I can hardly wait for Tuesday! I hadn't realized how much the riddle had been affecting my life.

Grandfather always gave me riddles to solve while we were working. He would never give me the answers. I had to solve them myself. Well, it looks like Grandfather and his pies is the biggest riddle of all!

Finally, Tuesday came, and as I arrived at Lynda's house, Lynda opened the door and showed me into the living room where she introduced me to her grandmother, Mrs. Robbins. Mrs. Robbins appears to be about my grandmother's age, and she has a twinkle in her eye as though she knows a secret.

"Lynda," Mrs. Robbins said, "Would you set the table while I bring the soup and sandwiches from the kitchen?"

"Can I help?" I asked.

Mrs. Robbins led me into the kitchen and showed me where the dishes and silverware were kept.

When all was ready we sat down and Lynda said the blessing, then we began to eat.

"Where did you hear about BetterBilt Pies?" Mrs. Robbins asked.

I explained about my grandfather passing away and about the memorial service. Then I told them about meeting Mr. Johnston who knew my grandfather as a young boy and how he had hinted at things I didn't know, and he mentioned the pies.

"What was your grandfathers' name?" she asked?

"Peter Harrison," I replied.

Mrs. Robbins choked, I jumped up to help her, but she motioned me back to my chair. After she caught her breath she said, "I used to know a Peter Harrison, in fact, I had quite a crush on him when we were young."

"Would George be Mr. Johnston's first name," she asked?

"Yes!" I said excitedly "Do you know him as well?"

"Yes, a long time ago in what seems another life and time, I knew both of them." She replied, "It's strange we all ended up here in Springfield."

"Do you mind telling me where you knew my grandfather?"

"In Ashland a hundred miles south of here," she replied. "When did Peter come to Springfield?"

"I don't know the year, but I know he was sixteen when he arrived here."

"Do you know when George came to Springfield?" she asked.

"From what Mr. Johnston said, he moved to Springfield at sixteen, three years after my grandfather. Grandfather helped him get a job. What does this have to do with BetterBilt pies?" I asked.

By now we had finished lunch so Mrs. Robbins suggested we retire to the family room, and she would explain about the pies.

In the family room Mrs. Robbins continued, "After the big war, WWI, the country was going through trying times. A lot of families had been broken up. Husbands killed in the war or gravely injured. Some never came home after the war because they were having a hard time readjusting to normal life. There were a lot of people who weren't able to take care of their children and gave them up to orphanages or children's homes until they could get back on their feet. Some parents came back for their children when they were able, but a lot of children stayed until the Home turned them out at sixteen years of age. I was one of the lucky ones. I was only there a year before my father came for me. Your grandfather and Mr. Johnston stayed until they were sixteen."

"The home was called The Biltmore Home. While I was there, sixty children lived at the Home. They ranged in age from newborn to sixteen."

"The Biltmore Home received funding from churches in the area and donations from private citizens. Some of the children's families sent money when they could, to help with the care."

"Every child had jobs to do each day, besides going to school. Older children took care of the younger children. Others did laundry, dishes, or helped to prepare the meals in the kitchen. Some cleaned the house. It was like we were one large family, everyone helping each other."

"Your grandfather helped George with his chores, homework, and whatever else he needed help with. He considered George his brother even though they weren't related. That was the way everyone was."

"There wasn't the conflict that you might expect with so many children from so many different backgrounds. I'm not saying that there weren't problems, but everyone was in the same boat, so unity was more important than conflict."

"The jobs most sought after were in the kitchen. There was plenty of food to eat and the work was light. Usually, the older kids got to work in the kitchen because of the knives, stoves, and ovens."

"On Wednesday afternoons, all day Thursday, and Friday were baking days. Everyone who was free to work went to the kitchen to help make pies. The older kids were responsible for cutting up the fruit and the baking of the pies. They also supervised the younger ones. They taught us how to roll out the dough for the pie crusts and how to dish the fruit into the pie plates. Some kids washed the fruit while others measured the sugar, flour, and spices for the pies.

"One group made pies while another made fruit cobblers topped with biscuits. This was the dessert to go with our meals. All the pies we made were sold to the townspeople, who started calling our pies The BetterBilt Pies."

"We got our fruit from local farmers and markets around town. It would vary from week to week. Depending on the season, we would get strawberries, blackberries, peaches, apricots, plums, rhubarb, squash, pumpkins, and of course in the fall, cherries, apples and pears."

"We sold them for twenty-five cents in a stall in front of the Orphanage each Saturday. We must have been doing something right because we sold all our pies every week. People began showing up at seven in the morning, even the cafes and restaurants came to buy pies."

"We felt like we were helping to keep the home going by participating in the making of the pies. It became a bonding of spirit and friendship to see those pies go from start to finish. We all took great pride in seeing the pies sell out each week."

"When the pies were gone everyone helped to clean the kitchen from top to bottom. It was considered a privilege to help with the cleanup. Everyone helping each other as we became brothers and sisters all working towards one goal."

"Those were fond memories. It was a trying time

for a lot of us, but it was made easier through the friendships we developed with the other kids."

"Well now, I'm sure I have bored you both to tears with my story," said Mrs. Robbins.

"Not at all," I replied. "Now I know what a BetterBilt Pie is. It appears the only way I'm going to get Mr. Johnston a pie is to make one myself."

"I will help you," said Lynda. "I'm not much of a cook but I can pare apples,"

"I'll help too," said Mrs. Robbins. "I haven't baked a pie in a long time. It would be fun."

"I'll need all the help I can get! I've never baked a pie! Maybe with us working together it will be closer to what a BetterBilt Pie was about, everyone working towards one goal, which is to produce a pie."

We decided I would get the apples "Good tart apples, preferably Granny Smiths, make sure they're crisp," Mrs. Robbins said.

Lynda will get the flour, spices, and sugar. We agreed to meet at Lynda's house on Saturday afternoon for the baking. Sunday afternoon the three of us will take the pie to Mr. Johnston at the Mission.

By Saturday I was nervous about making a pie. I'd seen my grandmother make pies on holidays and it looked like a lot of work. I looked in my grandmother's old cookbook and I realized I'd never heard of some of the ingredients.

At Lynda's house, I told Mrs. Robbins about looking up the apple pie recipes and about my concerns as a baker. She laughed and said

"Sometimes too much information is not a good thing. Some things are better learned by doing."

Lynda had the kitchen ready, so Mrs. Robbins delegated the tasks and started telling us stories as Lynda peeled apples and I made the dough for the pie crust.

She talked about her time spent at the orphanage and how they'd entertain themselves when their work was done. "We didn't have movie theatres, so we played games and read books. Books could transport us to other worlds where we'd imagine ourselves being there. By sharing the books with friends, we traveled to forbidden islands, attended grand parties in palaces, waltzed with the Crown Prince."

Lynda said she'd never heard her grandmother talk so much. She almost spilled the apples from laughing.

When it came time to put the top crust on the pie, Mrs. Robbins said, "Cut a B in the center of the crust because that's what we did at the orphanage, it vents the pie so it can bake properly."

Before long we had three pies ready for the oven, one for Mr. Johnston and one for Lynda's family and one for us to eat.

"What do you say to me getting burgers and fries? We can eat while the pies bake." I suggested.

"I have a better idea" replied Mrs. Robbins. "Why don't you two get something to eat. I'll stay and watch the pies. When you get back they'll be cooled enough to have a slice for dessert."

By the time Lynda and I had finished eating, we knew a lot about each other. She was easy to talk with and I needed someone to talk to.

At Lynda's house, I could smell the pies as I got out of the car. I know I've just eaten, but the smell makes my mouth water. I told Mrs. Robbins, "If that pie tastes half as good as it smells I'll be tempted to steal the second pie and take it home with me, forget Mr. Johnston!"

She laughed and said, "My mother told me the best way to capture a man's heart is to bake him an apple pie. That's what she did when she met my father, and I did the same thing when I met Lynda's grandfather."

"Grandma," Lynda said as her face turned bright red.

I laughed, "I am safe for now because we all helped to make these pies. I've been warned though, so I'll be sure to watch for any stray pies coming my way."

The pie was the best I'd ever eaten. I asked Mrs. Robbins, "What makes this pie taste so good?"

She said, "All pies taste better when you help to make them. It's as if each person puts a little of themselves into the pie."

The next day I arrived at Lynda's house at one thirty and Lynda and her grandmother were waiting. Getting into the car, Mrs. Robbins giggled, "I'm a little nervous about seeing Mr. Johnston. After all these years I wonder if he will remember me."

"Don't worry Grandma, if he doesn't, he will as soon as you both start talking about the Biltmore Home. I'm sure you have many memories to share."

We were able to find parking in front of the Mission, but we weren't sure Mr. Johnston would be there, so we decided to leave the pie in the car until we found out.

Entering the building I was surprised to see young people sitting at tables placed around the room. They were coloring pictures. Others were playing cards or reading books and magazines. Some were sitting around visiting. When I say young, I mean between the ages of four and eighteen. Some of the children appeared to be with their families, but a lot of them seemed to be alone or with friends their own age.

A lady approached us and asked, "May I help you?"

"Yes we are looking for Mr. Johnston. Is he here today?"

"Yes he is, May I tell him who is asking?"

"My name is Dwight Harrison."

"Oh, my goodness," she said as her face lit up. "Are you Mr. Harrison's grandson? I'm Miss Lucy. We miss him so much around here. This place isn't the same with him gone."

I said I was, and then introduced Lynda and Mrs. Robbins. Miss Lucy shook everyone's hands and then went to find Mr. Johnston.

It wasn't long until I saw Mr. Johnston come out a door across the hall. He looked thinner than I remember. He was wearing a suit that was again too large for him.

He walked up grinning, "I don't see any pie."

I introduced him to Lynda and Mrs. Robbins, he motioned for us to sit at one of the tables. As we sat down Miss Lucy came up and asked if we would like any refreshments. "We have coffee, tea, both hot and cold, and milk." We all settled for hot tea and Miss Lucy disappeared back through the door Mr. Johnston had come through.

Mr. Johnston was watching me, and he had an expression on his face like he was enjoying a private joke. When Miss Lucy came with the tea he asked me, "Have you had any luck finding me a pie?"

I laughed and told him about my adventures looking for his pie. When I got to the part about meeting Lynda and her grandmother, Mrs. Robbins took over.

"Do you remember a girl from the Biltmore Home by the name of Sylvia Temple?"

Mr. Johnston looked thoughtful for a minute and then said, "Yes I do, she used to help me with my schoolwork. She was nice to me. I was sad when she left, but happy for her when her family came to get her."

"I'm that Sylvia Temple," Mrs. Robbins said. "I have to admit at the time I had ulterior motives as I was quite fascinated by your friend Peter Harrison."

"I had suspected that might have been a possibility, but a friend was still a friend!"

I asked Lynda to accompany me out to the car. We excused ourselves, and left the building, Lynda said, "Did you see the young people here at the Mission? I've always imagined these places full of derelicts and winos like you see on the streets asking for handouts. There are families, elderly, young people, and preschoolers all staying here."

"I know, I'm surprised," I said.

Entering the Mission carrying the pie, Mr. Johnston's face lit up with a big grin. He called Miss Lucy to bring plates, napkins, forks and a knife. We removed the cover from the pie and Mr. Johnston's eyes got glassy as he saw the B carved in the top of the pie. After a moment he said, "You have no idea the memories this pie brings me. I never knew my parents. My earliest memories are of the Biltmore Home and all the children who lived there. They were my family. I always thought how lucky I was to have so many brothers and sisters."

"Today when I look back on those years at the Biltmore Home, the highlight of each week was always the making of the pies. We'd turn out one hundred to one hundred and fifty pies each week and it never seemed like work. We looked forward to those days when we worked together."

As we were eating, I asked Mr. Johnston about all the young people at the Mission. He said, "There are more than usual right now. There was a fire in an apartment complex over on Forrest Drive. Several families came here to stay until the Red Cross can find them a place to live."

"Some families are passing through looking for work. Sometimes they stay and find a job and a place to live. Others move on to other places. There are always teenagers passing through. Some stay a couple of days. Some just long enough to get a shower, something to eat and they're gone again."

"We try to find work for guests who want it. There are townspeople like your grandfather who periodically need help, and they'll hire people from here."

"We feed our guests and if they need clothes we get donations from several churches to help them out. We make sure the children have paper and writing materials for school, and we run a shuttle bus back and forth to the schools for them."

"Miss Lucy came here five years ago as a guest of the Mission. She ended up staying and working for us. We have six full-time employees on the payroll. Most of the people who work here came to us first as guests and stayed on to work for us. There are fifteen to twenty-five volunteers who come to help when they can.

"The guests help out with the chores such as laundry, housekeeping, and in the kitchen. It isn't required, but when they do it helps us because we're always shorthanded of staff."

"Some mothers help the kids with their

homework after school. We also have one lady who is a retired schoolteacher. She comes one day a week to work with the children that are having trouble with their schoolwork."

Mrs. Robbins said, "I'm a teacher myself. I taught elementary school for twenty-five years before retiring. I would love to come down and work with the children."

"We can use you. The children return from school at four. They study until supper which is served at six. For the kids who don't have homework, we have a playground out back where they can swing and play basketball."

Finishing our pie and tea, Mr. Johnston asked if we would like to see the facility. We said yes, so he led us into the kitchen where Miss Lucy and five people were preparing the evening meal.

Miss Lucy said, "Sunday supper is always chicken and dumplings with green beans and salad and tonight for dessert we have strawberry ice cream. A lot of the food is donated by various organizations, but we do have to buy some things ourselves. We get grants and some Government funding. We work on the fringes of our financial limits, but we're still open and that's what's important. If it wasn't for Mr. Johnston, I don't know how we could have made it. He's a miracle worker. A lot of the guests wouldn't have anywhere to go if we weren't here."

Leaving the kitchen we entered the laundry area.

Mr. Johnston explained, "On Sundays we have one employee working in the laundry, so guests come and help." There were four people folding towels and sheets as they came from the dryer.

From the laundry we pass an office. Mr. Johnston explains, "This is my office and where I live. It's easier being here twenty-four hours a day. I can help guests quickly and they appreciate the fact I live here like they do."

In housekeeping he explained, "Sunday is housekeeping's day off so there isn't any one here." As we were leaving a teenage boy came in asking for a mop and a bucket to clean up water the younger kids spilled while finger painting. Mr. Johnston showed him where the bucket and mop were and told him, "Thank you for helping," and sent him on his way.

"Everyone helps, even the children. That's what makes this Mission work as well as it does."

Mrs. Robbins remarked, "It reminds me of the Biltmore Home."

Mr. Johnston laughed, "I hadn't thought about it, but I guess you're right."

Miss Lucy caught up with us and informed Mr. Johnston it was time for supper.

When we got back to the common room they were setting the tables for supper. We thanked Mr. Johnston for the wonderful time and the tour.

"You're welcome to stay for dinner," Mr. Johnston said.

We declined but we promised we'd soon return.

Walking to the door Mr. Johnston put his arm around my shoulder and said, "The pie was the best thing that's happened to me in a long time. I really appreciate what you did, and I hope it answers some of the questions you had about your grandfather."

"It did," I replied. "But it opened up more questions. I'll have to keep looking to find the answers."

He laughed, "That's the way life is, Dwight. Answer one question and the answer will open a door to another question."

J. R. Reynolds

J.R has been writing stories for forty years. He has had numerous stories published in 'Stories through the Ages' over the last several years. He's had stories selected for on-line magazines such as 'Frontier Times'. He writes daily and has completed two full length novels, many short stories, and Novella's. He teaches classes on woodcarving bi-monthly at the local Cultural Arts Center, and is an Artist working in oils, acrylics, and clay. He and his wife of fifty-two years have four children, five grandchildren and three great grandchildren.

Balance
By Ken Sutherland

Excerpt from…

BALANCE: The 200-Year Journey of Andrew Crawford

In Ireland, the potatoes came up black again, so we had no money, not that we'd ever had much. When Ma got the influenza, the doctor wouldn't come.

"Would have made no difference," Pa said. She'd have died anyway, even if he did come.

It was the three of us, me and Pa and my older brother Sean, two boys with shattered hearts, unable to stop crying about Ma.

Pa lost the house, which was never ours anyway, and we moved to the streets, our belongings in a sack. We'd sleep with dozens of other bankrupt and destitute potato farmers in filthy alleyways, sometimes fighting over a dry space under an awning.

Then the British, who owned everything that should be Irish, gathered up the people with no place to go, and told us they would *give* us a new farm that we can own ourselves. A land grant. But we would have to move to Canada and become frontiersmen. They promised to pay to move us. Pa was doubtful. He didn't trust the British, but we had no other choices and so he agreed.

We spent a month fighting the wind aboard a leaky wooden ship, filled with pain and stink and hunger and fear the whole way. Some of the poor farmers were not able to finish the trip, and the English captain simply stripped them naked and dumped them over the side with no ceremony, not even a prayer. Even as a five-year-old, I knew this was wrong.

When we eventually arrived in Windsor, Ontario, the British wouldn't talk to us. Other Irish who were already there said it was all lies, we'd been dumped there just to be rid of us. This is how the English deal with their poor.

Pa got scutwork to survive, cleaning manure out of stables and whatever other manual labor could be found. There was no money in this work, because someone would always do it cheaper. We worked for scraps of food. We ate it fast, so we wouldn't have to fight to keep it.

Then Pa made the decision to sneak across the river into America, only half a mile away. He said there would surely be work there for farmers like us. Pa wanted to buy a boat to cross into Detroit, but couldn't afford even a leaky old one. Not that any self-respecting citizen would sell a boat to an Irishman, even for a handsome profit. But there was no handsome profit to be made, because there was no money at all.

Deep into winter, just after a bleak Christmas, the

three of us were living in an Irish camp near the river. We huddled together for warmth, nothing but our hats to keep the snow off our heads. Pa sat us in a tight circle so he could wrap his arms around his boys, and we shared each other's body heat. An older man attached himself to our family. He introduced himself as Michael O'Leary. I told him my name was Michael, too. "People call me Mickey," he said.

Then we heard folks buzzing over how the Detroit River had frozen over. The Irish campers, most of them in the same condition as us, started to test the ice, to see if they could walk across. There was a lot of debate about "a short walk" versus "certain death in the freezing river."

Eventually, the promise of America, with all its imagined prosperity, only a half-mile across the ice, won the argument. Pa took me and Sean, one by each hand. With Mickey holding my other hand, we began the cautious march. Dozens of poor Irish stooped low in the dim moonlight to avoid the American police, knowing they would beat us and send us all back if they found us. Everyone nervously hurried to cross the river. Someone said to *slide* our feet forward, rather than walk, so our footfalls wouldn't penetrate the fragile ice. Near the center of the river, word came back from those in front not to bunch up, because the ice was thinner here. If too many of us stood too close together, the ice might crack, and we'd all plunge to our deaths in the frozen water below.

Someone in the dark made a joke about how happy such an event would make the British, who only smile at an Irishman's pain. But the response to the advice was mixed. While some people did spread out, we felt a crush from behind us. The warning stimulated a new urgency, and the people in the back began to press forward, crowding to pass.

We found ourselves in a cluster of people, sweeping us along with them. Someone said the river was fifty feet deep. If we were to go down into the freezing water, we might not come up until Easter. As we approached the center, thought to be the weakest part of the ice, we heard a profound cracking noise, loud as nearby thunder. I saw people ahead of us disappear, dropping straight down through the ice. A woman screamed for help, but there was no help, because we were all sinking into the frozen water.

The sudden shock to the system was devastating. I could not move. I could not see Sean or Pa, who only a moment ago held my hand. I felt myself slipping into the icy water, screaming and flailing my arms even before I was fully wet, trying to keep from sinking. Just before my head went under, I called out for Pa. Then a large hand pulled me by the collar, up and out of the freezing water, and threw me roughly over a wide shoulder. Crying and shivering, I slowly came aware of my surroundings. People were screaming and the loudest among them was Pa, calling again and again for Sean.

But Sean was gone.

It was Mickey who had me, and he continued the dogged march across the river, until eventually, we found the American shore. He wrapped me in his arms to warm me and waited for Pa to come ashore. Finally, the three of us lay freezing in the bushes on the riverbank, keeping low to avoid the American police, Pa crying for Sean. Wet and frozen and broken, we made our way into Detroit and slept in an alley until a shopkeeper ran us off.

Detroit. Just like Windsor. Just like home. People here wouldn't pay the Irish to do work that local people could do.

We'd made it to America, our third country in a year's time, and it was only another disappointment. Nobody liked the Irish here. Nobody liked the Irish in Canada. Even in Ireland, they didn't like us enough to keep us.

Pa spent a great deal of time weeping for Sean, but I did not. I'd wept and wept for my beautiful mother when she died, and it brought about no changes. I expected only the same if I cried for Sean.

Pa learned about farming to the south, so we said goodbye to our only friend, Mickey. Pa thanked him for saving my life, and told him he wished there was a way to pay him back.

Mickey said there would be another time for that. He squatted down to look in my eyes and promised we would meet again. He said, "It is guaranteed by Irish legend, lad, that we all return to visit one another. Perhaps, even, as angels."

We didn't know what he meant by that, so we smiled at him and thanked him again, and began walking south.

Later, after Pa'd been silent for a long time, he muttered, "Irish legends, indeed!"

Ken Sutherland

PHOTO: *Lisa Kirkman*

Ken Sutherland, author of three novels and several short stories, lives in Reno, NV with his wife, Alene. This August marks their 55th wedding anniversary. He is a true Baby Boomer and Beatles fan, born in Oakland, California in 1947. He served in the US Army from 1965-1968 as a Medic.

In 1969, the Sutherlands were married and Ken began a 53-year career in radio as a DJ, newsman, program director, salesman, sales & general manager, network executive and, eventually, owner of 10 Nevada radio stations. He is a member of the Nevada Broadcasters Hall of Fame.

In 2022, he retired and concentrated on finishing the stories he'd quietly started over the years.

In his debut novel, now available from Amazon, "BALANCE: The 200-Year Journey of Andrew Crawford," a young man trips through time, re-living his own past lives. The story in this anthology is excerpted from this novel.

The Chuck Donnegan Mystery Series is well under way, with HEARTBREAKER and THE HOLLYWOOD DIAMOND MURDERS, also available from Amazon.

Ken Sutherland is accessible. Reach him at: KenSutherlandAuthor.com.

Love & Apples
By Elaine Thomas

Groggy, still in her pajamas, Grace sat at the kitchen table and ate slowly, annoyed that she had to get out of bed.

Her grandmother urged her to speed up. "You and I are going with your Aunt Sharlene over to Mrs. Albright's this morning, remember?"

"No!" Grace dropped her spoon. It hit the side of the bowl with a clang. Milk and cereal splashed across the table. "I don't want to go to Mrs. Albright's. I don't want to go anywhere with Sharlene."

"Gracie!"

Her grandmother's sharp tone shocked her. At his end of the table, calm as always, her grandfather sipped his coffee.

Grace jumped up and ran from the kitchen. She heard the chair hit the floor behind her.

Alone on the front porch, she regretted her behavior. She knew better.

Sometimes you know it's wrong, but you got to do it anyway.

Through the screen door she heard her grandmother's voice: "Honestly, I feel like I don't know the child anymore."

"Don't take it personal," Papa replied. "She's just

homesick."

He wasn't wrong. Deep down Grace knew her grandparents cared for her, but she missed Mama and Daddy. They'd been gone so long. She wasn't where she belonged. At home she'd be settled in, watching Saturday morning cartoons, laughing alongside Daddy as the Road Runner outsmarted Wile E. Coyote. Instead, here she stood, outside and alone, her parents all the way across the country. *Did they even miss her?*

The morning they dropped her off, Grace stood on this same porch and watched their car pull away. This morning felt different, air cooler and drier, fall just ahead. Their return kept getting pushed farther and farther out. She'd thought it would be fun to spend the summer with her grandparents. For a while it was, even now at times. Her parents sent postcards, pictures of broad bridges and big trees. Once a week they called on the telephone. As soon as they hung up, she missed them even more. They seemed so far away. She hungered to lay eyes on them. She wanted to touch them. She wanted them to hold her.

Her grandparents' front yard was familiar, yet still not home. Two tall rows of elms ran the length of the lawn. A maple and a crepe myrtle marked one end. Next to them began a dense semicircle of pines that wrapped around behind the house and all the way out to the other side of the yard. Grace squinted toward that end, noted the large holly tree and her favorite apple tree. The base of the apple might be surrounded this morning with fallen fruit. Grace did love apples. She knew the best path across the yard to get to the tree, how far to the right she could veer before the painful points of holly leaves, dead and dried on the ground, cut into the tender soles of bare feet.

She also knew her grandma would have a fit.

As if she could read Grace's mind, her grandmother called out: "Come on back in here. Your Aunt Sharlene will be along any minute. We need to comb those tangles out of your hair."

Grace sighed. She turned to obey and almost bumped into Papa, quietly pushing through the door. The screen squeaked shut behind him. He placed a calloused hand on the top of her head, slowed her to a standstill.

"Gracie, you mind Big Mama today," he said.

She tilted her head back to look up into his kind grey eyes.

He winked. "And your Aunt Sharlene."

Papa headed down the steps and out toward his battered blue pickup. Grace wanted to run after him, beg to go with him out onto the farm. Most days he would've let her, opened the truck's heavy passenger door and lifted her up into the cab. Not today. Between her grandmother and Sharlene, he wasn't about to wade into what she knew he would call "women's business."

Instead, Grace endured the agony of a hairbrush

through her long, disheveled locks.

"Go finish getting cleaned up," her grandma instructed.

Grace obediently headed back to the bathroom to brush her teeth, wash her face, and take one last pee.

Her grandmother helped her change into a clean beige shirt and matching brown shorts, an outfit appropriate for the start of the fall season, even as the weather remained warm. Ordinarily Grace could've chosen her own clothes, but not this time, not to wear to Mrs. Albright's, where appearances so clearly mattered.

Grace loved her grandmother. She really did. Always had. Other family members often commented how much she seemed to take after the woman they all called Big Mama. Yet the air between them these days hung thick with expectations that neither seemed able to meet. Add bossy Aunt Sharlene into the mix and it all just felt too heavy for Grace's little-girl shoulders.

Her grandmother cautioned, "You know how important today is to your Aunt Sharlene. You need to watch your Ps and Qs."

When in a better mood, Grace liked Mrs. A, as she thought of the elegant older woman. Sharlene was married to the Albrights' youngest boy, Bryce.

Before she could ask what Ps and Qs were, Grace heard Sharlene's fancy creamsicle-colored Oldsmobile pull into the yard. She rolled her eyes. She found her mama's baby sister ridiculously car-proud.

They took the back way to Mrs. A's. Sharlene's choice of the dirt road surprised Grace. This County Line Road was one of her own favorites, but she couldn't believe her prissy aunt risked covering her precious vehicle in dust—especially enroute to visit a mother-in-law they were all going out of their way to impress.

Her grandparents lived in an area that tucked into a corner formed by three adjoining counties. Portions of Papa's farm were officially within one county or another, but the land itself seemed unable to choose among them. It moved quickly from the sandy soil loved by pine trees to black dirt so deep and rich that it smelled alive, to red clay reminiscent of the former pottery-producing communities just to their north.

The road ran past some of Papa's fields. Although their farm wasn't a particularly large one, it was spread-out, hard-won acreage acquired over time. Generations of their family had farmed here. Papa called each field by an individual name, patches identified by purpose or appearance, such as "the red field," "the old cotton patch," and "the low grounds."

They drove through a shadowy section, the sun's light dampened by tall pines lining both sides of the road. Signs posted at intervals indicated this land and these trees, destined to become pulpwood, belonged to an international paper company. Grace remembered being in the crossroads store near her grandparents' house, hearing two big-bellied men in coveralls talk about these trees.

"More'n more land's being grabbed up by outside paper companies," said one. "They don't know or care anything about the old families here."

"You're right about that," responded the other. "It just keeps getting harder'n harder to make a decent living. One tobacco barn fire and you've got no choice. You have to sell off land, it's the only way to get through a bad year."

"Yep, and them in the next generation that don't want to farm just sell out when they inherit and move on."

Grace couldn't imagine her grandparents, or any of the families they knew, selling property they'd owned and farmed for so long. Their connection to the land was too strong. Yet that connection hadn't stopped Daddy from taking what he called "a great-paying job" with an out-of-state paper company. The job was the reason her parents had left her with her grandparents this summer. Daddy needed to go all the way out to California for meetings and company training. Right now, she hated outside paper companies as much as the big-bellied men at the store did.

For anyone from around here to fly clear across the country on business was rare. For Mama to go with Daddy...she'd told Grace she wanted to see for herself those enormous redwood trees she'd heard so much about...amplified the significance. Together, her parents built a short business trip into a long vacation.

"Go!" her grandmother had urged. "Gracie can stay with her Papa and me. It'll be fun for us all."

A song from the car's radio pulled Grace out of her memories. Elvis's smooth voice, low but unmistakable, came through Sharlene's fancy rear speakers, asking if anyone was lonesome. *Just like Sharlene, listening to an Elvis station now that everybody else likes the Beatles.*

In the front seat her aunt and grandmother carried on their own conversation. Grateful to be ignored for a change, Grace rolled the window down far enough to slide an arm out. Cool air felt good on her skin. She extended her arm to its full length, palm parallel to the ground, and envisioned the stiffened hand as a saw blade like the ones she'd seen when Papa let her go with him to the sawmill. She pictured the finger-blade slicing down trees as they passed by, until she grew tired of that game. She pointed her hand forward and waved it slowly up and down on the breeze, like a soaring airplane.

The car pulled out of the shadows and back into sunlight. An abandoned, weathered-board farmhouse appeared on the left, the old Woodruff place. Yellow streaks ran along the grain of the wide gray planks, knots visible in spots. Weeds grew up the outside walls and through broken windows. Scrub growth had taken over the yard. Although the house remained standing, its rusty tin roof intact, the surrounding outbuildings sagged. Some had given up completely and collapsed.

Grace searched the sky. Hawks often flew above the Woodruff place, flew as if flying solely for the joy of it. They floated in lazy circles. With their wide wingspan they looked like little airplanes. *Did young birds wait somewhere for the big hawks' return?*

Her grandmother and Sharlene continued their rambling conversation, not one word of which interested Grace in any way. She spread her body out across the backseat, lying down and stretching out her legs. She rolled the window all the way open and leaned her head out like a puppy, enjoying the wind across her face.

Spotting no hawks, Grace scanned for any sign of heavenly life. No face of God to be found there. Nor wandering angels. But within a few minutes her vigilance paid off. She heard geese honking in the distance. Their V came into sight. They flew with determination, wings pumping furiously.

Her grandmother turned toward the rear. "Look, Grace! See the geese?"

Sharlene flicked her eyes toward the rearview mirror, checking on her niece. She saw the child's head dangling out the window. She also saw the fine mist of red clay blowing up from the dirt road through the open window into her car.

"Grace!"

That's my name, don't wear it out. Grace thought it,

but didn't dare say it out loud.

"Pull your head back in the car and roll that glass up. Right now! And get your dirty shoes down off that seat."

"Sharlene…"

Grace took a moment to savor her grandmother's choice to reprimand Sharlene instead of her, then moved as slowly as she could manage and still look compliant. She sat up straight and rolled the window closed, all the while hating Sharlene with the fiery passion of a thousand burning suns.

On they rode. No one spoke again. Soft, tinny radio songs about lost or damaged love provided the only sound for three stubborn generations of female family locked together in a now dusty car moving along over the isolated red-dirt road.

***

After an eternity they reached the Albright place. Sharlene switched off the ignition, hopped out of the car, and strode toward the front door.

Grace dawdled behind. From her view Sharlene appeared all ass-cheeks and elbows.

Mrs. A opened the door, her smile wide.

"Come on in!" She ushered the three visitors toward her living room.

Right before Grace's eyes, as if witnessing a magic act, Sharlene turned into a completely different person. A pleasant person. Friendly and smiling, almost elegant. New Sharlene acted more like a mirror image of Mrs. A than the fussy, irritable aunt Grace knew so well.

Grace sat down on one end of a slick-surfaced sofa, her grandmother at the other end. Mrs. A and New Sharlene settled into two graceful armchairs across from them. A low, sleek coffee table filled the space between. A glass fruit bowl there, on that table, right in front of her, immediately captured Grace's attention. Suddenly she felt hungry. She hadn't finished her breakfast. She recognized some of the fruits in the bowl, a banana, a pear, grapes. Others she couldn't identify or remember ever seeing.

A large, shiny red apple called out to her. She'd never seen such a perfect piece of fruit. Without bruise or blemish, its size, its shape, its surface glow exuded an appeal even beyond the red delicious apples Mama bought at the grocery store.

Grace loved any apple, even the knotty little ones that fell from the tree on the edge of her grandparents' yard, the ones her grandma baked into pies, their homemade crusts filled with a fragrant blend of cinnamon and butter.

But this apple…*this apple was something special.*

No matter how badly she wanted to ask for it, she knew she couldn't. Doing so no doubt fell outside those Ps and Qs she'd been warned about. She'd have to distract herself.

She pulled her eyes away from the tempting fruit and looked around the large living room, everything so clean it sparkled. The mahogany furniture gleamed, as if mocking her own dark mood. She felt wronged by all the restrictions of the morning. Had they *really* wanted her in top form, Sharlene and her grandmother could've done a better job not upsetting her. Bored and fidgety, fighting the urge for the apple, she examined the lacy pattern of Mrs. A's floor-length drapes. Curtains could occupy her restless mind for only a few moments. Her gaze moved on to shelves filled with those many small items old ladies love, knickknacks and whatnots, ornate figurines covered in hearts, flowers, and depictions of romantic love or Jesus. She quickly tired of those.

As a last resort she decided to try to be polite, to listen, maybe even participate in the adults' conversation. The effort proved useless. They talked about family, about the church they all attended, about the latest community gossip. Their words floated over Grace's head, as unreachable as any hawk or goose in the sky.

With the three women absorbed in intense talk about what was right and what was wrong with the preacher's latest sermon, Grace took her chance. She gave in only *partly* out of spite. She really did want that apple.

She slid forward. She snatched up the apple and pulled it to her lips, sank her teeth into it, realized too late the enormous mistake she'd made. She'd anticipated the pleasure of the apple's soft, juicy flesh, its sweetness on her tongue. Instead, her teeth sank into hard, cold, tasteless wax.

Grace pried the fake apple loose from her teeth. She stretched out her arm to return it to the bowl, turning the bite mark to the underside. Trying to turn the apple just right to hide any damage, she stretched too far forward. Her butt slid off the slick couch and hit the floor with a thud. As she fell, she dropped the apple. It rolled across the table, spinning her bite mark into prominent visibility. The apple fell to the floor and rolled a little farther, stopping only when it bumped into the fancy open-toed shoe on Sharlene's right foot.

Grace kept her face down, attempting to hide her shame. She didn't want to see the disappointment in her grandmother's eyes or the glowering anger of her aunt. She heard nothing, only stunned silence. Then all three women erupted in laughter, loud laughter begun by Mrs. A.

Grace looked up. She saw Mrs. A hurry to her kitchen, where she pulled a real apple from a cabinet.

She brought it to Grace. "Here, honey, I think you might like this one better."

The yellowish-green apple was not like the red ones Mama bought, nor like the knotty ones from her grandparents' tree. She took a bite. It was as tangy as it was sweet, but as she chewed it, the apple tasted awfully good.

Maybe it was Mrs. A's kindness. Maybe it was that no one had uttered her name in disapproval. They'd only laughed, and not in any mean way. Maybe it was that the taste of the apple was so different from what she knew or expected. Or maybe Grace was just flat-out exhausted. She'd certainly been working overtime all morning to feel wronged. Whatever the cause, after a few bites she set the apple down. Still on the floor, wedged between couch and coffee table, she pulled her knees in tight toward her body and folded her arms across the tops of them. She dropped her face back down onto her arms and began to cry. Tears she'd been fighting so hard not to shed flowed freely.

Just as she had with Papa an hour or so before, Grace found comfort when a hand touched the top of her head. As her grandmother stroked her hair, she felt claimed. It'd been a rough morning, but all seemed forgiven. She crawled up onto the couch and let Big Mama hold her.

Elaine Thomas

Elaine Thomas grew up in rural North Carolina. She's a retired college communications director and on-call hospital chaplain. She enjoys cross-country travel by train, takes long walks on the beach, and is proud these days to be considered a childless cat lady. Her creative writing has appeared in numerous publications including the 2022 Stories Through the Ages Baby Boomers Plus.

Swampin' in '63
By Bill Weatherford

The summer had passed. I had just begun my senior year of high school, and in a few days, Leo would follow the work back to Texas. I thought I had seen my friend for the last time two weeks before, but my father had him stay to help finish our raisins. I had come home for lunch, but when I saw Leo sitting in our side yard eating with his family, I parked the car and walked over, newly self-conscious and uneasy. As I stopped near him, he smiled slightly, and gesturing with his head over his left shoulder, he spoke.

"This, my wife Agrippina, my son Miguel." The quiet introductions focused on a young wife, baby in arms, seated on an overturned lug box under the shade of a cottonwood. I watched as she fed their son with full nursing breasts. I remembered getting my hand inside a bra twice in the back row of the Rivoli Theater, but this was different. It was like seeing a pair of big ones in National Geographic and being ashamed to really look.

A little flustered, I took off my hat, pretended to adjust the sweatband it didn't have, and, squatting on my haunches, looked away from those breasts. Finally, Leo's uplifted eyebrows made me say the greeting he had me rehearse many times in Spanish.

Yet my, *Buenos dias, Agrippina y Miguelito,* were just words that tumbled out somehow, hardly the thoughts, the meaning, the real language I had learned from our three months in the fields together.

We sat silently for a while, becoming painfully aware of what I had sensed since we said our earlier good-bye. Now as Leo's family looked at me, I became the son of the *patron.* He was *bracero* and I was *guero,* names he had never let anyone use, but words that stood for us just the same. Our simple and generous friendship could no longer keep the distance from us, a distance of minds and experiences unseen before in the eyes of a sixteen-year-old boy and a grown man, our only bonds having been the weighty dust, the searing summer sun and the heavy work loading fruit from the fields of California's San Joaquin Valley.

I stood up and shook hands with Leo. "Next summer we'll work together again like five demons instead of just four." Leo smiled and said he'd rather look for quail, and we agreed. I nodded a good-bye to his family and mumbled some Bob Steel 'B' movie western, *Vaya con Dios.* My ears burned at my awkwardness, and I almost wished for my winter pruning cap with the flaps to pull down.

Instead, gratefully sliding into my '55 Ford, I hid behind the baby shoes and fuzzy rear view mirror cover, drove out of our yard and down a back ditch road well off the avenue. I parked; I wanted to think and remember.

I slouched down in the seat of my pride and removed the working hat that I now wore just for show. It was a Mexican hat, cowboy styled, but with the two little tassels that hung down over the back brim for luck and good fortune. I had always thought luck and good fortune were one in the same, but Leo said there was a fine line of difference between the two, and I believed him. I had learned to always believe Leo, and I had good reasons. He was the only field worker that always carried his own personal roll of toilet paper; he could make a cigarette from start to finish with one hand, and he saved me at least six times from getting a tattoo.

A man in our crew named Candolario always tried to give *free tattoos.* He would say, "How about a nice Virgin on you shoulder, or, maybe a crow with a cigarette and a top hat on you leg? I got one of those myself." Among the other offers were a cross on my forearm, a coffin on my back, two twisted serpents on my right thigh pointed at my privates, or the *Last Supper* on my chest. "Besides," he would say, "half the fun is getting drunk enough to do it. I'll see you Saturday night." It was manly to get one; I was tempted . . .until I found out, through Leo, that it was the *tattooer* who got drunk.

Hiding out on those Saturday evenings was how Leo and I really began our friendship. We would play pool in the cool basement of the Methodist Church and drink warm cream sodas. Our talk was always unhurried, easy and no matter how we began, would always return to our work. We were both proud to be *swampers* and in the eyes of a very physical world, special among all others that labored on valley ranches.

A good swamper had to be strong enough to lift as many as a thousand-plus, thirty-to-fifty-pound full boxes of fruit each day, once from the ground to a vineyard wagon and once again from the wagons to the trucks going to town. Not only did he have to be strong enough to lift the boxes but also fast enough to keep the trucks on time to the packing house loading docks. Somehow, he must remember to do all this and yet remain gentle enough to not bruise the delicate harvest. Swampers got paid an extra dollar a day over pickers, and that dollar often meant who drank first from the water cup or held the steadiest gaze when two glances met over a smoke.

Leo was too small for this work, but because he was in such a hurry to bring his family from Mexico, he pushed himself brutally to get the extra pay and longer hours. Even though he knew what would happen to his body, he kept trying to stay on the wagons, rushing a time that would put him back on the ground, a picker again. Then he would not wear his cowboy hat. Instead, a sombrero or stained gray pith helmet would mate with a bandana to keep away flies from his ears.

"Que brazos, amigo," he said, as I gave him a hand up to the wagon the first day we worked together. We were to spread empty boxes for the pickers who would be arriving in half an hour at 6:00 when it would be light enough for them to see the ripeness of each plum: To pick or not to pick. Still, in the early dawn I could see his gold front tooth, even before the sun rose, and shoulders so slender, I wouldn't have believed the thirty-seven years recorded on the *green card* he had to carry for immigration. I had been a swamper for a week now, but this was to be his first day.

"You are wrestler?"

I laughed at his question but could feel the muscles along my back and shoulders swell with a boy's vanity. "No, I don't wrestle. I work the fields to get in shape for football."

He nodded vaguely, then went into a long monologue in broken English and pantomime about how he was to help me on the wagon that day and that he was glad to work with someone big and strong.

"I am, Leo," he said. "Soon you see I work like demon. Three month time, my family come to me here. Then, I work like two demon." He reached up for the top box to put on the end of the wagon, and, straddling it, turned to watch the sunrise made amber from the harvest season dust. I figured he was setting up for an easy time, me doing the heavy lifting while he got *lost* going to his car for cigarettes. I was used to this; I was the *guero*, the most *blond* of all *gringos,* so I waited.

As we began to spread the empty boxes down the plum rows, I watched him from the corners of my eyes. He always threw his empties so they hit flush on their bottoms instead of an edge or an end where they would be weakened or broken. He did this all morning, even when he tired as the sun grew hot at 10:00 and the easier way becomes very tempting.

He whistled too and turned to wink occasionally, jingling the tassels of his hat as he resumed to gracefully arch empty after empty into the drive. If you listened carefully, you could hear, over tractor noise, the lush, satisfying sounds of those boxes as they cushioned themselves in the deep watergrass that ran down the middle of each row.

Later, when we began to pick up and load fruit, he started to name things in Spanish and would prompt me to repeat the words after him. Pointing at the ancient, heavy-laden trees he said, *arboles,* and then, giving a sweeping gesture to include the whole orchard, he said, *el campo.*

***

Days passed and I found that, to work, was *trabajar,* and those who did little were *huevones.* The vocabulary got bigger, the sentences longer, the accent more precise and our friendship deeper. Often, he would stop and quiz me on words I learned that day; he was a gentle friend but a demanding tutor.

When I asked him if I, in turn, could teach him

more English, he merely shrugged and said, "When a man be a teacher, he helps to make another man. Already for me, I am enough man so, until my family come, I help make you." There was nothing airy or smug or even matter of fact in what he spoke. It was only that truly simple promise one hears once, maybe twice in a lifetime.

We both sat back, our legs dangling over the edge of the moving wagon while our feet made earthen wakes in the newly worked ground. Since we were caught up to the progress of the rest of the crew, we simply savored the quiet wait for lunch.

***

When noon would come, while the rest of the workers would search for the nearest shade, we swampers needed only to relax under our vineyard truck. Because we only had thirty minutes, lunch was precious and sacred, much more than just a time to eat, and we were devoted to its enjoyment. From our sanctuary we would watch the daily entertainments of wrestling, boasting of fighting cocks or daring each other to eat chili peppers, the deadly green ones that made your eyes water just holding them close to your face. The half hour was supposed to be a rest, but we sometimes worked harder than we ever did for pay.

Our wrestling matches were a combination of Greco-Roman freestyle and a *beer only* tavern brawl. You won by either pinning your opponent on his back or making him *give* with a torture hold. The holds and crazy moves were silly imitations of how Pepper Gomez or Luis Martinez had won their Wednesday night matches on TV. Pepper and Luis were always the good guys, especially when pitted against sneaky other racial types and arrogant white guys with long, bleached blond hair.

I went with Leo to a few of these televised fights, which were really just promotions for the paying exhibitions in Fresno on Saturdays. The free ones were held in a big three-walled corrugated iron barn on the outskirts of the city. The *open wall* was so that the only cameraman could turn his equipment around to do commercials for Honest Sylvester's Used Car Lot in downtown Selma. Honest Sylvester always had the head of his *Spanish Speaking Department* with him, Adolpho Moreno: three hundred pounds of electric green suit, white pointy shoes and a slide string tie.

Once the bouts began, the crowd was the best part of the show. Some cowboy would throw beer on Ray Stevens every time he got out of the ring and an elderly lady with blue hair would jab *The Alaskan* with her cane. One night, someone hit *The Great Pompero* with an Eskimo Pie as he was being interviewed. Being very hairy, the effect on the wrestler was rather amazing.

About halfway through the last match of the evening, when I was yelling my loudest for Red Snider to murder Don Manukian, Leo nudged me. Like a kind of gracious monarch, he gestured confidentially at the crowd and said, "Guellermo, don't you sometimes wish you could believe all this too?" I was stunned and unsure of what to say. Carefully I asked him what he meant.

"Well," he began, "where but here can you see such pure good fight such pure evil, and everyone can be together to not like what they know for sure is bad. This is more holy than most church. It's too bad to know so much that you can't believe."

He turned back to the match and I just sat there thinking. If we bought beer on the way home, I wouldn't drink much. I was afraid I might confess how I had thought every moment real, from the *Japanese Sleeper* to the *Bombs Away Atomic Drop*.

***

Once I had the heart taken out of me about wrestling, there were really only two other noon events to get interested in: bragging and arguing over the weekend cock fights and the chili peppers. I never went to watch the fighting cocks because the birds were not well trained, and the owners only spent the time getting the animals pissed off for a Saturday night match. If this were happening, Leo and I would walk deep into a field and look for young birds and cottontail rabbits.

My schooling would continue during these walks, not so much now about learning Spanish but about the animals we sought. Leo didn't know a lot about nature especially, but he would make analogies about how animals and plants and people lived, what they needed and how they got it. It didn't seem very important at the time, but he would always find a way to bring it up later.

Once, two men almost got into a fight over who took whose place at lunch. Leo reminded me how we had seen two mockingbirds square off the day before over a peach branch perch. "Remember, amigo, the animal never want to be equal, only better." Evidently, to prove his point still further, he stood up and addressed our whole company with raised voice, "I can eat four chili peppers, and any man can eat more is muy hombre!"

No one took up the challenge since the record was three, but they all rose up as one to make him hold true to his boast. He walked to the center of the grove where Lalo slipped him four huge green ones, and the crew laughed in anticipation. Taking the four, Leo taped their ends together like a fistful of cigars, sighed slightly, closed his eyes and bit all their tips off at once.

He spent the rest of the day under a nectarine tree trying to keep a little bread on his stomach. When I asked him why he did it he said, to his knowledge, he had never before been a fool. Therefore, he wanted to get it over with as soon as possible. His words were brave, but he was only pitiful. He curled up and sat still in a muddy furrow among rotting fruit fallen from earlier pickings or knocked off by birds stopping to test their sweetness.

During the second month of summer Leo began

to show me off at lunch by having the rest of the crew test me on Spanish words and phrases. Usually, the questioning was friendly but rapid and tricky.

"What is the difference between a *cajon* and a *caja*?" asked Max; a clubfooted man who worked hard but took a lot of teasing abuse from the rest of the crew, especially when the day was very hot or the drinking water short.

"A *cajon* is a full box of any kind of fruit; a *caja* is an empty." I answered promptly and even thought it was a simple question, I did so with special respect because Max rarely got much. Leo noticed and hinted a smile.

"How do you say, 'It is a stinky dam hot day and I want to go home to my house?" Toro's question was sarcastic, but it wasn't pointed at me. Instead, he was simply acknowledging the bugs, peach fuss and cruel heat and the crew cheered the obvious from our oldest old timer.

"Hance mucho color y me quiero ir a casa, ahorita.

Fanning himself with his hat he critiqued, "You left out the *stinky damned*."

"You are the *Stinky Damned*," said Lalo beside him, and we howled and traded half a dozen dirt clods back and forth.

Once a big man named Megilio asked me how to tell a girl I wanted a piece of ass. I saw Leo put his hand over his pants pocket. Underneath, I knew he carried a *Pachuca's* knife, sharp, with a slight, angular bend halfway up its six-inch blade. Then, in the coldest and most controlled words I had yet heard, Leo said, "This boy speaks no trash, because he learns no trash, because he knows no trash. Speak this way some more, I fill your mouth with a slice of you."

The rest of the crew laughed, but it was uneasy laughter that acknowledged his message was meant, and that it would be so for them too. After a pause, Leo took his hand away from his pocket. Megilio said he wanted a drink of water, then retreated to the contractor's truck to drink, then, sit sullenly and begin counting the days it would take us all to forget that he had made himself a fool.

Of course, few days were this memorable. This was just an event that helped to separate one from the next, a bookmarker used to divide the routine tumbling of fruit into boxes, the rhythm of passing them hand to hand and the slapping sounds they made as they fitted like a very simple puzzle against the backboards of the truck.

***

As seasons changed with only table grapes left to swamp, I began to see a change in Leo too. The summer was taking much from him. I could tell he'd begun hurting inside. Sometimes I would refuse my shift of stacking on the wagon and took the harder job of handing up boxes from the ground. Leo thought I was insulting him, but I explained that I was hoping for a football scholarship to college, and the extra work might give me more strength and weight when scouts would come around in the fall. Sometimes too, when we loaded a truck, I would do part of his share saying that I wanted to work hell out of an especially lazy truck driver. I could hand up boxes faster than anyone in any crew, two, three even four at a time, and drivers hated it, because they had to keep up or be laughed at by the others waiting their turns. If he got behind or a loose nail from a box hung a driver up in his loading, I would hold my full box straight out, arm's length from my chest and whistle until he was ready. Inside, I would burn and quiver, but I would do anything to protect my friend and to have the other men call me by name when they spoke of me in private.

Leo would laugh at the struggling driver, but even his laughter hurt down deep, and he would go off into the fields a few rows to lean against an end post a special way. I would watch him and hope for mid-August. With it would come raisin work for my friend. Leo was waiting for August too because it meant that his family would finally get their passes into the country. He had not seen his wife or child for three months, and the boy was only days old when Leo had left them in Mexico. "Three more weeks, man," he would say and flash that brave gold tooth. As those weeks sifted into their final days, Leo's excitement became very personal, almost aloof. We were very quiet together. The Spanish quizzes were formal and about simple things: the heat, a covey of quail flushed from under a vine, the best ways to pick fighting cocks and *why you never bet against a Filipino!*

I didn't think too much about what was happening. School was going to start soon and an end-of-summer trip to Los Angeles with my school friends was in sight. We had been pointing toward that trip since the beginning of summer, and with it so close we got together to finish plans, boast of made-up summer sexual successes and count the money we could spare from our season's earnings. We would leave the following Monday, and, since Leo would be laying raisins on my father's ranch, that was where I would say goodbye.

When that day came, I didn't put on my usual work clothes or heavy boots, but a crew necked T-shirt and Bermuda shorts. I marveled at the dark tan on my back, chest and arms from a summer's work without a shirt and the unreal whiteness of my legs and feet, protected those months by *Frisco* jeans and steel-toed boots. Stepping outside I really felt the heat for the first time. I didn't want to get my new vacation clothes sweaty, but I climbed on our tractor to go look for Leo who was out back somewhere making raisins alone.

When I found him, he was laying the paper trays in the middle of a row. He would put a dirt clod on a corner so it would not blow away before he could lay a wooden frame on top. Then the frame was filled with grape bunches cut loosely enough for the berries to dry better in the sun. Yesterday he had made thirty-five, piece-work-dollars, and with the help of his wife, who would arrive tomorrow, he hoped to double that.

He stopped, stood up, and walked slowly to within arm's length of me, holding his side, slightly bent at the waist. We looked at each other a long time until he squatted down to the ground with a pencil stub he used to tally his trays. With some effort, and an earth-speckled hand, he wrote on the fresh paper before him. When finished, he carefully blew away the fine dust from the edges, rolled the paper into a scroll and tied it in the center with a shock of sour grass. Then with shoulders squared to mine, he handed me the paper, kissed me on both cheeks and walked back to resume, with earth-speckled hands, the filling of another tray. I opened my *certificate.* It had three written Spanish words: *Guellermo,* my given name in Spanish, *amigo,* for friendship, and at the bottom, in the biggest letters, with an attempt at a simple flourish, the word *hombre,* man…but sometimes, more than man. I shuffled around for a moment, unsure of what I was to say or if anything could be said.

Turning his head and resting his left hand in the soft dirt he spoke to me gently. "I now have my family; this is good. You have yours and your friend's, which, too is good. Maybe some summer we are again *amigos trabajadores.* In between then, we stay *amigos del corazon,* friends of the heart. This is more than good. This is best." I turned and walked back to the tractor. I wondered why I understood his words but not what he said. I wondered too why I had not asked him to explain; I wondered of the simple wisdom in his daily fables and I wondered why that simple wisdom hurt so very much.

***

Sitting there, remembering all this seemed like years had passed instead of two weeks. I began to realize how hot the car had become and how I was sticking to the heavy leather *tuck- and-roll* leather seats. I turned the engine over and re-crossed the ditch bank, louvered hood, *Baby Moons* and all. Thinking was done; I was ready to go. The radio came on in the middle of "It's My Party and I'll Cry If I Want To," and the DJ ended the set with the time; I checked my watch. I'd have to hustle to school for fifth period. From English, I would look out the window and see the girl's line up for P.E. I was in love with the girl standing on number 38, Nella Sue Pike, who wore the tightest gym suit of all.

I tossed my hat in the back seat and checked my hair in the mirror. I pulled out the noise control for my muffler when I got to the main road. Then I rumbled off like a boy will do sometimes, in too much of a hurry to become a man.

Bill Weatherford

Bill Weatherford is a native Californian. He grew up in a small San Joaquin Valley town and much of his writing has its roots in the central part of the state. He completed his undergrad and graduate work in Speech at UC Berkeley. In retirement, he has been an adjunct theatre instructor at Southern Oregon and Cal Poly State Universities and the University of Aalborg, Denmark.

Primarily a short story writer, he also wrote the YA novel, *Tilly & Turp (2024)* and the screenplay for the 2014 feature film, "Underclassmen". He hopes to produce another of his screenplays, "Killing Flies" in the near future.

He lives and writes in Los Osos on California's Central Coast.

Winter Squall
By Scott Winkler

Eugene tormented his wife and daughter. He sniped at them day and night. He was a fortress of fear and doubt behind the walls of which he sniped at them all day and all night. His ammunition was their trust and love. The more they loved him and danced around him on eggshells the deeper his assorted grievances against them lodged in the horizontal crevices that covered his forehead and the folds of his double chin. He was a closet miser who gave to charity only in an effort to purge the rot and darkness from his soul. the scant light that shone in his eyes told of his avarice and the mental gymnastics that plotted his gains and others' losses.

Being germ-phobic Eugene didn't shake hands. He threw his right elbow up in place of his hand and asked you to grab that. His attention span lasted only as long as it took for him to get his way and not a second longer. There was a friendship insinuated in his voice which turned sour and vaguely menacing almost imperceptibly. He hated you at first and then, if you didn't disrupt him or somehow challenge his grandiose opinion of himself, the hate mellowed to dislike, and then to a grudging tolerance which was as human as he got. To get a sense of where his head or mood was at, you checked his wallet and account balances. He was neither tall nor short, fat nor thin, young nor old, alive nor dead.

His daughter fled and his wife succumbed. The former got married and moved away before it was too late, cutting off all contact. That was 12 years ago. She had a few children, and they never came to visit; never was their car seen traversing the long driveway up to the house set back high above the main road or their children's laughter heard in the high-ceilinged hallways and great rooms of the gothic style mansion. Against all odds, she realized that the palatial home of her parents would consume her and bleed her heart dry. Headaches every day and terrible prolonged periods told her something was wrong, something fundamental, and that her life was at stake. She saw well the disquieting signs that her mother suffered daily, deeply and seemingly without recourse. Mother gained weight then lost it, then gained more and a few months later got skinny. She went to the doctor all the time. Her hair thinned and her eyes seemed to bulge. The frequent pill popping was obvious even as she denied that anything was the matter.

The young lady looked into her dad's vacant eyes and realized what it was. He hoarded everyone's love and good energy for himself. Into his vault of vanities went their cares, hopes and dreams where they swished around with his own juices and gases to form a kind of rancid effervescence that was difficult to detect but impossible to miss. He offered in return fine china, expensive crystal, sterling cutlery, fancy cars and affluence. On the living room shelves and in Eugene's study stood fine filigreed collectibles and impressive religious ornaments that reflected back his handsome face which he never once missed when he walked past.

Mother eventually collapsed: spiritually, physically, completely. Poor Sharon, still young, ten years Eugene's junior yet brought to the very brink. The timing made plain the cause. She was shattered by the loss of her daughter, her abrupt departure and the bitter isolation and loneliness left in her wake. She could hardly look at Eugene's closely shaven face anymore without losing her composure. His icy caked-on faux smile had a reptilian aspect that gave her the shivers.

Eugene didn't talk to his wife so much as hiss or sizzle at her like a coiled snake. She experienced panic attacks some mornings after he left for work and, when he returned, and she tried to talk with him, she almost swallowed her tongue biting back honest thoughts and words - the kind that bruised his fragile ego and kindled jealousy because they were real and someone else, because he didn't give her permission to have a life, or opinions, or tastes, and never would so long as they remained alive and married.

Her diagnosis was 'neurodegenerative disease' - etiology uncertain. The doctors were flummoxed, but that's how it is with the withering physical effects of chronic emotional abuse: no apparent cause, no cure, just head scratching, deep sincere looks at the patient and palliatives. Confined to a wheelchair, Sharon came to require 24 hour care. Her hair turned a ghostly white and her fingers froze in place. Her periods stopped and her teeth turned gray. Her eyes focus and her mind seems to work but when she tries to speak what comes out is a weak guttural effort reminiscent of a whale with a hangover.

Sharon loved her daughter in the worst possible way, but it was a bleak love, fraught, hedged inside Eugene's massive and domineering insecurity, and now physically separated by her departure, which kept asking: is it my fault she left? How did this happen? Is Eugene really that bad? She knew that he was but her mind played tricks on her, alternating between hyper-alertness and despondency, like a traffic light flashing green and red. Her parched soul saw in Eugene the mirage of an oasis of love and support that she crawled towards for a drink that never came. She had normalized so much fear she couldn't think straight. The prospect of facing him all alone every day without an ally exhausted her poise and decimated her immune system. She had nowhere to turn. Their son took after his father and was of no help. He was off at school getting a master's anyway. From her wheelchair Sharon wondered in her lucid moments what would become of her and how long she could survive like this.

Eugene was not the least fazed by the state of his

family. To the contrary, his daughter gone, dead and gone, basically, since he didn't miss her; after Sharon went down, he doubled-down on his charitable giving and grew his name in the philanthropic community. They were invited to all kinds of balls, banquets and openings. He was named Executive Vice President at his financial services firm. New clients poured in. He went from having six figures under management to eight in a couple of years. Everything was on the upswing. He seemed unstoppable. As Sharon sank he soared.

The disability insurance policies he purchased for Sharon some years prior for just such a contingency seemed downright prophetic. They paid out considerably more than the cost of her care. The Black and Filipino caregivers who pulled round the clock,twelve hour shifts taking care of her wouldn't miss being paid properly if he paid them in cash, so that's what Eugene did. Sharon's medicines were covered anyway by Medicare, so he double dipped there as well. The insurance checks arrived in his mailbox like clockwork, two or three a month, which he duly deposited and set to work figuring out how to put the money to work, for himself.

The recent turn of events left Eugene quite pleased. He congratulated himself on a job well done and combed back his dyed black hair in each of the several mirrors around the house. He smiled easily and developed a bit of a skip in his step. Success oozed from every pour. His son was coming along nicely as well. Having finished graduate school at a fine university, Peter settled down with a wife and some children of his own. He had his father's black eyes that expressed various degrees of disdain alternating with insecurity and feigned surprise. He didn't trust anyone. He bought a house even nicer than his father's and a gun to protect it. He reinforced his father's complaints about the breakdown of decent society and his asinine neighbors. The neighbors really hadn't done anything except water their grass and take care of their flowers and landscaping, which beautified their properties. No matter what Eugene did to take care of his lawn and landscaping, or how much time or money he spent on yard maintenance, no flowers grew and the grass turned yellow and died.

Peter didn't worry much about his sister or mother. He had precious little interest or insight into why one left and the other got so sick. As mother got worse, he visited her occasionally and always with the wife and children in tow, so he didn't have to be left alone with her. He was mostly busy running a business and building his fortune. His name spread in his field. His three little kids had to be driven here and there and entertained. Mostly his frazzled wife did that while he worked. Already their oldest, a 6-year-old son, began to develop the entitled arrogance and subtle sneer of father and grandfather. He routinely threw elaborate tantrums when he wasn't the center of everyone's attention, which led his parents to redouble their efforts to make him the center of attention. Grandfather Eugene approved of the boy's moxie. He had a generation skipping trust drawn up to avoid paying taxes that rewarded the boy but threw crumbs at his sisters. It was not personal against the girls; they just reminded him viscerally of his ungrateful daughter and wife.

One night in mid-winter Sharon dreamed that her daughter returned home with her husband and children. They all looked fresh, healthy and held their heads high. They embraced her and all of them cried tears of joy. When she woke bitter cold winds lashed the house and snow whipped around outside her window. She stayed in bed and the caregiver brought her tea and toast. As was his wont, mid-morning Eugene went to fetch the mail from the box down at the bottom of the driveway at the front curb. She heard the front door open and the wind tear into the house then open again, more wind and close a few moments later

In the mail he saw an unusual letter postmarked Boston where he knew his daughter had moved so many years ago. It was addressed to Sharon and Sharon only, not to him. He didn't care. He ripped it open. Yes, it was from their daughter, the first letter from her in all those years. This is what she wrote:

Dear Mom, I heard you are wheelchair bound. It breaks my heart all over again, but doesn't surprise me. Dad is a monster and a kind of psychological criminal. He has no business being alive but there he is, as formidable as ever, hovering and waiting for you to die so he can collect all the life insurance. If he ever goes away, I'll come home with the kids to be with you, promise. Until then, I'll try to write more often but only to you. I will not call the house and risk being on the phone with him. He is too sly. Love, Rhonda

Eugene sat down in his study to catch his breathe. For the first time in eons, he was dumbstruck, even dumbfounded. His hands shook, not so much from the cold outdoors as from being confronted, finally, by the honest truth, the ugly brutal honest truth, about himself, about his mendacity and cruelty. He ran his arm clear across his neat desk in a fit of rage, all the quaint knickknacks sent flying and crashing down around him. As the things hit the floor, a mirror in a gilded frame that hung in his study began to vibrate and come off of its flimsy wall support helped by the fierce wind blowing outside against the house. It hung up for a few seconds at an angle, turning and teetering, then fell to the floor with a thud and shattered into large,jagged pieces all knives and spearheads. From behind it, from a cavity in the wall, worms and rats emerged and slithered into Eugene pockets and house slippers. The desk lamp hung off of the side of his desk, swinging and flickering. His good looks contorted into a fearsome vampire-like sharpness. His hands were cold and white like a vampire and a little numb from his walk to the mailbox and back while the heat of his burning anger suffused his face with a dark glow.

He fondled and looked over the letter with a ruthless imperious gaze. He wasn't going to let Sharon have it or read it, no way."over my cold dead body." he knew what he had to do. Burn it....or? He went to his vault, dialed the combination, opened it and put the letter in the way back next to his will, the grandchildren's trusts and the life insurance policies on Sharon's life naming him as sole beneficiary. On the way out, his hand brushed against the gun that he kept there for boasting purposes but didn't know how to use. He ran a finger softly over the trigger and accidentally discharged the weapon.

His accidental aim was too good. Eugene was dead before he hit the floor. The miniature human mountain that was him lay there on its back bleeding out. One of his knees twitched for a second then went limp. A winter fly roaming the house since autumn landed on one of his eyes. The muzzle of the weapon peeked out over the front edge of the vault emitting tiny almost imperceptible wisps of smoke. It seemed poised to take aim, shoot again and finish the job if Eugene moved. The fly flew off.

Sharon was in the middle of a bite of toast. She remembered her dream in that instant like somehow the violent noise released it from her subconscious, rescuing it from oblivion. Her caregiver next to her dropped to the ground and lay flat. She dialed 911 from her cell phone from her prone position terrified for her life. The house phone commenced to ring and kept ringing, singing the praises of the single gunshot in all of its dazzling power and efficiency.

There was a wicked mess, to be sure, and a corpulent body swelling with a volatile mixture of toxic liquids and gasses that had to be moved and refrigerated until it could be buried. The bullet went clear through and through, through the front of his neck and out the back, lodging in the wall where the gilded mirror used to hang, where his dapper reflection used to appear on demand. The worms and rats scampered back into the wall where they came from in search of a meal.

The lashing winds outside subsided. The snow came down from a pinkish blue sky in a lovely gentle slow motion from all sides and angles reminiscent of a snow-globe after it is shaken up. The mailbox had frozen over with a long white snowy beard hanging down below it on a skeleton of ice like a presiding judge listening to all of the testimony. The judge ruled. The verdict was guilty. The penalty was carried out. Sirens could be heard closing in the distance.

Rhonda, her husband and children flew in for the funeral. They all stood behind and close to Sharon at the cemetery, surrounding her on either side. The sky was a steely winter gray. Sharon actually got up out of her wheelchair for the first time in years to shovel a bit of dirt on top of the coffin after it was lowered, as was the custom, then fell backward into the wheelchair with a weary satisfied expression. Peter cried briefly; then his cell phone rang and he walked away to answer it. His wife looked around sheepishly. Their children weren't there. No one else was either.

The elderly clergyman stamped out his cigarette, coughed a few times, bowed his head in mock grief and spoke briefly on the holy virtue of generosity which Eugene exemplified through his charitable giving. He opened a prayer book, but his cataracts were so thick he couldn't read from it. The grave diggers stood by impatiently in the cold leaning on their shovels. One of them pulled a small metal flask out of his pocket and took a hit, then passed it to his partner. After the service was over the clergyman walked over to them and took a hit, emptying the flask. As the family walked away, except for Sharon, who was pushed, the mostly bare cemetery trees rustled and quivered in the winter breeze as if to bid them peace and wave farewell.

Scott Winkler

The author is a semi-retired lawyer. He is a father, stepfather, grandfather, husband, brother and son. He has been writing short fiction in earnest for only about 2 years. during that time, his work has been recognized on several long lists, as well as Honorable Mention by the Creative Writing Society of New Zealand, semi-finalist among 23 others out of 'thousands' of stories submitted to the European Society of Literature Harold Bloom short fiction competition for 2023. Recently, his short story "The Milky Way" won first place in the 2024 Slippery Elm short fiction contest, with a cash prize and publication.

He loves to walk, read, play golf, occasionally travel and take care of his 2 best canine friends Pinky and Stella. He is a praying person and observes and practices ritual Jewish law on a daily basis. His late arrival to writing has to do with the need to make a living. definitely the law afforded him an adequate living. however, during and after the Covid crisis, he got quite literally burnt-out practicing law. it was taking too much out of him, wearing him down terribly, and he had had enough of it. As he dialed it back, he kind of accidentally turned to writing when an ad for a contest showed up on his fb page; and thus it began.

His passion for writing the Great American Short Story grows with each page written. But is a page ever completed? For Shakespeare sure, maybe, but for the rest of us? We will never know until we labor and keep at it until the sun comes up next morning. The human brain, heart and imagination, combined into one cannonball, know no force their equal for creating poetry, art, music and literature. The author regards this story as a sincere and credible contribution to the short fiction genre.

Living Springs Publishers

We hope you enjoyed this book. Please let us know what you think about it. You can leave a review on Goodreads, or wherever you purchased the book.

This is the eighth edition of our Baby Boomers Plus contest and book. The number of submissions to **Stories Through The Ages Baby Boomers Plus** has increased dramatically over the years we have held the contest. Each story is read by at least three judges. We receive stories from people just starting to write and from those who have won many awards. The competition is intense, and the judges agonize over their choice, realizing the heavy burden of being fair but decisive. There are winners and losers, that is the nature of a contest. We thank each and every author for the stories they submit and urge everyone to keep writing.

You can find information about our contests and where to buy our books at:
www.LivingSpringsPublishers.com.

Living Springs Publishers is a family owned, independent publishing company based in Centennial, Colorado. Our mission is to help authors, regardless of age or experience, share their gift of writing. Using our expertise in editing and publishing we help our clients bring their stories and manuscripts to life.